CHOKE HOLD

CHOKE HOLD

a novel by

TODD BABIAK

TURNSTONE PRESS

Turnstone Press
607 – 100 Arthur Street
Artspace Building
Winnipeg, Manitoba
Canada R3B 1H3
www.TurnstonePress.com

Turnstone Press gratefully acknowledges the assistance of the Canada Council for the Arts, the Manitoba Arts Council and the Government of Canada through the Book Publishing Industry Development Program for our publishing activities.

Cover photograph: *Insomnia 71*, by Mirek Weichsel

Design: Manuela Dias

Printed and bound in Canada
by Friesens for Turnstone Press.

Canadian Cataloguing in Publication Data

Babiak, Todd, 1972—

Choke hold

ISBN 0-88801-245-4

I. Title.

PS8553.A242 C48 2000   C813'.54   C00-920026-6
PR9199.3.B22 C48 2000

for Norman Collingwood

[TABLE OF CONTENTS]

Acknowledgements

Thanks to my family and to Leavenworth. Thanks to my kind and patient readers: Tandie McLeod, Terry Byrnes, Peter Eastwood, Zachary O. Devereaux, Jayson Cobb, Catherine Bush, and Mary DiMichele. Thanks to Susan Brown and Concordia University. Thanks to Sifu Michael Gregory and Sifu Brad Murphy for teaching me a bit about fighting, and to Carolyn Swayze and Turnstone Press for giving a fella a chance. Thanks to Moe's on the corner of Lambert-Closse and de Maisonneuve for cooking a turkey in the dark.

Thanks, Gina. You can read it now.

To know oneself is to study oneself
in action with another person.
—Bruce Lee

[CHAPTER 1]

Carl the wooden dummy has lost an arm. The men and women with notepads who represent my creditors have taken everything but Carl, and against the bare wall of the empty loft he looks like a little boy some mother has forgotten. How he came to be handicapped will remain a mystery.

On the second floor of this old brick warehouse not far from the Commercial Wharf, wind scatters the damp and twisted photographs that used to hang from my bulletin board; promo shots of me pulling arm locks and triangle chokes on long-limbed students, big-shot fighters from California in tank tops with a hand on my shoulder, smiling. Outside these open windows, the clammy mist that settles on Boston has settled on Boston. The rain doesn't fall, it just is. And I am a bankrupt. In my school, I can hear myself counting to ten, to 20, repeating everything I had heard, to move like water, hit harder, faster, to throw from the hip, and stop telegraphing attacks and weaknesses. Hide your weaknesses, students. Bury them.

The echoes of my steps crack against the walls, so I tiptoe. I sneak through my school as if something remained that I might insult. By the corner window with the broken latch is the hook where the red heavy bag swung and creaked. On the back wall, opposite the windows, are empty shelves where the boxing gloves and fake knives and pads and headgear would sit, and wait. On the hardwood floor near the central pillar is the blood-stain – my blood – now obscured by the accumulated dust and hair and other nastiness that has made its way in through the windows. Gone are the flags representing the origins of fighting systems, gone is the long wall mirror, the mats, and in the lobby my couch and desk. A small tornado whips some of the dust up so it hisses against the walls and rips at the yellow *Always Beware* sign stapled above the entrance to the studio. I realize it isn't the flashiest or cleverest thing to put above a door; it might as well be *It Hurts to Get Kicked in the Face*. Ellie once suggested I tack my Bruce Lee poster up there, the one from *Enter the Dragon* where he is bleeding from long slices across his chest and ready, ready. Of course I had reservations, suspecting she just thought he was sexy.

Why didn't they take all of Carl the wooden dummy? They might have sold him for $200, or more; if not at the auction, at the Kung Fu and Tai Chi place on Hanover Street. Even though he is an amputee, I would love to take Carl home, to Seymour. For repairs. But the hockey bags are already full of clothes, gloves, wrestling shoes, and other small remembrances, so I have no space for him. Carl is a sacrifice.

In the bus on the way to the airport, someone has dragged a finger through the condensation on the window beside me. The bus is full, and I'm sure it's been full all morning, half the city breathing and sweating that layer of wet on the window, so the valentine heart someone drew is a deep heart, dripping. I wonder if that someone washed up with soap and water before eating the chocolate chip cookie in his lunch bag. I wonder if that someone didn't, and the breath and sweat of four thousand secretaries and salesmen jumped into someone as he licked his fingers.

Monday morning and everyone is coffee and perfume. Through the lines of the heart, rain; a grey layer of Boston washes off the stone and bricks and into the sewers. I can't focus this last look at churches and Marlboro billboards because the rattling of the bus mingled with the heat and smell of us all will make me queasy and I'll have to ask the driver to stop, making America late. To obscure it, to make the city disappear, I take a deep breath and blow on the heart.

When I declared bankruptcy, I hid $4000 in an account my mom set up for me in the Seymour Treasury Branch a long time ago. It's still officially under her name so it can't be traced. After reading the list of books Ellie wanted me to read while we were still together, to help me gain a more sophisticated understanding of the world and the hearts of men, I planned on using the four grand to sit around in my apartment, rent movies, and masturbate into socks. To drink gin and tonics until my liver failed. Until I died or went so crazy the buzzing in the back of my head whispered away like an old balloon.

Last night my younger brother Denton called, and changed my mind.

In the customs line-up at Logan airport, I recognize a couple of men who trained with me in the Massachusetts Corrections workshop I used to run on weekends; actual cops never signed up, only little guys with poor eyesight or nervous conditions who couldn't make the regular police force. I taught them joint locks, mostly, and aggressive simulations. These two guys were pretty good students, smart enough, but since I can't stomach any stories today about how this cool Jujitsu move worked in that situation, stories about ass kicking here and crook busting there, I turn away from them. And I turn away from them because I'm ashamed of what has happened. To the reporters and everyone else, I said: I teach self-defence. What did I do wrong?

They had some pretty good answers.

Bye, Boston.

My younger brother Denton called me up last night to tell me about Nick Lozinski and the Plum House. About how it's spring in Seymour, ripe, and sweet-smelling. When he called I was in the process of getting drunk for the first time in a long time, one-ounce Bombay Sapphire gin and tonics with lime, and feeling very strongly about Chet Baker. Drinking is tough, I found, when you're living alone on the 11th floor of a studio apartment and trying to drink, truthfully only waiting for some great beauty to walk through the door and find you alone, and drinking, and listening to moony Chet Baker. You want her to see you as the sexiest black-and-white film star, maybe see how thoughtful you really are. And of course fall in love with you. But it was late when Denton hung up, and my door was locked, and I don't know my neighbours.

Two days ago, Denton said, Nick Lozinski ripped off a bunch of money from work, bought a black Jeep Cherokee Sport Limited Edition with an automatic sunroof and gold trim, drank himself nuts, seriously injured a three-year-old girl, and crashed into the front door of the Plum House. Nick Lozinski and I played Pee Wee hockey; he played centre and I was left wing on his line. Both years, he wore the C. I dropped a full glass of orange pop on the kitchen floor at his 13th birthday party and his mom, a kind and very fat woman who Nick liked to do impressions of in the dressing room, squeezed my shoulder with her soft hand just as I went for my mouth with my fingers in the nervous way I still have. "Don't you worry one red speck, Jeremy," Mrs. Lozinski said, over

Van Halen's *1984*, and she bent over and cleaned up my spilled orange pop. She didn't smell or pretended not to smell the vodka Nick had sneaked into it, and at that moment I was so glad I'd only taken one sip of that vodka. I was glad to be in her house, glad that Nick and I were on the same team and that it was October; that the Halloween light was getting low outside and that my birthday was coming up too.

With his explosive speed and deceptive stick handling, Nick was by far the best player on the team, and even though he didn't like to admit it, a pretty smart guy in school. He was tall for his age and handsome, with high cheekbones and hair short in the front and long and curly in the back. If any of the girls were going to write on any boy's arm in class – happy faces and skulls and crossbones and anarchy symbols and daisies – it was almost always one of Nick's arms.

The Lozinskis lived in a cream after-dinner-mint house on the shore of a manufactured lake in Seymour Gardens. On the day of Nick's 13th birthday party, the big house was warm and the heater gave off a comforting burnt-dust smell. So burnt dust and baking and cigars, and when the front door opened to let kids in and out, dead leaves. Gold-framed pictures of Nick and his two brothers were everywhere, and Mrs. Lozinski kept a room with leather furniture and white carpets that looked as though it hadn't been used in three years. A shiny piano, polished end tables, an impossibly clean fireplace.

Walking home as the sun went down, ignoring the rest of the team who claimed to be drunk on half a capful of vodka each, I was mad and jealous about Nick Lozinski being the luckiest kid in the world. I thought about my own loud dad in the bleachers during our hockey games, my dad whom everyone knew, and then I thought about Mr. Lozinski, who sat alone in his grey suits and never yelled, fat like his wife, smoking cigars in-between periods. My dad tucked his jeans into his big fireman boots and slapped us on the way out to the ice in a way that embarrassed me as Mr. Lozinski simply took his seat again after each intermission, ready to nod or maybe clap when Nick scored his goals. Nick always scored a lot of goals. He stayed in hockey, and I quit.

In the tenth grade, after not speaking to each other for a few years because he'd become a WHL prospect and I'd become other things, Nick Lozinski pissed on my head at the Safe Graduation party. Since they didn't want drinking and driving, the Seymour town council sponsored the Safe Grad every year, bussing every-one out to the secret location which always turned out to be a sandy pit in the flats east of town where a plane had crashed in the seventies. By the time the sun had plunged below the mountains, I was drunk for the first time in my life. At some point, I left my drama friends – who didn't seem to want to be at the Safe Grad and who weren't drinking near as much as I was – and wandered around before passing out. I woke up at around midnight and my Oilers cap was gone. It was completely dark, but the fire was massive. Football players were running through the middle of it and everyone was laughing about that. By the side of the fire, a brown-haired girl named Tracy with olive skin and a neck that made me want to lick it started telling me about what she liked and disliked about Duddy Kravitz, whom we had been reading about in English class. I knew who Tracy was and I knew I had no business talking to her.

Her lipstick was crooked, and she had a scar that ran from her top lip to the bottom of her nose. It was a fine scar. Tracy looked warm and familiar in the firelight, cozy, smoky. I'm not sure how I ended up kissing her but I kissed her and she dropped her big plastic bottle of apple cider and stared silently at me for a while. I picked up the bottle and took a drink from it. I told her I liked scars. Scars like hers.

Later, after I threw up for a while behind some birch trees and returned to the fire, a boy who smelled like rum and Coke picked me up from where I was slumped. As this boy held me, Nick Lozinski punched me in the face, calling me a faggot drama fag and some kind of rapist and a piece of shit. I remember the sound it made, those punches, how some of them hurt and some of them didn't. The thud against my cheeks and teeth. Then having no balance, being dragged into the dark of cowboy boots, short grass, and sand. Wanting to puke some more. "She Sells Sanctuary" by The Cult was playing. I remember liking the taste of my own blood, letting it comfort me as I crawled there, spitting to separate the pure stuff from the sandy bits gathered up from being face down in the plane-crash dunes. Nick Lozinski kicked me as I tried to stand up, and called me all kinds of things as his hockey friends stood around him, laughing with bottles of beer in their hands. I could see, and then I couldn't see, and then I woke up completely and Nick was pissing on me. Piss, the steaming raunch of it mixing with the smell of my own puke, and the blood – all of it in my hands like the innards of a horrible egg. Hot. On my hands and knees I tucked my chin into my collarbone and waited until he was finished. There was laughing at first, lots of it, but by the time it was over and I was kneeling in front of them all, spitting, and Nick was doing up his pants, the night was completely silent.

Two afternoons ago, Nick Lozinski walked into Gordy's, the bar my brother Denton manages. He ate two orders of chicken fingers with barbecue sauce for dipping and told Denton, after about eight rye and gingers, all about how his wife Tracy was as good as gone, her and the kids. That he was fairly positive she was going to take up with the Nip she'd been fucking in the city. Leaning over the bar, he whispered to Denton about how he understood why people murdered other people; he didn't understand it before but he understood it now. It was Friday night, and Gordy's is busy on Friday nights. Though it was loud, Denton overheard Nick telling some guys about his brand new Jeep, about how he was really looking for some good cocaine. At midnight, after paying his tab with cash and picking a couple of fights that didn't amount to much, Nick left. Denton called the cops and told them what Nick had said about the murdering and the cocaine, and half the bar went outside to see what would happen.

It's spring in Seymour, but winter habits are strong, so Nick let the Jeep warm up awhile as he yelled taunts and threats to a few people standing and drinking and smoking, waiting for him to do whatever he was going to do. The cops showed up, three cars with Chicken George up front, and Nick floored it. Gordy's is in the same strip mall as a Safeway, so shopping carts are everywhere. Nick clipped one on his way out of the unpaved parking lot. It flew and hopped in the dust and rocks, somersaulted, and smacked into the three-year-old girl whose mother was taking advantage of the midnight-madness pre-Rodeo Days shopping event. The cart hit the little girl, whose head smashed into the front of her mother's minivan. Her injuries turned out to be non-life-threatening.

Seymour isn't an old town by New England standards, but for the prairies it has some age because it was a freshwater stop on a trapline into the Rockies. After they expanded Black Gold Drive into a freeway, our street, the oldest street in town, became Kravchuk Crescent. The house across from ours, the Plum House, has been empty since 1990, the year I left Seymour. As Denton told me the story last night, I wondered: why did Nick weave his way through town, sirens behind him, only to settle on a dead-end?

A couple of years ago, Denton sent me a *Seymour Star* article about three generations of Kravchuk history, and the house they lived in. The article was a nice load of horseshit, and anyone who'd lived in Seymour more than two years would have known it, but they did include a before-and-after picture that I taped to the fridge. The Plum House in 1918, soon after it was built, strong and regal like a diamond on a plate of dirt; and the Plum House today, complete with the jungle grass and the boarded-up picture window someone had spray-painted RAD GRAD 92 across.

I can see Chicken George with his lights and his siren, squealing in behind Nick at the mouth of our crescent. According to the story Chicken George told Denton later that night, Nick didn't even slow down. He jammed that black Cherokee Sport Limited Edition with gold trim as if he planned on busting through the fence, through the dead-end. Then he veered right and smashed into the front door of the Plum House. The cops stopped on the street between our houses, lights flashing, and inched towards the house on foot, little black guns in hand. Chicken George stood amidst the high grass and weeds in the front yard of the Plum House. The two younger Mounties hung back. Without provocation, Nick staggered out of the house. He stood in front of Chicken George and pulled out a pen. "I'll use this thing," he said.

Though it has been years, when I think of Nick Lozinski and what he did to me that night in the sand dunes, a red and swirling pit of nauseous rage opens up in me and I want nothing more in this world than to knock him out quickly and gracefully, revive him, and knock him out again. This doesn't say much for my growth as a man, of course, and it doesn't point – sorry, Ellie – to a very sophisticated understanding of the world and the hearts of men, but I can't help it.

I want Nick Lozinski to be fat and ugly and pathetic. I want him to wake up every morning in various states of bloody, piss-soaked suffering, and to realize why he is being punished. So the story Denton told me last night about what happened in the front yard of the Plum House is entertaining to me. Especially this: when the cops approached Nick, he stuck the pen good and hard into his neck, an inch away from the carotid artery. Chicken George tackled and cuffed him.

Nick realized that Tracy his wife had been seeing Hong Park, a real-estate agent from the city, so he stayed at work over noon hour earlier that day to chat with the *Seymour Star* secretary. When she asked him to watch the phones as she used the washroom, he opened the company book and wrote himself a cheque for 35 grand. What had they been chatting about? According to the secretary, who was in Gordy's last night, Nick told her that a skinned bear so closely resembles a human being that a lesser hunter cannot bring himself to eat the animal. After lunch hour, Nick asked his press-room boss if he could take the afternoon off because of an inner ear infection. He drove into the city and deposited the cheque into a new account. After buying the Cherokee with one of his temporary Nick Lozinski cheques, he hooked up with a black call girl named Candace and spent a few hours with her in the Strathcona Hotel. He emptied his account just before the bank closed. Then he sped down Highway 27, where Chicken George pulled him over, admired the new truck, and gave him a warning for speeding and not wearing a seatbelt. From there straight to Gordy's, where he drank rye and gingers and ate chicken fingers dipped in barbecue sauce.

Nick resisted, screaming about his father and all the people he has in his back pocket before quieting down and leaning against the back of a cruiser as one of the younger cops bandaged his cut. When Denton got home, the thin orange tarp that covered the hole in the Plum House was flapping in the wind.

Dad bought us a Beta machine almost as soon as they came out, and the first movies Denton and I rented were Bruce Lee's and Ninja flicks starring Sho Kosugi. Even though Bruce and Sho sometimes used weapons and in-close fighting techniques, the kicks were what made the movies so good. A circle of bad guys would surround them in a bar or some kind of bad-guy compound, and they'd whup everyone's ass with spinning kicks and flipping kicks and incomprehensible neck-breaking kicks. Denton and I would tense up like wild rabbits and squirm in the peeling vinyl chairs Dad would never replace, squeezing our little hands into fists and cheering our boys, high-fiving when the battles were won.

Two weeks after Nick Lozinski pissed on my head, I joined the only martial arts school in Seymour at the time, Tiger Tae Kwon Do. The brochure said it was an ancient hand-and-foot fighting system known for its devastating flurries of kicks and rigorous training methods. As Dad drove me, I nibbled away at the skin around my fingernails.

"I wish your brother woulda come too. I mean, Christ. Your grampa used to take me out into the field and beat me until I bled from my ears. To toughen me up. Your Uncle Dan used to kick the bejeezus out of me too. It's normal about growing up, Jeremy. Maybe this class'll do for you what it did for me."

"Make me bleed from my ears?"

He shook his head. "Christ almighty. You know what I'm saying." Folding his bottom lip over the top to let me know he respected what I had to say, sorta, but I was wrong wrong wrong, he looked out his window. "You know, it's more complicated than bleeding, Jeremy, so quit your horse's ass talk. If your mother were here, she'd say the same thing."

I mumbled something under my breath, something like "Fuck you," or "Eat my ass" because I had no use for his *if your mother* stuff. On banner days, Dad would use my dead mom as leverage in as many as ten genres: bed making, food fixing, homework doing, lawn mowing, sarcasm ending, dish washing, temper adjusting, time managing, garage cleaning, and lottery ticket buying.

"Listen, I can take you home right now, and you can whistle on back to your fruitcake drama class and get your ass good and kicked ten or 11 times a day for all I care. If you wanna be a —"

"I don't want to be that. I just want you to stop summoning Mom every time I say or do something you don't like."

Dad turned up the radio, CIKN Country, and squeezed the wheel of the truck at 10 and 2. The song was about Saturday nights in Mexico. A few blocks later, he turned it down again, plopping his right arm up over the back of the blue seat, around the shoulders of the imaginary woman beside him. Where Mom used to sit. We were waiting for the train to pass, ding ding ding, and Dad looked over at the empty rail cars parked to the right of us underneath the north-end grain elevator. It was another hot afternoon, and the windows were open. The musty, smothering smell of the fields was everywhere, but in my nervousness I was still cold. The blinking barrier lifted and 50th Avenue opened up, and the ten drivers of the ten cars and trucks that passed us as we crossed the tracks waved and nodded and tipped their hats to Dad. CIKN Country enveloped the town, those Saturday nights in Mexico. When it was just the two of us again, turning right, he put his bottom lip over the top again, and wiped underneath his nose. "I just hated to see you that night, Jeremy. What if one of those boots to the head was a little over, in the temple? When I think of it I shudder all the way down to my toes, kid. It makes me want to cry out at night. Bleeding and sick, covered in piss, and I couldn't do a thing about it. There's no protecting you kids any more. I mean, *there you were*, covered in that little bastard's..."

"Yeah." I didn't want to hear him say it again.

Tiger Tae Kwon Do was in a strip mall at the far north end of town, near the car dealerships and the McDonald's. The bus depot was right next door, so there were lots of lonely-looking people wearing several layers of bread-coloured clothes standing around outside, occasionally peeking into the studio, breathing on the glass. Inside there were photos of skinny Korean men everywhere, posters of them jumping head-height, kicking each other, and chopping bricks and wood. Tran, tiny Tran with the third degree black belt, clasped his hands in the entrance of the studio and invited us into his office, which was decorated with photographs of tigers just about to pounce, and rice-paper drawings. We sat. After an inspirational speech about the martial arts being all about discipline and mind and body enhancement, he said my marks would certainly pick up in school. Dad cleared his throat. "I don't think Jeremy – not that I have to speak for him – is interested in the sport so much, or even the cultural aspects. Thing is, Tran, he took a decent beating a few weeks ago and he's really here to learn how to take care of himself. A few months, you know. He's already finishing grade ten so I suppose we should have had him in here years ago." Dad cuffed me on the shoulder and looked away, and said, slowly, "Even though I boxed as a kid, I never got around to teaching him much of anything on that side of things."

"What happened, Jeremy?" said Tran, standing up, waving at the incense smoke. His height hovered somewhere in the five-foot-two range. The tone was very us-against-them and I liked that, and trusted him immediately, imagining him and me knocking on Nick Lozinski's door, knocking him senseless, and having a nice piss swordfight over his teary carcass before hunting his cowboy-booted associates.

"Nothing much. I just got beat up by some guys."

"They *urinated* on him is the shit of it," said Dad. I had asked him not to mention that, ever, to anyone. If half the town knew, I didn't need the other half finding out. I wanted to leave.

Then Tran told us a story about how he was in a Vietnamese concentration camp as a young man. He lost his entire family. With some friends, he escaped and ended up in Korea, where he began training. "I started training serious because I knew, I had learned from the camps."

"Knew what?" said Dad.

"That no one, no one in this life would take care of me. Not God. I was alone, and I would have to fight to live."

I knew what Tran was talking about. It wasn't only remembering the taste of Nick Lozinski's piss that had kept me up every night. It wasn't only the imagined scenarios of his destruction making my heart beat too fast. It was, more than anything, a tightening in my stomach, a pillow-pounding clench all through me, the realization that I was essentially single, an adult, a free agent in a world that was not beautiful, not kind or funny or happy like the one on TV. These were the saddest days since my mom's death. No one was looking out for me.

Through the walls, as Dad signed some forms, early students yelled and kicked. I could see them kicking the air, me kicking the air, making the air around me dangerous, increasing the distance between me and everyone.

Tran gave me my white belt uniform in its plastic package, and showed me how to bow to the studio before going upstairs to change. Travis Many Fires, a short Indian guy I recognized from Rapid Arcade, showed me how to tie my belt. And downstairs he showed me how to do the preliminary stretching. Travis was a green belt, the cut-off for beginners. With his blue stripe he would be off to the advanced class, where I was certain the kicks and punches were at an esoteric level of devastation I would never, ever reach. As I stretched, I could feel the rest of the class sizing me up. And every time I looked through the doorway, Dad gave me a thumbs-up and a smile from where he sat on a couch in the lobby.

Without warning, Tran came out and yelled something in Korean. Everyone lined up. In the chaos, I slipped around on my bare feet, confused and forsaken for a moment before finding a place in the back. Tran yelled again and everyone bowed and I bowed. Completely lost, I looked over at Travis, who had scuttled across the room to complete some arcane formation based on rank, and he mouthed, "Just follow along." Axe kicks, front snap kicks, roundhouse and sidekicks. With the heel, no, with the instep. I was behind everyone, trying to gimp along, catching a glimpse of myself in the mirror now and then, bitten with intense shame, hyperaware of Dad watching me. The other white belts around me scowled with disgust as I bumped into them, off balance. After some hand-clapping, we were practising forms. Forms, as I understood them, were just rehearsed sequences of kicks and punches against an imaginary attacker who you had to pretend was in front of you, getting the beating of his lifetime. Just as I was starting to get it, someone behind me, a girl of all people, farted and excused herself. I laughed and looked around for some support, and a thick cloud of desolate, dusty, western-saloon silence descended on the Seymour Tiger Tae Kwon Do Club.

"Jeremy," said Tran, smacking me across the head, "no laughing. On the ground."

I sat down and Tran kicked me lightly in the stomach. My eyes gushed up.

"On your stomach. Push-up position. Twenty push-ups, on your knuckles. Count out loud."

Through the legs, past the doorway, Dad shook his fist in encouragement. He nodded and shook it some more, as I began to count.

I told myself, tears falling, that I hated Tran and all Asian people, that I was never coming back to this bamboo-smelling piece of shit, that Dad could go fuck himself, and that that very night I would slice my wrists in the tub and write slogans against my family and town and country and God in my own blood on the wall before taking a no-more-martial-arts bath into hell.

Seymour sits on the last stretch of prairie before you hit the foothills, an hour east of the Rocky Mountains. Eight thousand people live here, mostly families who got out of farming 20 or 30 years ago when the consolidated operations wiped out the small landowners. And oil people. Some Seymour Gardens types commute to city law offices and brokerages in Jaguars, but for me, this town feels too remote to be a suburb, even if the view is pretty.

There are hotels, bars, restaurants, and bakeries like in any town, and there's a museum, and even some tourist shops for the odd family who takes the secondary highway by accident. Germans, mostly, who buy just enough postcards and Inuit soap carvings and moose t-shirts to keep the stores opened. It's cold in the winter and hot in the summer and now it's both, which is better than either.

"Different, eh?" says Denton.

On the secondary highway that the Germans take by accident, the one that connects Seymour with the airport and therefore Germany, we are bouncing around in his 1976 red Ford truck, the rustmaster, and he is conscious that I am studying him as he drives. Thanks to beer and bar food, his neck and face are pudgier than the last time I saw him, manlier. Stubble. The eyes are somehow bluer, maybe he's using coloured contacts, and his hair is shorter than it ever was. He's very handsome, more handsome than me, and sweeter in the face, friendly. I used to be jealous of Denton when we were growing up, because he was always funny and good-looking. He never went through the slouching, nerdy phases I did; his teen years were relatively pimple-less, and people were always calling him up, especially girls. With the windows opened and this good-smelling spring air blowing through the cab, he looks a little like a cowboy ought to look, relaxed and tough but not in a brand-new denim or sequined way. Three years ago, at Christmastime, he flew out east to meet Ellie, who was then my almost-fiancée and best compadre other than him, and he hated Boston. No sky, no stars at night, too many people and languages, and old and dirty, too fashion-oriented, all these mean people wrapped up, worrying about everything that doesn't matter.

"Yeah. It is different." The McDonald's just inside the town limits has a covered playground attached to it, with plastic tubes and big buckets of red, white, and blue balls for kids to jump into. More Ford and GM car dealerships, a bigger MacLeod's Hardware, a Taco Bell and a Wendy's, new-looking gas stations, a colourful sign for the Judo school, and now there's a liquor store on almost every corner: Scotty's Liquor, Seymour Liquor, City Centre Liquor, Rocky Mountain Liquor, Klondike Liquor, Big Dave's Liquor. "Lots of booze."

"We should get some. I got Louis to cover for me when you called, so we can get cranked if you want."

"I shouldn't."

"Why not, Jeremy? It's not as if you're out of shape, and you don't have to work."

"I am out of shape. I haven't been in the gym since Bobby Bullas. I feel like a blimp."

Denton sticks his head out the window and takes a big whiff. "Ahh. Smell that, Jeremy? You smell home?" He takes a couple of rights, off 50th Street, and pulls into Klondike Liquor. A big, black felt marker on orange construction paper in the window says, RODEO DAYS GOLDRUSH! "What are we drinking?"

"Whatever you like, Denton. You're the expert."

He raises his eyebrows at me and gets out of the truck. Across the street, at the Fas Gas where I worked one summer, are two versions of grade-12-me in red coveralls, sitting on stools just outside the door. Everyone walking in and out of the liquor store is dressed for summer, shaking hands with each other and praising that setting sun and *how sweet it is* to not be bundled up, freezing cold, slow and ornery. Banners hang over the streets, advertising the carnival and rodeo this weekend.

In the rear-view mirror, Denton drops a case of Pilsner into the back of the truck, passing a paper bag under his left arm and shaking some guy's hand. Laughing at something, maybe Nick Lozinski, who must still be the going concern, gossip-wise. There's too much glare and I can't see who the other guy is, but he's wearing the same jean jacket as Denton, the slightly faded Lee Stormrider with a corduroy collar. There are more trees than I remember, trees everywhere, and huge lawns. Lawns still wet from the snowmelt, still brown.

Back in the truck, Denton turns back on to 50th Street, and the anxiety hits me. The fear of seeing my dad, thoughts I've been putting off all day. In the plane and in the airport, and really for the last seven years. When I first got into black belt competitions I used to wish, on the drives to the arenas and gyms where they were held, in Spokane and Missoula and Calgary and Regina, that the drive would last forever, that I wouldn't have to get out and fight at all, that I could somehow be a fighter without fighting, that I could separate the mind from the body in a certain way, and the fighting-body-me could take care of business and then come back to the real-mind-me, and we could get together after all the hard work was done and drink a pop and reflect about things. I'd love to take a break from my mind for a while, let my body deal with Dad, and then come back in a week, fresh, purged, ready. "Hey, Dent. You know it might be easier if I hole up in a hotel for a couple of days. Ease into this."

"No. It's about time you and Dad talked."

"But it might be easier if I –"

"No. No hotel. You'll sleep at home, in your bed. Where you belong. You can quit shitting your pants, by the way, because he's not even home right now. He's working graveyard tonight."

"I guess I'm just a bit scared. That's all I mean."

"Yeah. Well."

Down Black Gold Drive, we take a right past the Rapid shopping centre, where all the welfare families live above Superior

Video and the arcade. Everything here looks the same, just worse.

"Notice they tore down the grain elevator?"

Little pockets of filth-covered snow refuse to melt underneath random piles of scrap wood and metal in the empty lot. There is a thriving grain elevator north and east of here, near the fire hall, where the train tracks turn towards the city. But this one, the old, white, peeling-paint grain elevator used to be one of the best and spookiest places in the world. The rail connection has been ripped up too, and rotten old ties lie scattered among some trees in-between here and the hospital. When we were kids, we'd sling-shot rocks at the mice who lived around the tin silos. Mice were always zinging around everywhere, doing whatever it is mice do all day. Eating, I guess. Sometimes, if you were running in the right place at the right time and you scared some, they'd stam-pede right under your feet and you'd step on a head and it'd cry and your heart would jackhammer and you'd scream and jump and tell your brother and friends about it and you'd all crowd around and watch it die.

At the mouth of Kravchuk Crescent there are stains on the pavement. "Nick was really moving," I say, because Denton is going slow, to show me.

"I wasn't lying to you."

The little wartime houses at this end of the crescent are bright, as if someone has been buffing at the aluminum siding. Since I remember the crescent with leaves on the trees, the houses seem exposed, naked. Abandoned tricycles and wagons and tiny BMXs with training wheels litter the sidewalks, dollies too, all good news. American family cars and trucks in the driveways, with older Camaros and El Caminos and shortbox Chevys – dwindling youth – parked on the street. These are young families; the seniors who used to live on this end of the street are gone. Glowing TVs tell me it is dinnertime in Seymour, and everyone is watching Oprah Winfrey as they eat their baked ham and tuna casseroles.

In contrast to the colourful bungalows at the mouth of the crescent, the Plum House is huge and the colour of briquettes. In this flat, still wintry light, the wooden house looks as if it'd been built with strips of ash. The boards are sparse and blackened on the second floor, where the fire was. We roll past the house and turn around to park across the street and I feel cold, wrong, so I look to Denton, who has been watching me for a reaction. I raise my eyebrows lazily, to show Denton it's nothing to me, and as we park I look back. Thick tire tracks have ripped through the high, brown grass in the front yard, and it looks like Nick may have bounced off the big elm tree that I was never allowed to climb. Around the tree and the tracks, the yard is littered with beer cans and plastic shopping bags. The big double doors have been smashed to splinters, and on the plywood covering the picture window, someone has painted over RAD GRAD 92. The front balcony that used to jut out hopefully from the attic looks as though it is ready to come tumbling down; what kid didn't secretly want to play up there, when it was healthy? We park in front of our place, and the monstrous house across the street looks as though it's tired of being here, sinking shamefully into the ground, into nowhere, so something fresh can be built on top of it and everyone can have some mercy, and forget.

William Kravchuk, father of Joe Kravchuk and son of the man who built Seymour with the money he made running booze into Montana during prohibition, bought all the little houses on this street, ours included, from the city after World War II. Some people said he sold them for cheap to make the Plum House seem bigger and more beautiful than it already was, to make his car brighter and faster than it already was, his wife prettier and his kid smarter, his laugh louder.

Our own little brown and white house with, yes, aluminum

siding, looks nice. The pine trees Mom planted when I was a baby are taller than two of me now, and the garage has been recently painted. Denton points to the Plum House. "Dad had to drive the Jeep out of there. Chicken George wouldn't do it, he was afraid it would fall on him. Plus, there's always Satanists in there, so he was probably worried about stumbling over a dead goat or a German shepherd with its paws cut off."

On the driveway, Denton carries the heaviest hockey bag and the case of beer. I've got the light one and the bottle of Scotch.

"Funny what you said earlier about being scared," he says, putting down the case and the bag, and fishing a flat-looking basketball out of the pathetic shrub that's been beside our back steps forever. "For years I couldn't imagine you scared. Maybe it's a big-brother thing, even though you're only two years older and actually smaller." He kicks some thin gravel at me, lining up his shot. "But it seemed like all the fighting would make you, you know . . ." He shoots and the ball arcs and hangs heavy on the rim above the garage door before falling in. It lands on the concrete with a plop and doesn't bounce. "Invincible. Isn't that the point?"

The house smells like nothing. But I'm sure it smells mysteriously like me, like us, like Littles. We cart the bags downstairs, where Denton's room has expanded to include almost all of what used to be the basement TV room where we'd watch movies all day every rainy summer day when Dad was at work; the room where Dad watched NHL playoff games late at night a few months after Mom died so he could be close to us and sleep with Denton if he had to, because of Denton's nightmares. I'd stand right behind Dad, biting my fingernail skin through overtime when I was really supposed to be sleeping. He never knew I was there, or if he did, he secretly approved.

My room, though, is just as I left it, only cleaner. I hoist my bags up on to the bed and check things out as Denton sits on the stairs, watching me. I stick my thumb towards the TV room and give him the old I-didn't-know-you-were-a-carpenter face.

"Your room is always the cleanest in the house. Dad actually cleans it."

After Dad got out of the hospital, Denton explained to me how fragile he had looked, and helpless. He couldn't understand how I could stay away, how I could *go on living* in Boston knowing our Dad could die. What kind of person was I? What did I think living was all about?

My Tae Kwon Do belts, from white to black, are still nailed to the wall in sequence, and my medals are hanging from a big silver hook above the headboard, where Catholics hang crosses and pictures of Mary.

"It is clean."

"Well, Jeremy. Drinks?" I nod and he turns and stomps up the stairs in his shit kickers, banging the wall as he does it. I think: my brother is 23 years old. He yells, "Come on up." I do, but he stops me as I walk through the kitchen into the living room. "Close your eyes."

Just before I close them, I peek into the living room and spot the watercolour painting of my mom and me and the little garden she used to have on the side of the house. It's a poorly done painting of bleeding pastel colours, but I can see and smell and taste the day it represents, the days. Sun glitters off the bumper of a Datsun you can't quite make out. Mom kneeling in the dirt, one of her hands underground and the other one scratching her head, looking back and up at me in the painting, about to say something. Jeremy, are you helping or what? She's wearing a blue halter top and long, dirt-stained pink gardening shorts. Her legs are plumper than they really were, and the bottoms of her feet are filthy. She is tanned, with blonde hair way up in a messy bun getting messier as she scratches it, and these huge white-framed sunglasses darker at the top and lighter at the bottom. I know silver stickers in the corners of those glasses said her name: Linda. Not much older than I am now, 28 or 29. She looks up at me and you can't see my face but I'm holding a garden shovel full of dirt, wearing uneven cut-off shorts and no shirt, sticking my belly out, evidently considering worms. Considering worms and maybe spaceships like any proper seven-year-old does most sunny days alongside carrot and tomato plant gardens.

"Can I open my eyes?" Something is panting, Denton is whispering.

"No," he says. "Put out your arms."

I do, and there's a puppy in them. A supercharged Jack Russell with a brown head way too big for its body, blinking and shaking, licking at the air and whining.

"We got him two weeks ago. He still lives in the porch and shits on paper, he's so small. Is that a surprise or what?" Denton's hands are cupped in front of his chest.

"What's his name?" I put him down on the light brown carpet; they ditched the green shag.

"Panther." Denton's new blue eyes sparkle.

"Panther?"

"Good name for him, eh? I mean, just give yourself five seconds and take a good look at him and you'll see what a perfect name it is." Panther runs head-first into my ankle, rolls on his side, and bites his paw.

"It's a pretty good name."

"Yeah. We were watching a nature show one night, and we figured it'd be perfect. Jeanette doesn't like him so much."

I was waiting for him to mention Jeanette. "Is she around a lot?"

Denton walks past me, into the kitchen. He takes two glasses out of the cupboard and pours two Scotches. "Dad's happy, Jer. He's happy."

In Gordy's, Denton looks huge. After the Scotch and some discussion of Gwen, we decided the bar was the best idea. Gwen is another one of the bartenders, a student, and Denton is in love with her. They dated for a couple of months and then they stopped because she felt Denton – her boss – was smothering her. According to Gwen, he was in too deep. Right now, he stands on the public side of the bar, chatting with her, making fun of the karaoke singers, shuffling his feet, drinking his beer slowly. She has a rounded, sympathetic face and big eyes over which she wears Lennon-style silver-framed glasses. Tall, almost thin. I imagine wedding pictures.

I am sitting at a wobbly table in the corner. The bar is about half-full, dark and smoky, with an empty dance floor at the back surrounded by some video lottery terminals. In the middle, standing in something like a DJ booth, a skinny guy in tight jeans – the karaoke host – tells a joke about fat women and almost everyone laughs. There is a lot of smoke in here, and the windows are fogged. The host reminds us that we can either fill out the cards or come right up and request something, anytime, and then he breaks into a Motley Crue song. I look over at Denton and lift my beer. He lifts his. Gwen lifts hers.

A big screen displays the lyrics at the bottom of a crappy video inspired by the song. Just below it, Diane Bélanger, a woman I recognize from high school, stands up and waves. I wave back. Denton brings me a fresh beer and tells me things are going pretty good with Gwen. He asks me if I think Gwen is pretty and I tell him, yes, she is very pretty.

When the Motley Crue song is over, the karaoke host urges us to please request some songs and get up there and sing so he doesn't have to do it all night. Then he leaves the booth and there is silence for a while before The Tragically Hip come on. Karaoke on hold. Diane comes over and looks down at me.

"Hi Diane."

She smiles and butts her cigarette in the clean ashtray on my table. Nodding, she blows the last puff of smoke she'd been holding inside. "I was just telling the girls, hey, that's Jeremy Little over there."

"Yep. It's me."

"You back in town for good, or?"

"I don't know yet."

She nods some more, and pulls her shoulder-length black hair behind her ears. "You're in business or something, right? In the States?"

"No. I was living in Boston. No business, though, not really. For the last few years I ran a self-defence school, but I failed at that. Did you want to sit down?"

She smiles and teeters a bit. It's obvious that she's been drinking for a while tonight, but so have I, so maybe it's me who's teetering. Tracy Lozinski walks behind her and pats her on the shoulder on the way to the bar.

Once Tracy is safely past, I say, "She seems to be taking things well."

Diane nods and starts a new cigarette. "You look different."

In my three years of high school, I think I spoke to Diane Bélanger four times, all unavoidable encounters involving line-ups or group presentations. Diane was the good-looking girl with brains, the Students' Council President, starting forward on the senior girls basketball team. For several very important reasons, I was afraid of her; she was too pretty for me, too smart for me, too *taken* for me, and she was Tracy Lozinski's best friend. All of this aside, I act as though we are old pals, or at least acquaintances or minor associates, since that's what she seems to be doing. Unless she has me confused with another Jeremy Little. "I'm seven years older."

"Don't remind me," she says.

"You can sit, if you want."

She's definitely smashed, making eye contact with a spot in

the middle of my forehead. I check for a pimple, but everything's okay up there. She reaches out for me, for my face, so I lean back and take her hand. A reflex. It always amazes me how clumsy and obvious people are, when they try to touch one another. "You have a scar above your right eye," she says.

"Yeah." I give her hand back. In chemistry class, where I sat in the desk behind her, I was forced to shield my crotch area with a textbook when I thought about her too much.

The karaoke host begins talking again, and Diane turns away from my forehead to look at him. She claps, even though no one else is clapping and there's nothing to clap for. The faded Levis fit her very nicely, they always have. From the side, I remember that Diane has a long, attractive horsiness about her face. I want to ask her, again, if she'd like to sit, but before I can do it she walks back to her table. To join Tracy Lozinski.

The microphone squeals and the skinny host pumps his arms and says, whitely, "Are y'all in da house? Don't diss our homey Travis 'cause he's in da house."

Travis Many Fires gets up from a table where he has been sitting alone. Most of his table was blocked by a pillar so I didn't see him, not that I would have recognized him anyway. His head is shaved dark and shiny, and his right ear is riddled with earrings. Someone, another woman but not Diane, claps and says, "Woo!" Although he was always short, Travis seems shorter than he used to be. He's wearing baggy blue jeans and a black t-shirt with a snowboard logo. I smile at him but he's under the spotlight so he doesn't see me.

To an orchestra background, Travis sings *Fight the Power*, the Public Enemy song, lounge style. He changes his voice for the Flavor Flav parts, and points at the crowd, smiling and winking and thank-you-very-muching as he says the damning white-people stuff about Elvis and John Wayne being racists and suckas. I'm glad to see Travis and I'd like him to notice me. The odd hip thrust, lots of winking, some jacket swinging, and at the end he's down on one knee, covering himself with the leather jacket, whispering into the mike. I can't understand what he's saying. A few people clap with me and Travis is out the side door, blowing kisses, before I can get his attention. I look over at Denton and he's smiling. He comes over and leans beside me. "Many Fires has left the building," says the host.

"Travis."

"Yep," says Denton, "that's Travis."

"I thought he was on the west coast somewhere. What's with the shaved head?"

Denton looks back at Gwen, and turns slowly to me and shakes his head. Adjusting her glasses with one hand, she throws a wet rag at Louis, the other bartender, with her free hand, and laughs. "I don't know. We don't talk too much."

"I gotta call him tomorrow."

"Yeah." Denton punches my leg, crouching now. "You know, Gwen and me are great chums. We've been chumming it up like wildfire over there and do I ever fuckin' love it. Hoo, boy."

"That's sarcasm, right?"

He stands up. "I guess my sarcasm needs some work. You never used to check with me about it."

"It's the Americans," I say, finishing my beer, which is wet on the outside of the glass, the way beer looks in commercials. "They just aren't a sarcastic people. I need more practice. It's not you. It's me."

"How about you and Diane, tiger?" He smiles, and blows a *herm* out his nose.

"She looked at my forehead for a while, it was pretty intense. Why? What's wrong with her? Is she married?"

"No. Just a barfly, kinda. Drinker, sleeps around a bit, I think. She has a kid though, her and this guy Trent from the city had a kid. The kid lives with Trent. Her parents support her, as far as I know. They have money."

"I remember."

"Yeah." He watches Gwen, who pulls some glasses out of the dishwasher. Off in Gwendale, interim capital of Dentonness, he walks back to the bar. Gwen looks up at him sweetly, so I stop looking. He returns with another beer that I shouldn't dare drink, and the tireless karaoke host starts into an AC/DC song. The booze plateau I suspected I was on hasn't proved to be too rock solid; if I drink this beer, someone will have to call an ambulance. Everyone in here, as I look around Gordy's, is as drunk as I am or drunker, and they all seem so very comfortable, as if their seats are *their seats*, talking about trucks and men and women and babies, a few of them probably picking through some up-to-date Nick Lozinski stories as Tracy sits a few feet away from them, drinking vodka and sevens. Most of these people are my age or a few years younger or older. If any of them have jobs, they should have been in bed at least two hours ago. I can pick out the oil-rig roughnecks in their sweats and running shoes and jean jackets and hats, looking like Denton but tanned, more worn out, far fatter than when I knew them in high school. Looking for what, here? Tonight? The women sit in the corner, around Diane and Tracy. Some handsome guy with a deep, raccoon-eyed skier's tan has ventured into the women's section, and he leans over one of the tables, and the women are being coy with him. I wish Diane would come back over here and be coy with me.

In contrast to the smokiness of the bar, the air outside is crisp and fresh, with a hint of pine and snow from the foothills and mountains. There are no stars above an eastern city, and no absolute dark like this. In cities, each light seeps into the overall yellow haze that is inescapable, a city lie that you forget is a lie. It is nice to understand a place again, to order it in my head, to feel as though I could walk home blind if I had to. I know in the south, behind Corinthia Elementary, it's nothing but hills and ranches, and that north is the city and east is the prairie. West, the hills. I know these houses as I pass them and I recognize the names on the mailboxes beside the front doors. Behind the Black Gold Centre where I learned to play hockey the strangers are sleeping in trailers, waking up in a few hours to set up the midway for Rodeo Days this weekend. The Civic Centre pond is completely thawed, the lights glittering off the water and off the long glass windows protecting the palm trees in the foyer where I studied for high school exams. I cross the weir. Cold and already smelly water laps at my feet, coffee cups and condom wrappers that had been buried in snow for months now floating dumbly beside the fountain sprays that will be turned on this Thursday afternoon – during the opening ceremony for Rodeo Days.

I take the long way home, the car way, and as I turn into our crescent I spit in the lawn-lover's yard; a man who poisoned my Siamese cat, Sam, for poking around in his garden. In one of the young family houses at the mouth, I can hear through the open screen door that some guys are listening to Led Zeppelin. They sing along.

There are yellowing real-estate signs in the front yards of the two houses beside the Plum House, with recently placed "fantastic deal!" stickers at the bottom of each, under the agent's name. I'm suddenly overtaken by an urge to walk on my hands, something I've only been able to do confidently for about a year now, so I go down. Of course I give myself too much momentum and my feet fall forward and I'm on my back, and the stars spin, and this is where the Northern Lights will be in six weeks. The fun part of being drunk is over, the rest is regret, more spinning. After years of hard work perfecting my balance, it feels queer to stumble on the way to my feet, to be uncoordinated. Once I am standing, I say, "Led Zep" out loud, just to say it, and then laugh at myself for saying it.

The bright police tape dangles in front of the Plum House. The old tree has a red Dutch Elm Disease ribbon tied to one of its branches. I walk around to the back yard. Street lights on the crescent and on Black Gold Drive throw trick-or-treat shadows into the overgrown grass surrounding the wispy skeletons of the old plum trees and shrubs that Joe pampered like newborns. The back porch has slumped in, the wood rotten and soggy; winter-dead weeds droop between the boards. I step on it and it gives, like skin on cooked pudding. A mean family of wild cats lived underneath this porch. Jeanette used to feed them.

Planks have been nailed across the massive back door where wreaths of wildflowers used to hang, and a DANGER: KEEP OUT sign is attached to one of them. If Dad put up the sign, Denton should have reminded him that for teenagers, these words translate to, "Hey, everyone: come on in, it's a blast!" The burnt mattress and box spring and a few old chairs and couches that were also partly destroyed by the fire still sit near the dark garage. Thin twigs cover the garage, and some climb the trellises up the side of the house. Sheets of plywood and two-by-fours cover all the windows, so the house feels impenetrable from back here, yet a sour smell sneaks out through the cracks, a spring smell, the smell of active ruin, a dead thing.

I walk softly around the house, as if I don't want to wake it. Standing in front of the tarp for a few minutes, which shimmies in the wind, I debate going in. The smell from here is more powerful, somehow embarrassing. Since my stomach is already feeling prickly and brittle, since I am drunk, I tell myself to wait. This decision brings enough momentary relief to bring on another attempt at a handstand as I cross the street, but I'd rather not throw up. Instead of a handstand, I just smell the cigarette smoke on my fingers and on my sleeve, to clear my sinuses.

Water before falling asleep is recommended. But first I walk downstairs into Denton's room. His birthday was a few weeks ago, and he has some cards arranged on the headboard of his bed. *The Far Side* one I gave him is in the middle, and cards from Dad, from Gwen, and from people whose names I don't recognize, are all in a row. There is one from Ellie, with a recent picture of her propped up against it, a picture I haven't seen. Her thin lips are pursed in a controlled smile, and her sleepy blue eyes have the half-squinting squeeze of concentration they always have in pictures. I haven't seen this haircut, shorter, with a few strands pulled down at her ears for that feminine sideburn look. Of course she's wearing that black shirt I love, one button undone at the top with a flash of her gold necklace sliding down the front of her neck. Ellie and Rob Palford must have gone to a photography studio together to have the new pictures taken of themselves and each other. I'm glad she spared Denton the 8x10 of them cuddling. *I'm thinking of you*, she writes, in calligraphy, *and I'm sure we'll see each other again soon. I hope your father is well. Happy 23rd.* There is no joke or bad poem. The front is a black and white photo of a little boy peeking between two pillars, his pudgy face and hands covered in filth. It looks a little like Denton if he was a fat little boy – or at least that's what Ellie would have thought. They had a lot of fun together when he visited Boston. In the evenings, while I was teaching, they'd go out for drinks at an Irish place on State Street, and by the time I'd showered, locked up the school, and rushed out to meet them, they were already hammered. I just sat on the outskirts, sipping juice, laughing when they laughed. I listened to my brother's stories, realizing that Ellie, who'd been hearing them all night, knew more about contemporary Denton than I did.

His bed is comfortable. Snooping around might be fun, but I'm pretty lazy. I'll get up and look around in a minute or so, because I still haven't had any water. For now, I close my eyes. And even though things spin and I should probably go make myself throw up and get this over with pronto, I'm too comfortable here, in our warm house without smell. I'll wake up when Denton gets home. He can help me out.

[CHAPTER 2]

In the summer, while I helped her trim the front-yard pines she planted when I was born, Mom would sometimes wave to Jeanette or Joe Kravchuk, the people who lived in the Plum House. Our family called it the Plum House because Mom called it the Plum House. According to the kids in the neighbourhood, who called it the Kravchuk Mansion, it was a bloody place where children in search of overshot orange street-hockey pucks were snatched up and thrown into computerized raping machines before being sliced into thin strips for tenderizing.

Dad and most of the town called Joe Kravchuk 'Crazy Joe Kravchuk' because in the late sixties he lost his fortune on trifles. Until I learned what the word meant, I was sure trifles were robot dishwashers that rusted – their batteries too expensive – in the corner of a black and white kitchen. Joe was crazy because he never drove his 1963 Corvette convertible, and because he was allowing the most beautiful house in the county to decay. He was crazy because he played an organ on the back porch in the middle of the night, and because he grew a field of plum and cherry trees in his back yard, for *experiments*. It was rumoured in the schoolyard that he had been abducted by UFOs, that his brain had been replaced with energized alien clay. Mom said that after 50 years, Seymour was glad to see a less-enterprising Kravchuk, glad to see the family lose some of their money and all of their power. People were unfairly hard on them because William Kravchuk had been a ruthless and dangerous man; something neither Joe nor his pretty young wife Jeanette could help. Denton and I were always happiest to believe the stories we heard, and to lip off Crazy Joe, especially because Dad was on our team whenever the subject came up at the dinner table. Mom wasn't. She figured the Kravchuks weren't crazy at all but special, victims of strange times, the sad king and queen of Seymour.

When I was 12 and Denton was ten, Mom got sick. She had been visiting the doctor regularly, and things had been odd in our house – Mom would leave the room suddenly to lock herself in the bathroom and Dad would follow her and knock softly on the door until she let him in – but it was not something that worried me. I wasn't stupid. I was convinced they were holding back the news that Denton and me were getting a brother or a sister, and I wished they would just tell us and quit with the whispering. One day I got home from hockey practice and no one was home. I made Denton and me some Kraft Dinner and we watched TV until late that night; a Steven King novel had been made into a mini-series. At around midnight, Dad got home and told us Mom had a tumour that couldn't be fixed. We had been watching the horror movie so the news was unbelievable at first, like part of a story I could just watch, or listen to. Then he made us turn off the TV and he explained that she would *never* come home again. That night and the days following were chaotic and terrible. Dad was hardly home, Denton cried violently and wouldn't go to school some days and Dad didn't make him, and I wasn't interested in talking to either of them. Visits to the dark, moist hospital room didn't help. Either she was so drugged up that she could only talk nonsense if at all, or it hurt so much that she cringed and huffed and pounded at the sides of her bed, sweating, telling us to leave her. It wasn't her; I wanted to see my mom.

The week after she died, Dad was very calm. Then, for a while, when Denton and I were downstairs, we would sometimes hear him talking to himself and breaking things in the kitchen and living room at night, lamps and picture frames and glasses. He stopped talking to friends for a while, and it was my job to console Denton. The bed and the upstairs furniture he gave to charity, so we had to use the old stuff from the shed.

Simply this: my mother was gone and not coming back. It happens to everyone, but that didn't make it any less confusing for me, any less wrong. I was able to think of her alive somewhere, to think of times when she and Dad were out at a party and Denton and me were in bed, waiting for them. Until they got home there was no sleep, because what if something happened? A car crash or a random killing, news of a nuclear assault and I'd never get to hug them before it hit. But nothing ever happened, and they always made it home, and as soon as I heard the car in the driveway, Mom's voice upstairs, then, yes, sleep.

After she died I thought of her in this nervous way, as if she were late coming home from a party and I was waiting for her to open the door and whisper Hello, Hello sweetie, to the cat, so I could turn over and stop my heart from beating so fast, and breathe. Of course I knew she was dead; I had seen her so wild and so sick in the hospital that I had secretly, shamefully wished for it more than once. The school forced me into the counselor's yellow office once a week, with its dusty plastic plants and posters of sunsets and happy faces and quotes from the Bible, and the counselor told me about it, again and again, about how Mom was alive in my heart and in my memories yammity yam yam. I listened to the counselor – it was better than social studies – but what she had to say was pointless because I knew what I knew and I didn't need any help knowing it. My mom was dead. But when was she coming home?

For a couple of years after she died, I watched a lot of TV and ignored my homework because I knew the teachers wouldn't say anything; all they ever did was murmur and mouse around me as if I myself was dying. I stole chocolate bars and threw snowballs at passing vehicles from grater piles in the Rapid parking lot as the welfare families stood on their balconies and smoked and laughed. In social dance class I lifted Michelle Hadsworth's skirt and when she screamed I pushed her and called her a bitch. After a wrestling match, I punched Denton in the face and gave him a monstrous shiner on his left eye. Dad wasn't around much.

Halloween was always a big deal in Kravchuk Crescent because we had the closest thing to a haunted house in town. Every year teenagers got drunk and terrorized the Plum House, and no one ever called the cops. Joe would come out on November 1st, my birthday, and quietly clean things up. On the night before my 14th birthday, to prove something to Denton – who was genuinely afraid of Jason and Michael and Freddy – and for other reasons I can't quite remember, I toilet-papered the elm tree in the Kravchuks' front yard.

The next day, even though it was a Saturday and my birthday, I was outside washing our picture window because some kid had thrown eggs at it in the excitement of the Halloween vandalism spree. Dad was at the hall and Denton was at piano lessons. I was at the top of the ladder, trying again and again to reach a spot beyond my grasp, cursing the injustice of work on a birthday. There was a tap on the bottom of the step. "Excuse me, Jeremy."

And there was Crazy Joe Kravchuk. I'd never seen him close-up before. His nose was big and purple, and his black-grey hair was slicked back, wet. A black trenchcoat over a black suit. "Yes?" I was beyond thinking he was going to grab me, haul me across the street, and toss me into an anal raping machine, but I figured

I was minutes away from a lecture in the back of Chicken George's police car. I climbed down the ladder, politely refusing his help, and smiled as naturally as I could. At the bottom I wiped myself off and looked mournfully over at his white-striped tree. Had he stood inside while I violated his elm, watching me the whole time? Why hadn't he opened the door or a window, and yelled?

Crazy Joe held a canvas shopping bag, the kind Safeway was handing out to promote environmental awareness. Over six feet, Joe was taller than I expected, and underneath the suit, thin like a cricket. He stooped, and his eyebrows arched way over his eyes. "Joe Kravchuk," he said, offering his hand.

"Jeremy Little."

"Pleased to make your acquaintance, Jeremy." He held my hand as he stepped back and half-bowed. Cautiously, he switched bag-holding hands and wiped a red leaf off his shoulder. His wedding ring shone. "Wonderful autumn day, no?"

"Sure." I looked around to see if anyone watched us. It wasn't a wonderful day at all, cold and windy and on the verge of snow.

Pointing up at our window, Joe shook his head. "Disgusting and irredeemable behaviour."

Since he didn't make eye contact, I didn't feel as though I was included in that group. With conviction, I said, "Bastards."

He smiled at me. "I am here for a reason, Jeremy."

So he did know who'd done his tree. I was disgusting and irredeemable after all. "If you want some help cleaning it, I could –"

"I'm not here about the tree, son. But thank you for the kind and generous offer. Honesty is godly." He turned his big nose down and patted me on the shoulder. "I'm here because I want to tell you your mother was a fine and admirable woman and I'm terribly sorry you lost her."

"Oh. Thanks." No one had apologized for Mom dying in a while.

"I've been having the occasional discussion with the Chief, your father. He comes by the house from time to time, and –"

"You have?" This was hard to figure, since Dad still made regular reference to Joe as *the looney*.

"I have. And unless I'm mistaken, today is your birthday." He looked down at his shiny black shoes. His head trembled slightly. "Well, I thought it was high time you and I became better friends, Jeremy. Would that be all right with you?"

"Sure." I felt as though I should have said more, but I couldn't think of anything else.

"Good news." Then he pulled a wrapped package out of the bag and passed it to me as if it were too hot to hold in his hands. As I took it, Joe shuffled his feet as if he had to go to the bathroom, and looked over at the sun. The Kravchuks weren't rich like they used to be, but I knew they still had a lot of money compared to us, so I relaxed, suddenly happy and hopeful. "I hope this is suitable. I debated with myself about whether or not it was. Please, open it."

I did, slowly. The wind picked up and blew some of the wrapping away, and Joe went after it. The gift was the painting, in a gold frame, of my mom and me by the side of the house. Summer, with the sun so high, small shadows, lilac wind; her skin strong and her hair. Since Dad had busted or hidden the pictures of her, the memory of Mom in the hospital bed clenched and spitting, wearing a chocolate-coloured wig, had been winning a fight with the other memories of her, the everyday ones, memories of gardening at the side of the house.

Joe waddled back with the clump of wrapping paper in his hands, doughy-faced and warped, and I didn't know what to say. "I painted it," he said.

I thanked him and left him there in the front yard, so I could stand in the kitchen and look at the picture alone, and think about Mom. When I gathered myself together, feeling like the devil himself for toilet-papering Joe's tree and for saying all the things I had said about him over the years, I went out to clean it all up. But the elm was just the elm again, and our window was washed too. The ladder was tucked along the garage, where it belonged, and the ball of crumpled paper, with trains on it, was gone.

Joe presented himself at our back door one Sunday morning in February. It had been months since he had given me the painting, and out of fear and shame I hadn't made good on our friends arrangement. Denton answered the knock because I was still eating breakfast and Dad was at work. Pale, Denton walked into the living room – where we ate in front of the TV since Mom died – and said it was for me.

"Hello, again, Jeremy." Joe looked tired and he trembled more. His hair wasn't nearly as perfect as it had been on November 1st, and his nose was more purple.

"Denton, meet Joe."

"Charmed," said Joe. "Good-looking boys, aren't you? Strong."

Denton looked over at me with his mouth opened. "Crazy Joe."

I wanted to hit him for saying that, but Joe just laughed and nodded. "That's right, Denton my boy, that's exactly right." Joe stepped up and leaned against the kitchen counter and the three of us looked into our reflections in the linoleum for a while. "Cozy house you have here. Safe." Joe pulled his jacket around himself. "A place needs a good feel." He smiled at Denton.

Very uncomfortable with this, I wanted to take Denton aside and tell him not to laugh at Joe's nose or the way he talked. Making me proud, Denton just smiled warmly. "Thanks, Joe," he said.

"Denton. Jeremy. Is your father about?"

"No," I said. "He's working."

"He's always working," said Denton. "Dad's the fire chief of Seymour."

"I am quite aware of that. A noble thing, too. An adventurous career." Joe made a fist and shook it in the air. "Adventure, *life*."

"Yep," said Denton, grabbing himself a few Oreo cookies from the bag under the counter and unsuccessfully offering them to Joe before shovelling a couple in.

"Well, that's a shame," said Joe. "I'd really hoped he'd be home. To invite the three of you for dinner tonight. I'm planning on some Indian cuisine, and –"

"Pemmican?" said Denton.

"No, young sir. *East* Indian cuisine. South Asia." Joe's hand quivered as he unbuttoned his jacket.

With cookie crumbs flying out of his mouth, Denton said, "Yeah, we made pemmican in social class. It's not so hard. All you need is some dried meat, and berries, and some other stuff. The Indians made it because it didn't get rotten too easy." He looked over at me for approval, stuffing another couple of cookies in. I shook my head. He opened his mouth, displaying the chewed cookies. "What?"

"Dad gets off at noon," I said. "He usually sleeps a while before dinner when he works nights."

"Dear old Dad works shiftwork, doesn't he, boys?" Joe's smile looked pained, everything about him looked pained. He couldn't have been as old as he seemed. "In and out, shifting schedules, sleeping when he can. Sure, sure." He turned around and looked out the back window, moving to lean on the basement door. It was a cold, still day; the bright sun shone hard on the snowdrifts in the back yard. "It's Sunday."

"Yep," said Denton.

"You boys aren't churchgoers, then."

"Nope." More with the cookies. Since Joe looked away from us, I took the opportunity to slap Denton on the arm. He slapped me back and shoved one more cookie in just to spite me.

"Just as well," said Joe. "Jesus was a fine prophet but he wasn't a god. He didn't die on the cross, like you learn in Sunday school. Pontius Pilate and Joseph of Arimathea, they were in on a big scheme to help Jesus get away. His bloodline still exists today; it's one of the greatest-kept secrets of western history. And I'll let you in on a lulu if you two can keep a lid on it." He bent over Denton and whispered, "I'm one of the living descendants."

The sun disappeared for a moment and the kitchen shadowed as Denton coughed and stopped chewing. The last cookie he'd rammed in dropped into the shirt pocket of his pajamas. "Really?"

"I'm afraid so," said Joe.

"No way!" said Denton, slapping me with one hand and digging for his wet cookie with the other. He blew the fluff off the cookie. "Jesus."

"Dad comes home at noon and it'll be noon soon," I said. Obviously, Joe needed some air. I thought that Jesus stuff was an irresponsible thing to say to Denton, who was only 12.

Nobly smiling down on us, Joe took out his handkerchief and wiped his shoes, which looked as though they would be slippery on ice. "Sorry to interrupt your breakfast, boys. Enjoy your cookies, young Denton. Just wanted to invite everyone before I sent Jeanette into the city to pick up ingredients."

"Thanks," I said.

"Would you like to join her for the ride, Jeremy?"

Joe made me think of a car jack when the car is way up in the air. If anything slips, the ground or the car, *zing*. "I can't. Homework." Since Denton knew I didn't have homework, I gave him a glare to make sure he wouldn't be piping up about it.

"That's too bad. I'm sure you'll get along, though, just excellently. She'll be pleased to meet you both."

"We'll be pleased to meet her," I said. "And so will Dad."

Joe smiled. "Eight sharp, boys." He slipped his hands into black leather gloves and walked carefully out the door.

"Wow," said Denton, when the door was closed. "Our neighbour and Jesus."

"He was joking about that," I said, taking the bag of Oreos from him.

"No, he wasn't." And Denton was right. Joe didn't sound like he was joking. He sounded like a descendant of the bloodline of Jesus. Jesus Kravchuk.

Since it was only his second night shift in a row, Dad had insomnia, and he was angry. There was no way in hell, he said, he was going to the booby hatchery across the street. I told him that Joe said he'd been a regular visitor over there and Dad squinted his eyes at me and scratched his chin and said, "That man is so off his ass, it's scary."

Denton convinced Dad that we had to go, and he wisely held back the information about the bloodline of our Saviour; I had asked him to keep it as our secret, and he agreed. Dad asked what Joe had said about Jeanette, if she would be there or what. I told him that she would and that she was looking forward to meeting us and he said, "Cocksucker," and went into his room to try to sleep again.

Just as we were leaving, Joe knocked on the door, yelling, "Escort, sirs!" as Denton opened it. Dad wore thick, smoky cologne. Joe bowed and shook Dad's hand as if it were the best-feeling thing in the world, holding it for a long time as he told him how fantastic it was to see him on this fine winter's night and how winning the evening would be. Dad smiled and went quiet. Crossing the street, I watched Joe ahead of us, his hand on Denton's shoulder, hair fine like it was on my birthday, black suit again, black shoes.

Around the side of the Plum House and into the back door,

which opened into the kitchen. The windows were steamed and the cooking smells were round and spicy. A silver fridge had been built right into the wall, and pots and pans hung over a wooden island where silver bowls of mysterious food sat waiting. Joe took off his jacket and tied on an apron, calling Jeanette. In the entrance to the main room, she met us, reminding me of older movie stars with famous names, whose faces I didn't recognize at the Academy Awards shows. Younger than Joe. In the white high-heeled shoes that strapped around her feet and ankles, she was almost as tall as Dad. She tilted her head and said, "Welcome," smiling with dark eyes so small I couldn't tell if she was looking at me or Denton or beyond us both, at Dad. "Mr. Little," she said, and took Denton's coat. "Mr. Little," she said, and took my coat. She took Dad's coat with a nod. Red dress, silver necklace. The hot smells everywhere seemed to originate with her, all energy in the house with her.

Above the door that faced the street was a stained-glass window. The other side, the inside face of the brown curtain I had been looking at all my life, blocked the picture window. Everywhere in the warmly lit foyer was the reddish-brown of thick wood. Black and white photographs in carved frames. In the study, walled with religious books, a soft-voiced singer said something about the silver lining. I asked who the singer was.

"Chet Baker. My husband is nuts for him. Thinks they're secretly related."

We followed her upstairs, and she identified the faces in the old photographs, three generations of Kravchuks and just as many of her own relatives, who came from Poland. As she opened the doors to each bedroom, save one, the one that would eventually burn because of all of this, Denton asked questions about who slept where and when. I looked at Jeanette's legs, in nylons, as much as I could. Dad hung back. He said nothing.

Dinner was shrimp butter masala and lamb curry, with mango

liquor and nan bread stuffed with a paste I didn't understand. Suddenly aristocratic, I became careful with my posture. I pretended I belonged, I ate slowly, and I avoided second helpings even though I wanted more. Denton ruined my daydream by bringing up his concerns about pemmican, the Indian hunting staple. How could pemmican be left out in an Indian meal? Dad held a napkin in one hand and a fork in the other, sitting beside me, across from Jeanette. The table was heavy and wooden, the cloth pretty and complicated, the china and silverware old, etched.

After dinner, we sat in the study and listened as Joe explained his plum and cherry experiments to us. The idea was to fuse the plumpest and sweetest plums to make the perfect plum whose taste, he said, would be the key to *the mysteries*. We were all quiet for a few minutes after that. I squeezed Denton's arm so he wouldn't ask about *the mysteries*.

The three adults drank a lot of wine. Joe talked about music and dancing and food, about decency and a quiet love for life that comes with appreciating these three essentials. He told Denton and me that we might never experience true delight. Looking across us to Dad and Jeanette, who were in two antique chairs, their faces lit by the orange lamp, he said, "Somehow we have lost romance."

"Yes, I know, Joe," said Jeanette. "It's sad, isn't it?"

He stood up, fixing his red bow tie, and waved Jeanette over to him. "Let's show them. Let's show them how we dance."

"No, sweetheart," she said. "I'd rather not."

He turned up the music, slow jazz music. "I've stood up here, Jeanette. I'm waiting for you to dance with me. Please, dear."

"Later, Joe. We'll dance later."

"Excuse us, Jeremy, Denton, Glen," he said, and took her up out of the chair by her arm, hard but not so hard that it appeared to hurt her. They went into the kitchen together. The horn blew, piano in the background, then the singer – old feelings, sighs.

Denton sat back in the sofa, looking tired. Dad crossed his legs and looked into his wine. A few minutes later, Jeanette backed out of the kitchen, Joe danced up to her, and they clasped hands and moved around the foyer, the main room, together. Joe in his black suit and shiny hair and Jeanette tall and syrupy in her crinkling red dress, a peeled fruit wrapped in a picked flower – spinning. The music wasn't so loud that I couldn't hear their shoes clicking and sliding on the wood floor. When I saw her face, Jeanette's eyes were nowhere. After the dance, Denton and I clapped, and Dad clapped, and Jeanette sat down. I smiled at her and she smiled back. A warm, heartbreaking smile. I remember hoping, all night that night, that Jeanette was looking at me, noticing me, thinking about me and what I might be thinking. I wanted her to know I was 14, halfway to 15, not a kid, spry, and smart in school.

Not so long before we left, Joe put on an old waltz record. It was fuzzy but it still sounded good, honest. Romantic. Joe and Jeanette danced close for a minute, and then she stopped to take off her shoes because they were bothering her feet. Dad leaned against one of the bookshelves in the main room, now looking past his empty wineglass, at the dancing. I wanted to ask him what he was thinking about; he had to know, now, that these people weren't really crazy, that Mom had been right. Denton said he wanted to try, so Joe showed him.

In bare feet, Jeanette was about my height when I was 14. Just as I moved to ask her to show me, she walked right over to Dad, took his empty glass, put it on the table, and squeezed his hands. Joe called me over and he showed me how to waltz too, then I led Denton and he led me. Joe said, "Good, good, guys, that's fantastic," over and over again. A new song started up. I looked up at Joe, for encouragement or advice, but he wasn't watching us. I noticed that Jeanette stared at Joe with her little eyes as he stared at her, as she and Dad danced close and silent. Denton and I waltzed across the room.

On the way out the door, I saw Dad whisper something in Jeanette's ear. With his left hand on her right shoulder, his thumb brushed the front of her neck. He moved in close, not smiling, and said something into her ear. She placed her hand on the back of his neck and closed her eyes and leaned her head back. As he said what he said, her lips came forward as if they were considering something, those lips. Dad looked strong. I saw all of this over Joe's shoulder, as he gave Denton and me a basket of plums. Right away I bit into one, juice dripping down my chin, warm there in the cold, as the three of us walked across the street to our own dark house.

A squirrel makes an argument just outside the window, and there's a comforting house hum when I really concentrate, but our house and Kravchuk Crescent are so quiet I can hear my body ticking and thumping and gurgling away, talking to itself, reminding me that I'm a weak mechanical thing. It's completely dark in our basement and there's no clock radio beside the bed, so I can't tell the time. My skin smells like cigarettes. I have a headache, but not a bad one; just a dull, hollow reminder, like my sound, that I am here. Under my head is a towel, and when I slide out of bed I step on the rim of a garbage can. The taste of puke in my mouth.

Once I have made some coffee, I locate some vinyl chairs in the garage – where my white canvas heavy bag still hangs – so I can sit on the back deck. It is a cool morning, metallic and clean, dry enough that I might need some moisturizer around my lips until my skin adjusts to the lack of ocean. A train clickety clicks, wailing away across the street behind the Plum House. Dad always hated the conductors for blowing the horns all the way through town.

The sky is wholly blue and the Rockies are out, still quite

snowy. I sit a while, and I walk out on the driveway with my coffee. The Plum House is in silhouette, the sun directly behind it. The roof has partially caved in up front where the fire was, so the upper floor looks like an old man with his false teeth out. Here, the patch of grass at the side of our house where Mom's garden used to be should really be a garden again. Tomato plants for sure, and carrots and flowers. Maybe rhubarb and a raspberry plant on the east end, and even a plum tree somewhere if I can find a decent spot to grow one. A paperboy slouches up the driveway and sticks the *Seymour Star* into the mailbox beside the front door even though I tell him I'll take it. When I tell him thanks, flexing my sarcasm muscle, he turns and takes his Edmonton Oilers cap off and puts it back on again, and smiles, and takes off on his bike.

Above the *Star* banner is information about Rodeo Days, with some cowboy boots and snorting bull clip art, and a faded photo of the rodeo queen. Ellie is a graphic designer, and she would smile and shake her head at a front page like this, at these cowboy boots. The headline is, "Lozinski Hearing Monday." My heart doesn't go out to the man who pissed on me, and I take special comfort in the fact that although I'm not in the greatest position regarding accomplishments and future prospects, at least my here and now has nothing to do with prison.

From the driveway I can hear someone opening and closing the back door, walking on the deck. Panther barks. Hopefully it's Denton. Hopefully he'll be able to refresh my memory about how I woke up in my own bed with a towel and a garbage can set up for me, with the taste of regurgitated Pilsner in my mouth. As I approach the deck the Molson slippers tip me off: it's Dad. And I am caught without a strategy. He leans forward and looks back and sees me, and smiles. I smile back and he stops smiling. I wave. "Hi."

His light curly hair is up in a sleepy pompadour. In a blue

terry cloth robe tied off with a white belt from another robe. "Hi there."

Panther spots me and runs up to stick his nose between two wooden supports and bark. I give him my hand to lick. "Hi, Panther." Since there's no avoiding it, I make my way up the steps and on to the deck. And I unfold another chair and sit beside Dad, who has an early tan. Clean-shaven. "You stole my chair," I say.

"You got it from the garage?"

"Yeah." The sun is on my ear and neck now, perched just above and to the south. I look over at Dad, who takes a pull of coffee and crosses his legs. No potbelly. While the going's good, I could whip up some excuse about a package at the post office and hop over the rail, over the fence, to the Seymour Bakery on 50th Avenue for a doughnut. I would run the risk of Chicken George picking me up for wearing pajamas in public, but at least it would allow me some time to evaluate my position. My stomach bubbles and croaks. Should I be dumbly polite? Silent? Should I make some jokes? Invite him to pour coffee on my head and get this over with? A great man would never be in my position.

The back yard, I notice, has undergone some changes. They have gotten rid of the pussy willow tree whose leaves often clogged the eaves on the garage. The big circle of dead grass in the middle of the yard where our round trampoline used to be every summer is still dead, but somehow not as dead. And the fence is now completely chain-link. Since the grain elevator is down, I can see the big white H of the hospital from here, and the sign for the new Protective Services building. I look over at Dad to say something, anything, but the whistle of another train interrupts me. Panther begins to howl along with it, because dogs everywhere are howling; the Dobermans across the alley in the yard with the big fire pit, the old Rhodesian Ridgeback two doors down named Stone, who was a pup when Mom was still alive and who I'd hoped was still around, and some newer dogs I can't place. The train, obviously a little one, is almost out of Seymour now and the other dogs have stopped, but not Panther. He continues along, howling unevenly, looking straight up with that Easter Island head into the sun. I pet him and he finally gives it a rest; he ought to be embarrassed, like someone who claps too late at a play, but he isn't. He just gives the air between us a big lick. And in the stillness, the silence between my dad and me is as loud and stupid as it could possibly be. "I sure missed the mountains," I say.

"Was the train that loud when you lived here? Has it gotten worse or is it just me? All the way through town, that's no warning." He clears his throat, sleepy voice. "Blowing it all the way through, that's just dirty."

I nod. "Yeah. I can't really remember."

A bad engine on our street, parking. Someone walking up the driveway, maybe the paperboy apologizing for being short with me, or an Amway salesman; maybe someone with The Church of Jesus Christ of Latter Day Saints is coming for me since I'm back out west and they probably have a computer full of big shots like me who have failed, who crawl home feeling wounded, maybe, and open to salvation. Whoever it is, welcome. Welcome. Please, break up the party.

Denton. "Hey fellas," he says.

"Where were you?" I say. "When did you get up? Didn't you put me to bed?"

"About half an hour ago." He winks, and heads into the house.

Dad rubs his hands together. "I put you to bed last night, Jeremy." He sits back and rubs his hands some more and taps his feet, the slippers saying shlit, shlit, shlit. "I assume Denton stayed with Gwen."

"No."

"Yes."

"Oh, man. I'm sorry, Dad. I'm not usually –"

"It's all right. I do it for your brother all the time." He whispers, "Since this Gwen business started turning sour he's been coming home like that three, four nights a week. I went to check on him and there you were. Hell of a surprise."

"I bet. Sorry."

Denton comes out with coffee. I'm not so thrilled with Denton for letting me leave Gordy's alone, for staying at Gwen's so Dad had to put me to bed. "Did I get sick?"

He nods. "You gained some weight. And a scar. You *look* seven years older."

Denton laughs. Someone across the alley turns on the radio, the end of a country song. There is nothing to say, which is crazy because I've been gone for so long. I really can't think of anything to say, or ask, without making things uncomfortable. There are topics we can discuss and those we can't, and the topics we can discuss will inevitably web into those topics we are avoiding. Maybe that is why we don't talk. Or maybe we just don't feel like it. Denton laughs again and Dad looks over at me, his eyes sparkling and stern. To him, none of this is funny, and he's right about that. "So how long you," he begins, and takes a drink of coffee. "How long's a guy planning on staying in town, Jeremy?"

"I don't know. This might be a holiday."

"*Holiday*, eh? Sure, why not?" Dad stands and folds his chair before leaning it roughly against the rail. He opens the door to go into the house, then closes it again. "No. How's that? Denton said you lost your school out there a few months ago. What's waiting for you back in Boston? That isn't here? That gal there, what's her name?"

"Ellie."

"You two back together? That it? You American now?" He looks over at Denton and he must get some kind of signal, because he stops there. He does something behind me to make the broom fall over, then he says, "You had her picture on your chest last night. I wake you and you get spooked. Then you get sick, right there."

"In my room?" says Denton.

Dad nods. "I cleaned it. It was all over himself, mostly."

"Yeah, well, many thanks," I say.

The door opens, and he is in the house. After a minute, Denton unfolds the chair and sits beside me. He twists his toes into the mushy boards that need replacing. "There's good there, can't deny it. That's what you got wrong about Dad. He loves you is the most of it."

A plane flies overhead. When it is gone, I say, "What the hell does that mean?"

Denton doesn't answer.

Ten minutes later, Dad opens the door and asks if I might want to walk him to work later. He'll treat me to a hamburger on the way. He says it like it's his job to say it, which it might be. Denton says yes for me.

We sit at a damp, splintered picnic table behind the Burger Baron parking lot, and chow down.

Running blindly into a fight is a great way to ensure defeat. If there is a fight floating around between two people, there should either be avoidance or strategic attraction; drawing, feinting. With some people, the *topic* is unavoidable. Ellie would stare and stare at me if there was something to be discussed: fighting in general, a party I refused to attend with her, my intimation of her flirting in the office, me being too silent, maybe, or too frivolous and evasive about our future together. And our fights would be unnecessarily ugly. It's best to avoid talking about Jeanette, so at the picnic table Dad tells me about when he lived in dorms in college – all the crazy stuff he did like get together with his buddies and light up farts with Zippos.

I haven't had a burger in a while, and this one is wonderfully greasy, mustard and mushroom soup sauce and mayonnaise and fat dripping out of it, and processed cheese food hopping on to my fingers like wax. It's full of onions and a red sauce that is sweeter than ketchup. Chocolate milkshakes. Before McDonald's and Wendy's, this was the only real burger joint in town. All parking lot, with intercom menus that don't work and only one table inside. A little kitchen and a big sea of gravel in the centre of town.

Dad's hair is combed back with some gel that smells like Fruit Loops, something classy he must have learned from Jeanette. His khakis and his windbreaker fit him well; he looks good, better than I expected. After his stroke, Denton spoke about him as if he was almost dead.

He and Fred Carpenter, the New Sarepta Chief, are the only two paid firefighters in the County of Seymour. They work in shifts, Dad here and Fred in New Sarepta, because the phones are connected. They coordinate everything, keep the trucks and equipment in good order, and work with the Emergency Rescue people. They get, on average, one call a night from external sources and three a night from Emergency Rescue. There's hardly ever a fire. They open up quite a few pickup trucks after accidents, talk worried drunks out of killing themselves – Dad has taken courses – and rescue old people from non-life-threatening situations when the emergency meds refuse to respond to the stuttering repeat callers without any problems other than loneliness and maybe a misinterpreted doomsday warning on *Unsolved Mysteries* or the 11:00 news.

Dad asks if I think I'm going to give self-defence another try. After that, he asks me about my scar and tells me he wishes it had worked out. I admit to him that I sometimes hoped a bunch of people would get killed in Boston, people you wouldn't expect to get killed, rich people who could pay big fees for whole families to take all my classes. He tells me he thinks people, on the whole, feel safe, and I agree with him. Even Americans, with all the city troubles. He tells me people figure if they are going to die or get hurt, they are just going to die or get hurt. And he's probably right about that. He reaches over to touch the scar, and I let him. People love to do it.

And I tell him about the scar. About how Bobby Bullas was cocky and athletic, a bit bigger than me. On his registration form he wrote about boxing in school and about all the street fights he'd been in. The first night he was in class I explained that *it's possible* to defeat an attacker with soft motions, even though it's always better to throw everything at him, to make sure you get out of there alive. Bobby put his hand up and asked me to show him how *it's possible*. Because I didn't want to look bad in front of the class, I asked a big, clumsy guy to stand up on the mats and come at me with everything he had. I knew he wouldn't come at me with everything; some people just lack the bone for it. Very simply, I locked him up and choked him out. Then Bobby jumped on the mat and said he wanted to give me everything he had. What could I say? Fourteen students sat waiting. Bobby went into a boxing stance so I knew all I had to do was evade his punches and go downstairs on him. As I took him down, he caught me above the right eye with an uppercut elbow. The doctor told me afterwards that it was a one in a million shot, cutting as deep as it did. It healed bad.

"And he's the one who killed the kid?"

"Yes. Bobby Bullas."

"It's hard, that." After chomping away on my onion rings for a while, Dad looks up. "These are addicting me," he says. "Get them away." He dips them in ketchup and looks at his watch and I look at mine. "We'd better get on. I wouldn't want to have to fire myself for being late. Sorry, Glen, you're fired. I appreciate your frankness in this matter, Glen. No hard feelings?" Standing up to empty his tray into the garbage, he breaks into a deep, wheezy laugh, staggering around, picturing himself taking himself aside and firing himself. I can't help laughing too. He's addicting me. The sun is warm even though it is almost evening. Cars with their windows open are playing contemporary country hits, awful stuff. What happened to real country music? Everyone listening to the same song, the work of CIKN. A tiny woman wearing a baseball cap drives by in a pickup, singing along, loud enough for us to hear. "I sure like this song," says Dad, wiping his eyes with the clean half of a mustarded napkin. "Jeanette hates it." A little yellow spot transfers to the bridge of his nose and I decide not to tell him about it.

We walk through the downtown core of Seymour, the intersection of 50th Avenue and 50th Street. Banks and a Dairy Queen and a PetroCanada station. Down the Avenue, main street, we pass the hair salon, the old Waldorf Hotel that is now a Chinese restaurant and a bar, a liquor store and a video store back to back, and a couple of women's clothing shops, one discount and one not, flanked on the corner by the old McClelland's drug store. At the railroad tracks, we turn right to get to the fire station. A couple I don't recognize walks up the street, their hands in each other's back pockets, and the man waves to Dad. As the paved road ends and gravel begins, we walk alongside the tracks, the weeds, the fence, street lamps, electricity poles. Only the sound of crickets now, and some other cricket-related creatures who must be hanging around on the other side of the tracks, on the shore of Belvedere Lake – the real lake in Seymour, which is a swamp. Dad unlocks the station. "You wanna come in for a second?"

Shrug. Nod. I do. The air inside is rubber mat, dust, coffee, oil. I remember Saturdays when Denton and I would help Dad wash the trucks, Mom in a lawn chair on concrete with her Linda glasses, facing the railroad tracks and the north-end grain elevator that said SE MOUR because the Y had faded. The sun would be out, full and thick and lazy, then suddenly behind a cloud. We would be soapy shadows then, watching the street two neighbourhoods away bathed in it, lucky *there*, the horizon shimmering with heat like it does everywhere in the prairies. But it would not last long. The sun would be back soon enough. Truck-washing Saturday always turned into big waterfights, but Mom was usually off-limits because one time Denton got waxy water in her eyes.

The trucks are smaller than I remember them, colours have faded. Dad takes off his jacket and calls Fred in New Sarepta, so I clomp up the stairs and lean on the pole, looking down at the cement one floor below. It occurs to me that this pole is useless since nobody sleeps up here and the lockers are all on ground level. It's a storage room. Oxygen cannisters and boxes and hose. Dad hangs up. "Jeremy?"

"Up here."

He walks underneath me and looks up through the pole hole. "Fred says hi."

"Hi to Fred. Dad, why is there a pole?"

He kicks at it. "There's always been a pole. It used to be your babysitter. It's for sliding, you know that."

"But nobody's ever up here, to slide down it in an emergency. All the volunteers live –"

"We used to play poker up there, on Friday nights."

"But that's only one night. Otherwise it's useless."

He kicks the pole harder, without looking up. "It's history, tradition. Firemen slide down poles. What's so hard to understand about it? They don't have fire poles in Boston?"

"No, I'm sure they do."

"It's no dumber than making a job out of training people for a bunch of fights that'll never happen. Unless they make them happen, like your boy Bobby."

I'd like to mention something about him making a certain fire happen, but I don't. Instead, I say, "Beep, beep," and I slide down the pole. It is fun. In his big fireman boots, Dad is a bit taller than me. I follow him into his office, where he sits behind the metal desk. The box of sugar cubes, the smells, the crappy radio in the corner. I put on his helmet for maybe the 200th time in my life.

"If you're planning on staying awhile, we're starting a new volunteer training program in a month." He takes some papers off his desk and stuffs them in a drawer. "Not that you're staying." More papers, some into the garbage. He turns on the radio, CIKN, and folds his hands on the desk. "Looks like Dents is gonna give it a shot. Remember watching the guys jump into Alexandra pool with full gear on? You get to do that."

After returning the helmet to its spot on the door, I smile at him and leave the office. To inspect the firetrucks in the dark of the garage. "I'm gonna go home now," I say, after a while, from the garage.

"Take it easy, then."

"I will. Have a good night at work." A heater clicks on above me. I can hear him sliding something around on his desk.

"Probably won't be any calls. Tuesday."

"Well. Have a good night anyway." I open the door.

"I will. Thanks. You too, eh?"

"There's mustard on your nose, Dad," I say, before I'm all the way outside. He says something else, but I can't hear it.

It's cooler now, but pleasant. The sun has eased below the tips of the mountains and the still-leafless trees have a cautious and awkward look to them, as if they're preparing to dip their toes in the water. I jump the rock-scraped hopscotch in front of the second-hand clothing store that used to be the Masonic Hall before they built the new one near the Willow Ridge Elementary school. The tree I used to climb in the yard surrounding the boxy United Church is as inviting as ever, and the old theatre, where

Dad tried to take Denton and me to see *The Empire Strikes Back*, is now a dog-grooming school. The Native Friendship Centre has some posters on it, advertising a sun dance next month. I run across Black Gold Drive and down the bike path, all the way home.

Because of a phone call Mom couldn't take for him, we were late for *Empire*. The line-up was already around the corner by the time we showed up. Dad tried to make it up to us with some ice cream cones and jokes.

Since I was that kind of eight-year-old who would, under pressure, sometimes say, "I hate you," to the people I loved, I probably said it that night, to my dad. No, not probably. I remember. I said it.

[CHAPTER 3]

When I was 18, what kept me up nights was the magical possibility of flying far, far away from Seymour. I applied to universities in Vancouver and Montreal and Halifax, and my drama teacher – Sandra Keating, whose twin daughters I babysat twice – convinced me to take all the American tests because her brother was a dean at Boston University. He could get me a fee remission, and maybe a scholarship of some sort.

They actually burned witches 20 miles north of the city! When I was 18, Canada was an unpopular blob, a cold Nowhere to the people who really mattered in this world: Americans. No wonder I couldn't sleep.

I got into Boston University with a modest scholarship and free tuition. Mom's parents, the grandparents I never met because they died in 1970 – the year before the year I was born – had been relatively successful architects. With some of the inheritance money, Mom and Dad started an education fund, and by the time I left it was well over $100,000. It was enough. And Dad wasn't denying me much in July of 1990.

Seymour does not have: cobblestones and spiderweb street patterns, a waterfront and an ocean, anything Victorian, magnolia trees blossoming pink and white. Part of the scholarship was a guaranteed part in every junior play in my first year, so I had a lot to think about with that and my regular academic classes. Twice a week I went to a nearby Judo club to keep in shape. Judo, a grappling sport, was a nice change from Tae Kwon Do, which is all about kicking.

It was hard to concentrate, and difficult not to think romantically about the Charles River and Paul Revere's tomb. But I did my work and I talked to a few people in the play – a student-written piece called *As I Lie Dying*. One day in November a girl named Pascale asked me out on a date; all semester she had been poking fun at my accent and the fact that I lived in an igloo. I had never been asked out on a date before, so I was both terrified and happy. Like almost everyone else I met, she was rich, smart, and loud. Pretty too, but I can't remember her face. Hair dyed popcorn-butter blonde, nice perfume.

Pascale drove us to the movie, *The Doors*, which I didn't like so much. It played in a downtown cinema and afterwards we went for a beer in a pub that didn't card students, with real wood inside and dartboards all over. Jim Morrison was the topic. I truthfully figured he was an ass and I hated the music outside of a few songs, but Pascale thought he was "deliciously radiant" and poetic and a genius, so I agreed completely. Listening to her go on about him, I somehow convinced myself that I'd liked the movie too.

Pascale said she'd willingly die young to live a life like his, and that she'd do just about anything to find a man like Jim Morrison. This bothered me, at the time, because no matter how hard I tried, I couldn't fancy myself anything of a Jim Morrison. As we drank beers, she asked me about Seymour and I didn't say much because Seymour, in my view, was an embarrassing place to come from, and my family was poor and simple and a huge mess at the time. Boston made these thoughts powerful. I told her, angrily, that I hated my dad, that I wouldn't care if I never saw him again. Then I heard about the great and perfect life she had lived, even though she didn't consider it so great and perfect, and her future plans for stardom in film and stage.

On the way out to the parking lot, arm-in-arm, walking in the light rain to her fast blue car, we saw a guy in a Red Sox cap pushing his girlfriend around. Slapping her against a car, calling her a bitch and a fat slut. Her hair was soaking wet. Pascale stopped and said, "Hey, you bastard. Stop that."

The guy looked over. "Yeah, mind your own business."

"Want us to call the police, woman beater?"

He leaned forward and his lips shot out as he walked towards us. It looked like he was ready for a smooch or a spit. He threw his arms up and cussed. It was dark, and as he splashed under the two or three street lights his shadow got longer and shorter, longer and shorter, faster and faster. He slipped off his jacket and threw it on the wet pavement. Moustache. He pushed his chest out, and he went right past Pascale. I backed up a bit, arms out. He rammed into me, shoved me back. "What's your problem, there?" Turned and spit and gave me the kill eyes. The girlfriend or wife ran up behind him, her hair shining. "Hit him, Rory. Smack the little shit."

I hadn't been in a real fight since Nick Lozinski beat me up and pissed on my head. Every opportunity I'd had to avenge myself, to fight Nick, had been lost. I would walk up behind him and a group of his friends where they stood against the lockers in the high school hallways during lunch hours, and Nick would be demonstrating a body check he'd thrown on some guy in the New Sarepta game, and he'd be so noisy and so tough and sure-looking that I'd hurry right on by, shaking, hating myself like Hamlet. I knew what it was; I was weak and he was strong. Nick would succeed and I would fail. Society stratified itself naturally; there were lawyers and there were janitors; there were Nicks and there were Jeremys.

And there were Rorys. In case I hadn't heard, Rory pushed me and asked if I had a problem again. Tiny red eyes, his nose twisted up and pumping as he asked me, to make triply sure, what my problem might be.

Looking back on it, as I have done hundreds of times, there are many things I could have done. Most generally, I broke a huge rule: never let an aggressor walk unchecked into your space. I allowed Rory to cross the first three ranges of combat without preparing to defend myself, without intercepting him. In the seven years since that moment, I've practised every possible manoeuvre to stop Rory, to trap Rory, to lock Rory up, to blind him, to break his bones and skin so he would never consider asking me about my problems again.

"No," I said, looking away, at a puddle. Big waterdrops from an awning splashed into it. I didn't even try.

"You sure?"

"He's sure," said Pascale, behind him. "Go on now, Rory. Big hero. You too, smart Suzy."

Rory blew a few more hot breath clouds into my face, garlic sausage and beer breaths, water dripping off his cap, before turning around, picking up his soaked jacket, sliding his arm around smart Suzy, and hunching away.

In the car, after changing a gear, Pascale put her hand on my knee. "It's okay," she said. "It's better that you didn't fight. You might have gotten hurt." Of course she was thinking about Jim Morrison, what he would have done. I figured she'd be thinking, hmmm, smart Suzy isn't so dumb after all.

I pushed her hand off my knee. A coward. As Rory threatened me, I had felt nothing but fear, fear of punishment from one of the strong men. I said nothing to Pascale, not even good night when she dropped me off.

Suddenly I hated Boston. I missed Denton. After finishing *As I Lie Dying*, I started missing classes to be at the Judo club more often, to fill every available hour with defensive throws and take-downs. I hadn't learned my lesson; I had allowed someone else to piss on me. If this continued, my life would become a long string of humiliations and robberies. No one could possibly admire or love the Charlie Brown, the Gilligan I was becoming.

I missed most of my Christmas exams, and when my drama teacher saw me on campus, she asked questions. As I stood in front of her, waiting for my turn to talk, I decided a few things. School wasn't for me. After something like a pep talk that I wasn't paying attention to, she shook her head and asked me what I thought I was doing here then. Good question, I told her. "Pot head," she said. So I started packing.

I didn't tell Denton about dropping out, so the education money continued to flow from back home. To my new address near Boston Garden. I saw ten movies in the span of the holiday and treated myself to hamburgers for Christmas. It wasn't hard to find a job in Boston. I cleaned offices in an ugly brown building full of real-estate and telemarketing companies from 10:00 pm to 5:00 am so I could learn how to fight all day long every day. That was my first Christmas without snow. In Boston, everyone was happy and healthy and full of good cheer. I started work January 2nd. Jeremy Little, janitor. Virgin and janitor, in America.

The first light of morning meant quitting time. The sun would roll over the ocean into the big window on the ninth floor and I would sit in a leather office chair and watch until it hurt my eyes. I made it home at 6:00 am, slept a little, did Savate from 11:30 to 2:00, practised Muay Thai from 3:30 to 6:00, went home, slept another hour or two, ate dinner, worked out, and off to work at 9:30. Weekends were Judo.

The Savate – French kickboxing – taught me how to read the chest because the arms and feet are too fast and can hypnotize. It introduced me to boxing, and helped my balance because the kicks are so fluid and precise, toe attacks. Muay Thai, with its cruelty, its elbows and knees and shin kicks, had something so savage and obvious about it that, if nothing else, it taught me not to be afraid of pain. Every now and then I'd get a knockout shot in Savate or Muay Thai class and I'd feel dumb for a few days. Once I stopped seeing colour for a whole afternoon.

I worked and I trained and I was miserable. Although I told myself there was no time for friends, I saw every major movie and I'd been around to almost every popular club in Boston, alone. Sometimes I rode the T and walked along the Charles at night, just to see if anything would happen to me. Provoking tough-looking guys with eye contact. Once I called a party line to talk to a girl and there were no girls on the party line, one older woman and a lot of guys like me. At work, I read fighting books. Signs of aggression were suddenly everywhere, boxing rings, wrestling squares. How had I missed it? Fighting was all. Every time I touched someone in martial arts class, I turned it inside out. What's happening here? Here?

After following my pattern for over a year, I passed out in the middle of a sparring match and Kit, my Muay Thai instructor, called my boss and said I was sick. Kit took me to my apartment and I slept 22 hours. I got fired.

Kit hired me as secretary, accountant, janitor, promoter, and training dummy. I slept nights again. Weekends were free so I could train at the Judo school. Out of weakness, I bought a TV and a VCR.

One summer Saturday I was the only one who showed up for Judo. My instructor, Yukio, worked with me all afternoon, teaching me locks and throws I hadn't learned yet, and we sparred to submission for a few hours, doing stuff you're not allowed to do in competition, older and meaner Jujitsu stuff. That afternoon, after showering and changing, I sat in the entranceway with Yukio, who was only a few years older than me, and we talked about fighting. I wanted to talk about women, about how anxious

I was about them and about everyone, really. About my life at that time. But I couldn't talk to Yukio about that.

Yukio looked and talked and acted so much like a martial arts instructor that it was difficult to see him as a man outside the studio. Judo was all he ever talked about; maybe it was all he ever thought about. I suspected this, when I looked closely at him, at the lines around his eyes. It's common, and an attractive way to live a life. If you want to be someone, why not become something?

A crewcut guy knocked and shoved his way through the glass door, wind chimes swinging, wearing jeans and a tight tank top. He asked if he could put up posters and Yukio very politely showed him where. His arms were covered in black, swirly tattoos and he had holes in his ears but no earrings.

"What's it for?" I said.

"Seminar with Steve Sutton." The guy, who had dark skin and big, black eyebrows, looked over at me and smiled. "You train with Kit, right?"

I nodded.

"I've seen you there." He pointed at me. "You're *crazy*, son. Muay Thai's evil. Evil like Iraq!"

"It is kinda evil," I said, leaning back and lifting my pantleg to show him my permanently lumped and purple right shin. My trophy.

"Evil!" He leaned forward and said, "You know, man. It's so hot out there my balls are drowning in a pool of sweat." Then he laughed and pointed at me and over at Yukio, who didn't think it was worth laughing about. "Tough room," he said, and tacked up his sheet, backed up, untacked it and retacked it. He repeated this a few times until he figured it was perfect. Without looking back at Yukio, he said, "So, Sensai, you own this place?"

"Yes," said Yukio. "Me and the bank, we own it."

"I hear you," said the guy. "I run a school near the

Commercial Wharf. By Columbus Park. I'm Garret." He shot his hand out and Yukio gave it a good shake and bowed.

"Judo?" said Yukio.

Garret smiled. "No, no. Not Judo. It's an integrated Kung Fu school. *Self defence.* I do a grappling class too. I'll be getting my Jeet Kune Do certificate from Steve Sutton before the seminar. Yeah, but I took Judo when I was a kid. It's good, *I guess,* if you ever have to throw someone or get some points or something."

Yukio cleared his throat. "Well, good-bye. Good luck to you."

After practically pushing him out, Yukio locked the door behind him. Martial arts communities are pretty ugly, especially among the mainstream city instructors competing for the same students. There's a lot of bitchiness, and always some patronizing comments thrown into otherwise pleasant conversations; which is funny, because so many of these same instructors never shut up about respect. Garret was new school. His kind of patronizing wasn't about who's the better instructor or who's had more training. Garret had no respect for Yukio because Yukio was in a Judo school. Worse yet, he was the head instructor and owner of a Judo school. And what can Judo get you? The same thing most Karate and Tae Kwon Do and Kung Fu schools can get you: a uniform, a hint of Asian culture, increased lung capacity, a few moves, and a false sense of security.

"Jeet Kune Do, eh?" I said, patting the back of the couch. I figured Yukio was pretty solid, he could take a jab here and there.

Yukio looked overdone, crispy. He lifted his stiff arm and tore the paper off the board. It hurt me to see him do it, because Garret had been so meticulous about putting it up. Yukio tore the paper into about 100 pieces. "I'll show him throws, the cunt." He crumpled the pieces into a ball and threw it at the garbage, where it hit the rim and bounced on the floor, scattered. Then he swallowed and looked down at himself and fixed his *gi.* Tightened his black belt. Swallowed again. "No, no. Not Judo, he says. What am I supposed to do? Close the school and run down to California to train with Inosanto? I can't do that. I can't afford it and besides I have students to think about. I'm a Judo instructor. What's wrong with Judo?"

The trick in fighting is to force a feeling of total relaxation on yourself so your instinct isn't hampered by tensed-up muscles and fear. When you're standing before your opponent a few seconds before a fight, it's pointless to strategize. Once the fight begins, training and experience have to take over. Nothing ever works as you plan it, and fighting, real fighting, isn't anything like it is in the movies. In the real world, guys can block your kicks and punches, and they're usually just as good as you are, or better. It isn't smooth, it's chaos, and it's hard to make your body do what you want it to do, what you imagined it could do the night before, because you're trying to protect yourself and hurt the other guy too, who is thinking the exact same thing you are. To reproduce relaxation, I always take a deep breath before a fight, and blow it out fast, choo. It works.

Yukio was as steamed, as emotionally out of control as I've ever seen anyone in my life. If he'd been a cartoon, smoke would have been blowing out his ears. Choo, I was thinking. Choo, Yukio. He fixed his *gi* some more. "What the hell am I supposed to do? It's too much." After a further stiffening, to what felt like the very brink of detonation, he slumped down against the wall, his head in his hands.

"You can't be an instructor of everything, Yukio. You're doing fine. You're a good Judo instructor. You've taught me a lot."

"Yeah well motherfuck that fucker and his Jeet Kune Do Integrated Kung Fu *self defence* grappling class. All these new shits. Walk in here, into my school, and insult me like that. I teach some grappling, he says. Well, let's hit the mats, I should have said. God, I wish I'd said that. Rip his arm out of its socket, the cocky ..."

I understood where he was. This was his whole life. I wanted to leave.

"What would you have done, Jeremy? If someone just stepped up to you and insulted your school like that?"

"I don't have a school."

"Say you did. And you poured everything into it. And then someone walked right in and made a big joke of it?" He looked up at me, his fists clenched. The soft-focus picture of his original master in the woven case above him, I realized, was crooked. "Of your life?"

Yukio wasn't talking about Garret any more. "It was over pretty fast," I said.

"One student today," he said, pointing at me as if I was a hunchback. "Not to belittle you, Jeremy, but one student?" He was silent for a minute before slapping himself on the head a couple of times, standing up, and fixing his *gi* again. Then he shrugged at me and smiled, probably embarrassed.

"I gotta get going, Yukio. It's my day off and I've got laundry. Dropping some stuff off for Kit later too." These were lies.

"Okay," he said.

As I slipped on my shoes, I looked back and Yukio stood with both hands under his chin, his rock-hard Judo hands, 12 years of Judo, crossed on his chest and holding his chin. There was a red spot on the wall just above the shoe mats; he may have been looking at it. I knew I would never come back to Yukio's school again. It wasn't fair of me to think what I was thinking.

"Hey, don't worry too much about it, Yukio. It's nothing, this."

"No, no. No. We'll see you next week."

"Sure," I said, and unlocked the door, and left. Pacing around the bus stop in the balls-drowning heat, I hoped Garret had left a pamphlet at Kit's gym.

Steve Sutton had a blond ponytail and a black sweatsuit with his name in yellow down the legs and across the chest and back. As we stretched, he played theme music. The Beastie Boys. In the sunlight that shone through the big windows in Garret's second-floor studio, Steve Sutton looked mean and dirty-faced, like a Hollywood bad guy. He used crew-cut Garret for all the demonstrations, and Garret cringed and yiped as Steve Sutton punched and kicked and elbowed him, and trapped him up and threw him into fierce chokes and leg locks.

Wing Chun Kung Fu is a Chinese system developed a few hundred years ago by a Buddhist nun named Ng Mui. She taught it to a young woman named Wing Chun, and the system stayed in her family for 200 years or so. Then, early in this century, Yip Man, a family member, moved to Hong Kong. A good businessman, he was the first to teach the system, originally developed to short-circuit the older Kung Fu systems, to anyone outside the family. It's short range, utilizing hand and foot traps to defeat your attacker as quickly and economically as possible. It looks vicious and simple, and it is and it isn't.

In boxing, two fighters hold their guards up, move around, and hit each other. They stay on centre as they stalk one another in circular patterns around the square ring. Wing Chun is also based on centre-line theory, but it is very different from English boxing. Since it is not a sport but a self-defence system, there are no rules in Wing Chun. If the attacker's arms are up, the instinct is to attack and trap them, to ensnare them – through one of several means – in the attacker's stomach or chest so he is momentarily immobilized and unguarded. If the legs are free, trap them with your legs and your in-close and very un-Hollywood-looking kicks so they can't be used against you. Then go on the offensive with a flurry of forward momentum until the opponent cannot attack you. The fist is most often held vertically, not like the boxer, and the Wing Chun fighter uses several open-hand attacks, like finger jabs and slaps, to stun and further disarm the opponent.

When someone grabs you, he gives you information. When he swings at you or blocks your real or feinted attack, he gives you something to trap, to lock, or to break. The empty hand system that Bruce Lee studied before he went on to experiment and fuse his own system based on improving *the system* – Jun Fan Gung Fu – and his own philosophy of fighting – Jeet Kune Do – was Wing Chun, under Yip Man.

Steve Sutton destroyed poor Garret again and again.

"Hit me, Garret," Steve Sutton would say, and Garret would take a breath and swing. Then Steve Sutton would back out of the way and say, "No, Garret, really. Really hit me." Garret would rub his scratchy head and buck up and really try to hit him and Steve Sutton would slip and move his hands so quickly and hit and almost hit Garret high and low, and smother and confuse Garret's tattooed arms and twist them and slap them around so many times that Garret would just crumple to the floor and put his guard up to make it all stop.

Kit and I went to the seminar together. Even though Kit wasn't nearly as serious and traditional as Tran or even Yukio, he was clearly embarrassed by Steve Sutton's profane and utilitarian demonstrations and lectures. By the Beastie Boys. This was not about meditation and life-enhancement, or about an interesting and edifying hobby for your kids. Steve Sutton was for blunt, calculated devastation. What works and what doesn't, strip everything else away. He borrowed shamelessly from several and mixed them up like a stew. He clearly respected Wing Chun and everything Bruce Lee did, but he was quick to make alterations and judgements about the old systems. It was all about the complexities of simplicity, about training to anticipate and intercept all attacks, about destroying the opponent before he has a chance to hurt you. Kit took me outside during the break and said, "This is sick, Jeremy. A bastardization. I'll have no part of it." He left. I got a new partner for the second half.

Sticking hands, *chi sao*, is simple, conceptually, but difficult to learn. Like all sensitivity exercises, you have to teach your arms to move and react based on pressure and momentum. Steve Sutton put on a blindfold and whipped Garret just as effectively as he did without the blindfold because a good fighter shouldn't necessarily have to see the opponent, only touch him, to get the necessary information.

After the seminar, dizzy with joy, with the intense beauty of what I had witnessed, I stayed to talk with Steve Sutton. Five or six guys surrounded him for autographs and I decided it was just as well because I had nothing to say anyway. Garret was in a corner, picking up some headgear and focus pads, moving like an old man who has fallen down the stairs. I walked over and introduced myself.

He looked down and rubbed his hand where it had been twisted too hard. "I'm Garret, this is my –"

"I know you. I met you last week at Yukio's Judo school."

"Judo," he said, as he bent over to pick up some fake knives. "Judo seems like a sweet and comfortable place to me right now. Just for five minutes I'm going to stand here and wish I was a nice, not-in-pain Judo instructor. Ooh, aaah. Judo. Counting to ten in Japanese. Stances. Aaah."

Once he was finished making fun of Judo, I asked him if he taught what Steve Sutton taught. He did, plus some Kali, Silat, Shooto, and Brazilian Jujitsu. We joked around for a while before I bought a three-month membership for a reduced rate, because I agreed to teach a Muay Thai class for him once a week. It was August, a heat wave, so hot and humid that all of Boston was out of breath and balls-drowning, seminar or not. Waiting for Kit to pick up his phone, looking out the window at the city below wiping its forehead and sighing, stumbling around in the heat, I smiled and decided that I was happy for the first time since leaving university. Kit's line rang and rang. I wanted to clear things up, so I wouldn't have to worry about how to clear things up. Breaking with a martial arts instructor in favour of a new one is like breaking up with a lover. There's no easy way to explain it. "I like this person better," is what we should say, but we almost never do. We make up excuses, webs of causality that make it look like we had no choice, really, in the decision – that it's beyond us and we're all victims in this crazy crazy little world. I hunkered down and told Kit I was going to train with Garret. He said he expected it and got quiet. I asked if he would fire me and he said, "No. Not right now."

In bare feet, I stayed in my studio apartment that evening and practised some of what I had learned, slipping around in the drops of sweat on the parquet floor. Listening to The Breeders. When people touch you, they give you information. What to do with it? Whatever it was, I vowed to do it, blindfolded.

That Christmas, Dad got an award from the province of Alberta for his good work in the community. Denton, who had decided to take an extra semester even though he'd graduated, finished high school and made the western Canadian all-star football team. They played one January game in a big, covered stadium in Vancouver. The Pacific Coast Americans beat our boys by eight touchdowns, even though they played Canadian rules.

Denton wasn't too hurt, though. He was going on to his fourth girlfriend. By January of 1993, my younger brother had slept with four girls; he was 19. In those days, my sex life consisted of the odd porno movie I would rent, shamefully, on the way home from the gym. The people above me screwed, it seemed, ten times a day; they filled me with it, frustrating my otherwise tolerable virginity. In a futon or another piece of wooden furniture, grunting, laughing, telling each other yes, and no, the woman's moans in rhythm with the hammering, crying out. Breaking my heart. They would stop and I could continue whatever it was I had been doing, watching TV or practising or reading a fighting book, and they would start up again, taunting me, smacking the floor and walls with open palms. I would imagine them in various positions, sweating, doing everything I wanted to do. Doing things I was afraid of.

The best attack is an attack by deception, so Garret and I spent hours and hours deceiving each other, manipulating each other's information. After the regular classes, he and I would swap techniques and ideas, and try them out on each other. We practised counters to every imaginable street attack: the pushes, grabs, punches, kicks, hair pulls and head butts, tackles, knife thrusts, eye jabs.

After some negotiations that I was a part of, Garret convinced a Brazilian Jujitsu fighter, Megachunk, to come to Boston for a seminar. Megachunk was tiny and muscular, a flyweight, and his English revolved around sex slang. Garret and I, by watching him, translated for the rest of the people in the room. Mount position was fuck position, 69 was 69. At one point in the day, Megachunk wanted to emphasize the fact that we should stay very close to our opponents at all times; space was bad, it created opportunity for strikes and counters. At one point in the afternoon, one partner was to be on top while the other was in guard position – a superior position a fighter can achieve while on his back – legs over his opponent's legs and hooked around him, above his ass. As in sex. The people who were unaccustomed to the intimacies of wrestling were uncomfortable with this. Megachunk stood up.

"I said the fuck. The fucking. The fighter, he wants to hurt you. Don't be afraid for fucking him." The studio went silent. Garret pulled me into him and the experienced students did the same. Six people left.

Every Saturday and some Sundays Garret and I practised grappling. The Judo was handy, but on the ground we fused Megachunk's Jujitsu with Shootwrestling; both incarnations of old Jujitsu, concentrating on top mount and side mount positions on the ground.

Since there was no air conditioning in the Waterfront Warrior School, Garret and I walked to the Common one Saturday. In a flat and open spot where no one threw frisbees or footballs or baseballs, we planted our bags and took off our shirts and rolled around together, practising our chokes, locks and other submission holds before sparring. After a couple of hours, when we were tired and not much good to each other, laughing and fighting for superior position on a hump of worn grass, someone threw a bucket of cold water on us. I rolled over – breaking the never-give-him-your-back rule – so Garret threw a rear-choke on me. After tapping, I flopped.

"That's really cute, guys," said a woman in cut-off shorts and a bikini top, spinning an ice-cream pail. "I thought I'd cool you off before someone was impregnated. Or was I too late? Anyone need a cigarette?"

Garret jumped up and stood over me, one foot on my chest, arms raised triumphantly. Then, to the woman, he said, in a John Wayne voice, "Come here, shnookicakes. You got what I need."

The pretty woman came over and rubbed the wet top of his almost-shaved head. "You stink," she said, and kissed him.

"That's what I do," said Garret, looking down at me, shrugging. At this point I was wondering why we didn't come to the Common more often, and how Garret had actually summoned a woman with the word *shnookicakes*. Before I had a chance to take

Garret down, he jumped off me. I stood up beside him and wiped some of the sweat and grass off myself. "Jeremy. This is my girl-friend Rachel."

Rachel said hi and gave me five. I told Rachel I'd heard lots about her, even though I hadn't heard much at all. Her dark hair was in corn braids, something I wasn't used to, and she was almost as tall as Garret, thin and birdy. Since Garret hadn't asked me for any money after the initial fee, and since he'd treated me more like a second-in-command than a student, I guess we were friends; but we didn't do much besides watching a couple of closed-circuit fights in sports bars together. How he felt about Rachel, how important she might have been to his life, what she looked like and what she did, these were things we didn't discuss. We talked fighting.

"Anybody here with you?" said Garret, poking her in the arm. As they talked quietly for a minute, I rolled over to my gym bag and finished my bottle of water. I made some notes about relaxed breathing and pulling your opponent down on top of you when he's choking you from mount position. Then, sitting back in the warm grass, I let the sun ease in on me. I wondered about Rachel and Garret, what they thought of me, since I was younger than them. If Rachel hadn't poured another bucket of water on me, I might have fallen asleep there, in the timelessness of a lazy sum-mer day. The water felt good. Because it seemed the thing to do, I stood up and pretended to be pissed off, and laughed. I took the bucket and was threatening to fill it at the fountain when Ellie showed up.

It was a set-up, I could see that. Garret and Rachel introduced us and walked over to the fountain to get some more water. I was nervous. The freckles that peeked out from above and below her sunglasses, over her nose, took away from the formal and intelli-gent air she'd developed at work. Hair very blonde, naturally blonde, and thin lips great for smiling. I told her I liked the blue

Guided by Voices shirt she wore, and she told me she wished there was a good place for frozen yogurt that wasn't too far away. We commented on the heat. She was pretty but not so pretty that I couldn't speak.

Rachel returned with Garret running behind. After dropping an arm around Ellie's shoulder, she said to Garret and me, "We'd like to take you two gladiators out to dinner if you'd consent to it." She was almost a whole head taller than Ellie.

"Does that mean we have to shower?" said Garret, wiping some blood off his chest. He'd given me a bloody nose earlier. Suddenly I felt like Garret and I were best pals, pals since grade two. It felt nice to have a pal, especially an immediately retroactive one.

"Can we go like this?" I said, highlighting the patch of dried blood on my shoulder framed by a long streak of grass stain. It was meant as a joke but no one laughed. I bent down and rifled through my bag for sunglasses.

"Of course," said Ellie, late, "it's only semi-formal."

With my pasty arms and chest, I wished I hadn't been such a vampire all summer. In the direct sunlight, I must have looked like Doc Hollywood or some other victim of consumption. No sunglasses, so I stood up. Subtle Garret and Rachel had abandoned us again, so I found myself thinking of something interesting to say. Nothing.

"You have blood on your neck," she said.

"I had a bloody nose earlier."

Then she did something. She licked her finger and wiped at the blood on my neck. Then she licked again and wiped more. She leaned in and breathed on my cheek. I thought of starving people and headless dogs to save myself some embarrassment.

"I'm sorry," I said. "Bad first impression. I need a shower."

She nodded and backed up. Smiled. "Don't worry about it, Jeremy. You look good, like you've been in the park all day, being a boy." One more lick and swipe. A relentless barrage. I had to get some pants on before she discovered my dink.

"Yeah." I took deep breaths, choo'd them silently. It would be nice if you'd lick at me some more, I was thinking. I was also thinking about how I was too nervous to think. I could still smell her, and I imagined some marvellous elixir was seeping into my pores, making things sweeter inside me. Even if it was just spit.

"You're a chatty one, aren't you?"

"Me? Oh, sometimes."

"You can't think of anything interesting to say?"

"No, I can't."

"Tell me about your grandchildren." She wasn't smiling.

"What?"

"Nothing."

"Did you ask about my grandchildren?"

"Yes."

"Why?"

"I thought it might be funny. You know the bumper sticker on old people's cars."

"Oh. Right, yeah."

"You're a quick one, aren't you? A major poet of some distinction." She punched at my shoulder and danced around a bit. Strong legs in soccer shorts, very tanned. "Are you as fight-crazy as Garret?"

I nodded. I guessed so. Smiling some more, she backed up and turned around and jumped in-between Garret and Rachel, who stood by a tree. I bent down and looked through my bag some more. Soon all three of them were standing over me. Garret dropped his foot on my shoulder. "What are you doing?"

What was I doing? Crawling into my bag? Looking for a disguise so I could Mission Impossible the hell out of there? I looked at my wrist for the watch I wasn't wearing. Smiling up at the three of them, I said, "Packing up. I gotta get going."

Garret dragged me away from them. "I asked you last night if you had plans tonight and you said no."

"I don't know." The sweat was making my hair itchy. Ellie thought I was stupid.

As if I was oozing pus from all orifices, he curled his nose up at me. "You don't know *what*? Are you blind?"

"I don't think she'd like me."

He pushed me. "Don't do this. We'll deal with your issues later. I was telling Rachel about you the other day, about how you never go out and how you're lonely and don't have a girlfriend."

"That's not true. I'm not lonely."

"Come on, Jeremy. You don't have to be Clint Eastwood around me. I know how it is."

"How what is?"

"Just listen. Ellie broke up with her boyfriend a couple of months ago, and she's sort of depressed about it. We figured you two'd be a good match. Don't you think she's beautiful?"

"Sure. But she called me a boy. And I'm not sure I like you talking about –"

"She's a girl with a future. Like you." He smiled and pushed me again. We fought so much, it was our default form of communication. "I don't see a problem here, sunshine. There's no reason for you to feel threatened."

"I'm not."

"Okay then." He cartwheeled back to where Rachel and Ellie stood, over my bag. I followed, just walking. "Well. He's changed his plans. He had these plans for a dinner with the mayor of Boston, but he's calling it off just to step out with you two ravishing lovelies." He put his arms around them and turned around again. The kind of guy men want in their clubs, Garret had a fine physique, an extensive knowledge of contemporary music, and an air of head-nodding effortlessness about him. He had *it*, the mysterious blend of moves and looks that makes one person in the crowd the very one who must be fixing you in the eyes when you have something to say, nodding sagely, the one who can justify you. A particular kind of power is what he had, and of course I wanted to have it; but I was okay feeding off him too, learning from him. Being his student.

Walking to her car, Ellie stopped me when I started to pull my t-shirt over my head. "No," she said, "don't do that," without looking at me. Garret and Rachel climbed into the back seat and Ellie pulled me around to the trunk. "You don't have to be nervous, Jeremy. They're not really setting us up. It's only dinner."

"Sorry if I get blood on your car."

From inside the 1984 Mustang, Garret yelled, "He always apologizes."

Sushi. My first time. Ellie wore a black dress with two crisscross straps across her brown, almost-bare back, hair tucked into a black comb like a dainty monster's hand. Hardly any makeup at all. As she watched me bite into the pretty flesh, I began to feel as though she were an accomplice; with the saki and wine, I ached for her in a way that made me want to go into the washroom and look at myself in the mirror for a while, to make sure of things. After dinner, we drove back to Rachel's parents' place. They were loaded and the house was enormous, like a castle. It was a warm, windless night.

We sat in a circle in the back yard. The lanterns shone off the little ripples on the surface of the pool. Once I started talking, I found it hard to stop, it rushed out of me. Shivering with my mom in Luna Lake just before sundown as she held me up before my first time waterskiing, telling me to stop being a baby and wait for the boat and thrust your hips forward but don't lean too far forward, Jeremy, or too far backwards. Yell when you're ready. You can do it, sweetheart. I told them she called me sweetheart, and regretted it afterwards. With my saying too much, the atmosphere changed. Garret went in to turn the music up, Pavement, and Rachel went in to help him. I was drunk. It took me a minute to realize Ellie was staring off into the fence, silent.

"You miss your mom?" she said.

And before I could answer, yes, I realized I'd made an error. Over dinner, she'd mentioned that her parents had "passed away." "I didn't mean to bring up families, Ellie. I'm sorry."

"I'm just drunk."

"Me too."

"It's sometimes easier when you're drunk and sometimes harder."

"I don't drink much," I said.

"Me neither."

There was some more fence watching, then. A few silent minutes of buzzing between us, over the music and the industrial coo of the pool. Even with the sad subject, I was wild for her. The lights shining off the water began to bounce with the music. "Do you want me to go away?"

"No," she said, and put her hand on my hand for a moment, and took it away. I wanted her to put it back.

Rachel came out of the glass doors in a yellow one-piece bathing suit. Another bottle of wine in her hand. "Last bottle," she said.

Ellie put her hand on my hand again, and stood up. Her bare feet ticked on the wet tile as she tiptoed into the house.

Swerving a bit, Rachel took a swig from the bottle before filling the four glasses. The music made me envy this life, this backyard pool life. It made me wish I had been a preppy too. "Where's Garret?" I said.

Rachel shook her head, whispered in my ear, "Oh, he's completely fucked."

Since *fucked* can mean so many things, I didn't know what that meant. It became obvious a few minutes later, though, when he screamed, "I'm the ruler of the lagoon!" from the roof of the house, buck naked, just before a backflip with an impossibly perfect genitals-first splash into the pool. I could see his twisted face even before he came to the surface. "Oh Lord," he said. "Lord."

Ellie ran out in a red bikini and dived straight into the pool. With a twisted expression of her own, she surfaced, splashing. "Garret's naked!"

"You betcha, baby," he said, apparently recovered.

Rachel and I drank another glass of wine each, and then she jumped in.

Ellie make a face and motioned me in with her finger. I took another swig of wine. The anticipation sent a shiver through me, betraying the fact that when we stopped at my apartment for a shower, there was no clean underwear in the drawer. "I can't."

"Why?" everyone said unanimously. Garret mumbled something about Canada that I couldn't hear.

"I'm freelance. No shorts."

"So?" said Ellie. "Stinky Garret's naked. Why can't you be?" What was with these people? Did they think this was a movie? I imagined my first naked experience with a girl to be in the dark, in a bed. Ellie took off her top. Then she went underwater and surfaced with the bottoms in her hand. "Now?"

I thanked God then, in my small way, for his blessings. As Rachel dunked Garret, who had begun to howl about Ellie's nakedness, I slipped my shirt off. Rachel crawled out of the pool and turned out the lanterns and we were shadows now, silhouettes. The glow of the city was just enough to keep the water sparkling. Under the surface, a dim pool light-blue that seemed to portend hope, possibility, sex. My eyes adjusted and I could see tall Rachel peeling her bathing suit off on the other side of the pool. Rah rah rah, Garret cheered. Ellie, with everything but her face and the magnificent brown of those shoulders half-hidden in the refracted underwater blue, sung the ba boom dee doom stripper music as I undid my pants in the dark, slipped them off, and jumped in. Cannonball.

When my mouth reached the surface, she was there. We floated to the end opposite Garret and Rachel, where I could touch bottom, and she wrapped her legs around me and I could feel her hairs, and she hummed through her nose and we kissed for a long time. Her legs and hips were hard and soft and we were both so hot the water around us began to feel lukewarm, like bathwater you've fallen asleep in. I wasn't sure what to do, but at one point I tried to slip inside her. She stopped me. "No. Not tonight," she said, and that was fine with me. Not tonight had a future in it.

After either five minutes or five hours, we separated. The CD skipped, juh juh, juh, juh, juh. I hadn't noticed the splashing around at the other end of the pool, Garret and Rachel going at it, Garret saying things like, "You like it? Huh?" and Rachel saying, "More, little man, more right there," and both of them growling and moaning and saying, "Yeah!" Ellie pulled away from me and out of the pool. I grabbed my clothes and followed her, admiring her naked in the light, stepping into her wet footprints, into the house, each step up the stairs worthy of another small offering to heaven. Standing behind her, kissing the back of her neck as she grabbed towels out of a fresh-smelling closet. Pulling me into a bedroom. Naked, smiling and drying ourselves carefully in the street lights shining in through the big window.

"Are you staying overnight?" she said, between kisses.

The clock radio in the corner said 3:22. I didn't answer.

"I don't want you to feel pressured."

I knew it wouldn't be the smartest move to make a big deal out of the fact that the most beautiful woman in Greater Boston might actually think that meagre, forked, and unfortunate Jeremy Little wouldn't want to sleep with her, lest she discover how meagre, forked, and unfortunate I really was. So I just smiled and knelt down and kissed the chlorine off her legs and the pelvic bones, the white line of her bikini just below the deep brown of her stomach.

"It seemed like Garret had to force you to come out."

"No. I can't think of anywhere I'd rather be. I'm so happy I could spit."

"Don't spit." She moved away from me to close the door. When I stood up she pushed me on the bed and hopped on top, the pale light shining between her legs, proof of divine intervention.

"Whose bedroom is this? Whose house?" I was struck with the fear that someone, someone far older and politically connected, would come busting through the door, demanding my name and passport. Telling me to get the hell out of his bed.

"Rachel's parents are in Europe."

"Oh."

She dangled her wet hair on my chest. "This isn't what I do. I've only been with four guys, all boyfriends."

"Me neither."

"How many partners have you had? Have you been –"

"None. None so far."

She smiled. "No fucking way." She stood up on the bed. "You're a virgin?"

"Yes." Shame. For a second, I wished I'd lied.

She danced around a bit, and flopped on top of me again. "Guess I'll have to be your teacher."

I nodded. Was any man luckier?

"Lesson one: everything but." And she moved on me before going down, before sliding up over my chest and over my face, easing down over my mouth for a long, important lesson. Before stopping me from turning her over for more lessons. "I want to sleep now. We're wrecked, Jeremy. We shouldn't do anything else or we'll kill each other's mystery."

She fell asleep on top of the covers, soft breaths. Of course I didn't sleep one minute; I wanted to wake her up several times, to ask about her last name and to admit to her that I was only 21. When the sun came up orange she turned orange, the freckles around her nose alive, secretive like stars, the rise of her hip a foot away from mine. A heartbreaking body a good fighting body and telling me nothing. I slid off the bed and into my clothes. A few blocks from Rachel's parents' house I found a bank machine and called a cab. I threw up out his window and he made me pay extra for a car wash.

To salvage some dignity after the virginity revelation, I waited a day before calling her. When I got the answering machine, I hung up. It took almost forty-five minutes to compose a satisfactory message, tidying up my apartment to beat the writer's block, mentioning the chlorine I couldn't get out of my mouth, the wine, the taxi. I went through my first-year English textbook for lines of poetry to impress her with, but after practising the Pablo Neruda quotations, I chickened out.

For a couple of days, no reply, so I tortured myself on the third day and attempted to watch rented movies before trying again. This time the answering machine used the we pronoun. The next morning, Garret informed me that Ellie and her terrible boyfriend were back together. He patted me on the back and told me not to worry, that it wouldn't last. Always the philosopher, he provided me with social, ethical, and psychological reasons for it, citing the natural fear that rises in a person when confronted with a powerful emotion; her first reaction was to retreat into the safety of familiar arms. I told Garret that it didn't matter. I was through with Ellie. Didn't even know her last name. Barely remembered what she looked like, actually. Garret called me the prince of all bad liars.

To waste time, I stayed late at the studio, with Carl the wooden dummy. A couple of weeks later, on a Sunday night, Garret called and asked me to take care of his classes for a couple of days. Since Kit had shortened my hours to weekends and holidays, it was no trouble. Garret had been paying me for teaching for the past few months, and the students were getting used to it. On Thursday of that week, during lunch break, as I ate yogurt without a spoon, Garret showed up wearing a grey suit, his hair visible. "Sunshine, our luck has changed."

"Our?"

"One of my old students is hooked up with the Red Sox, and they just hired a new head of team security."

"No."

"Yeah. I've been doing interviews all week. Found out this morning."

"That's great." I always knew he would end up a big shot.

He pushed me around some, smiling. "The money's awesome, Jeremy."

"Good." The pushing was starting to annoy me.

"The good news is I have to sell the school to you. A bargain. You'll be stealing from me. Do you know how easy it is to get a small business loan in this country? We Americans love an enterprising young eskimo." With Garret's pushy leadership I made some calls about my expired student visa, about landed immigrant status, and I secured some appointments with banks. On his cell phone, he told Rachel to get the champagne chillin'. Rachel worked at home, freelance technical writing.

That night I couldn't sleep. I was certified in enough of the disciplines to be head instructor, but I knew nothing about money. The idea of being in debt was not an appealing idea; I trained and worked and taught a bit, did all the things I wanted to be doing, but I didn't have to worry worry worry about every little thing every little day, because the responsibility was ultimately someone else's. Did I want to be the worrier? But risk is the American way, I told myself. Risk. I had to be a man. At 2:00 am I called Ellie and she answered the phone, groggy. I told her she should be ashamed of herself for messing with me the way she did, using me. That for such a smart girl she was stupid to get back together with her terrible boyfriend, that even though I was a bit young and a cherry I was nonetheless pretty classy about romance if someone gave me the chance to be. I told her I would never call her again, never bother her again, but that she was welcome to call me if she ever wanted to see how un-terrible some guys are, even if they are not quite 22. She didn't say anything. I told her she had broken my heart, said goodnight, and hung up.

A week later, she called. Garret and I had to cancel the Friday classes because I was at the bank and he was at the Red Sox offices, smiling at people and telling jokes and shaking hands. On the Waterfront Warrior answering machine, Ellie let me know where we would meet, alongside the Hancock, where Boylston and Dartmouth intersect.

Still in my bank outfit, I arrived early and stood in front of the old Trinity Church, thinking about churches and God for a while. I have always saved my thoughts about God for those times when I'm too nervous to think about the dirty business I'm nervous about. Whenever I consider it seriously, it becomes obvious to me that I am not a true believer. How could I be? I looked at the flowers in the nightlights, and stood in the wind-spray of the fountain. Until I realized Ellie might ask me something about the library if she found me there, I sat on its steps; I wasn't keen on admitting to her that I'd never been in the library. It's a strange area of Boston, with the glassy shine of the Hancock Tower on one side and granite ritual on the other, mirrored in the glass, fused, making you wish for both and also making you wish for neither.

Her heels clicked. Cars buzzed by, people here and there in their own clicking heels, but there was nothing but Ellie. In the strong wind, her silky pants and matching shirt outlined the body I knew. And took me over, sending a hollow thud of sweet, distant longing all through me. She stopped, took my hands, and kissed me on the side of the mouth. "Your hands are freezing," she said, peppermint breath. "You nervous?" I nodded. Like never before. With one hot hand, she dragged me down Boylston. For a long time we didn't talk, shuffling through the thin crowd, until she showed me the finish line for the Boston Marathon.

At a bar called Le Cirque. Some Québécois were in there, speaking French. Like all good Canadians, I took it in high school. But I was no master, even though Dad's mom was from Montreal. *Est-ce que tu est triste?* and she answered perfectly, a complex answer, with a fine accent. I decided to stop impressing her with my French.

After the first glass of wine she breathed comfortably and sat back in her chair. She had even more freckles and an even better tan. Since I had been self-conscious of my albino skin on the night we met, I had made more of an effort to be tanned and well-groomed. Her hair was carefully messed, and when the wind came in one of the windows and blew at her, it smelled like tangerines. "So. You called."

"I did."

"When you hung up I decided you were a freak and that I was right to stay away. But this morning I thought about it, and I realized it was romantic what you said, and brave. Even if it was a bit needy. When I woke up that morning and you were gone, the whole thing was unreal. I was confused. Why did you leave?"

"I didn't want to kill our mystery."

She smiled. A big part of me wanted to cover her up with

something and take her out of Le Cirque and lock her up in my castle. Or squeeze her too hard.

"I didn't want you to wake up and discover you'd done something you didn't want to do."

"I never, ever do anything I don't want to do. That's a decision you never have to make for me, Jeremy."

"Okay. I was wrong."

"You were wrong. I wanted to wake up with you, get to know you."

I took a sip of wine. I looked out the window. A couple walked by with a greyhound. What a world. How could I understand another person when there were people out there buying bony-horse greyhounds, on purpose?

She sighed and nodded. "Look, Jeremy, I'm here and you're here. What else do you want? I like you and you like me."

"Then why are you with him?"

"It's complicated." She flicked at the top of her glass with her fingernails. "I'm not with him, not in my heart. I don't think I am. Have you ever broken up with someone you've been with for a long time?"

"No."

"Well, it's complicated and painful. Please, Jeremy, don't think of it in a . . . simple way."

I smiled at her, but my lips trembled. It was simple. Yes or no, what could be simpler? I felt nauseous as I realized that in seeing her again, I had picked the thin scab off a wound. "Okay. I'll try."

"Good boy."

She told me about graphic design, about how it was hard to be creative, even in an industry that is creative by definition. Management was out of touch with current trends and design technology. The firm she worked for wouldn't buy new computers or software, they wouldn't shell out for copyright fees to get the best art, and they didn't realize they had a flaming genius on their hands. She smiled when she said the genius stuff. I told her she probably was a genius, and that the boneheads would figure it out soon enough. From Rachel, she knew I was in the process of taking over Garret's school. I told her how worried I was about needing another $15,000, since the banks had given all they were going to give and I was already *stealing from* Garret, and she wished me luck about that.

I walked her home and we stood in front of her house, talking absently about the differences between the Canadian and American judicial systems. Most of what I added to the non-conversation were guesses and half-remembrances from social studies classes in high school. She cupped her hands together as she spoke, shook her head in confusion, used pauses like an actor; I imagined that she would be a great manager. I wanted to kiss her. A long, smart, and sober kiss. So I did. Silk shirt sliding around up and down the skin of her back as I held her. With all my heart I hoped that terrible boyfriend wasn't inside waiting for her, peeking out the window or worse, lying comfortable in bed. Apart from what I understood was an occasional, complicated visit by terrible boyfriend, Ellie lived alone in the red brick house, her inheritance. Again, feeling an allegiance, I wanted to go inside that night and prowl the place and sleep beside her, but she didn't invite me. I stood on the sidewalk and watched her turn the key and open her door. She looked back at me before walking inside, and blew me another kiss.

It took me over an hour to walk home. The night was thick and muggy, since the wind had died, and halfway it started to rain. I thought of Seymour; the smells and the dust when summer is dry, hills and fields, grasshoppers, the first snowfall of the year. In the midst of money and brick I thought of our little house, of Dad and Denton. What would they be doing at that moment?

In the familiar hum of my apartment I stood dripping in the entrance, turning on lights and wishing I had somehow smoothed my way into Ellie's bed. As I brushed my teeth the phone rang. Ellie and I talked until 6:00 am as I twisted the cord round and round my arm, picking at the loose pieces in my parquet floor. The sun came up and I learned how terrible terrible boyfriend truly was, and I found out about her family and the accident. Her dad had been a lawyer, her mom a painter. I told her about Denton and Dad, and even some stuff about Jeanette and Joe. Before we hung up, in that sweet pause, she said she was falling in like-a-lot with me.

The next day was my last day at Kit's, so she came by and took me out for a picnic lunch. We ate on a patch of grass in front of a church, cold chicken sandwiches she'd made with tomatoes and mayonnaise, and orange juice that she'd blended with two bananas. That morning, while Kit and I were doing some light sparring, I had walked into a head butt. An ugly bruise thumped below my right eye. She touched it.

Some Anglican priests walked out of the church and down the steps in front of us. They smiled and we smiled and one of them, a woman, said to another one that we looked like a handsome couple. Handsome. Ellie and I looked at each other then, and said nothing. Once the moment had passed, she asked me why I wasn't spiritual. I almost made something up about the life force and surrounding energies, watch out for and accept the void, surrender to the inner cures of the eight-fold paths of Buddhism. Instead, I licked some mayonnaise off my finger and decided to say something serious. Something about harmony, instinct, awareness? Looking into the shadowy spaces between the big bricks of the church wall, I thought of some deep and impressive points I could make. After all, it was my life; she would be judging me based on what I felt about my life. "Fighting is everything," I said. "And everything is fighting. That's pretty spiritual, I think."

Nodding, she stuffed the garbage into the red vinyl lunch

bags. Then she yanked at some grass and tilted her head and said, "That's interesting enough, Jeremy. But it doesn't sound so healthy." With the light shining into her face, her eyes were small and quick.

Healthy? I licked at some more mayo. "It's safe. Isn't it healthy to be safe? Fighting has no rules, it's just timing and coordination and rhythm and balance. Honesty and lying are involved. Just like life. You win or you lose. I don't want to lose, that's all. Isn't that spiritual?"

She smiled. "It's something."

Some more priests walked out of the church. These ones didn't smile. "You think that's pretty stupid?"

"I don't know anything about it, Jeremy. But I always thought Garret was a bit of a kid about martial arts, and he recognized it. It's weird to hear you talk about it so seriously, that's all," she said, still smiling.

I was mad. "It is serious."

"Okay. Tell me about it."

"Do you really want to know?"

"Sure."

"Sure yes or sure no?"

"Just tell me, Jeremy, for Christ's sake. Convince me. To tell you the truth, I dislike fighting. I don't like boxing. I don't like wrestling. I don't like martial arts movies. But maybe I'm missing something."

"You are, you're missing a lot." The sun came out from behind a cloud. Both in shorts, our bare legs touched, hers brown and polished and mine pink and hairy. Since she wore sandals, I got a good look at her feet. They were okay feet. "The whole concept of interception is –"

"Like in football?"

"You intercept the opponent's attack. You can wait for them or draw them in, and then you stop their attack and take over. When you intercept an attack, you create a moment of imbalance and helplessness because their brains short-circuit for a second. Then you attack."

She drank the last bit of juice out of the plastic cup and stood up. "All right, show me. Intercept my attack. Draw me in."

Not sure if she was making fun of me, I stayed sitting. "I make it so you feel I'm nothing, that you can take me. I dance around a bit, feint, open myself up. There's lots of ways to draw someone in."

"Stand up. Show me. Show me how deep and important it is. Show me how much of a man it makes you."

As I stood up, she booted me in the ass. She bounced up and down, kicked in front of me. "How about I show you later, Ellie. I'll show you how to fight from the beginning. I have to explain a few things first. And we're in a churchyard."

"Come on, pussy. Draw me in. Intercept me." She spun her hands around and did a somersault and stood up and bounced more and kicked the air. "Let's go, bitch."

"Okay. Hit me."

She crouched and bounced and switched her feet around. She danced around a bit like on the Mohammed Ali videos. Now I was sure, without a doubt, that she was making fun of me. When she had said *bitch*, it had been in that mock-redneck way. I was the redneck. Fighting was everything to me; I didn't expect other people to understand it, but at least they could take it seriously. It *was* serious. At that moment, it was so serious that I seriously considered walking away from Ellie.

"I don't make fun of graphic design."

She stopped bouncing. "That's true, Jeremy. But no one's ever been killed while designing a magazine ad."

"Fighting's not about killing."

"What's it about, then? Beating someone so they're so bloody and broken that they'll remember you forever as the toughest guy in town? Do you need that, Jeremy? To be the toughest guy in town?"

"No."

"Then why, how is it so serious for you?"

"It's self-defence. It's so people can't hurt you. It's so you can protect yourself, that's all."

"Really? So the fights I see outside bars every Saturday night, with a horde of screaming guys circling two idiots pounding the hell out of each other, that's just defence?"

"No."

"What is it then? And why does Mohammed Ali shake so much?"

"A disease. And I'm not a boxer."

"What are you, then?" She starting her fighting routine again, bobbing and weaving like Balbo the Bear in *The Jungle Book*.

I realized, then, that my hands were balled into fists. It scared me, so I took a deep breath and allowed them to rest by my side. "I'm just a guy."

"Really?"

"Just a guy. Can we talk about this later?" The sun was behind Ellie's head. It was hot. Her shirt was riding up, from all that bouncing, and I could see her belly button. The shadow of her bra. "It's a pretty church, isn't it?"

"It is a pretty church," she said.

On the way back to the gym we passed a storefront where some guys drank from bottles of beer. Ellie dropped a dollar in a man's hat. We held hands and walked slowly, even though I was already late. A block from the gym, across from a construction site, she kissed me. "Jeremy."

I squeezed her hand.

"If it's what you really want to do with your life, I can loan you the money."

I shook my head. "No."

"I have a lot of money. Most of it is tied up but a lot of it isn't. My parents weren't poor, and they had a big life-insurance policy. I could spare 15 grand so easily, like nothing. A low-interest loan."

Two police cars and an ambulance blew by before I could say no again, so I stood and waited until it was quiet. Ellie held eye contact, letting me know she was serious about this. After a little while, I said, "Isn't it wrong to mix money and . . . liking a lot?"

"Ah, suck me."

"Sure. For hours. I've been reading up on techniques actually, to augment my first lesson. I have no fear in this area, and you'll find my lung capacity and muscle endurance are not wanting." Garret would have been very proud to hear me say these things. "Ellie, I'll do anything and everything longer and better than –"

"Do you want it or not?"

"Here? Now? Lesson two?"

She pushed me. "The money. How else are you going to get it?"

Couldn't we just talk about churches? Or Disney cartoons? I was quiet for a while as she dragged me down the block. Two black-haired girls in ragged dresses, sisters maybe, sat on some steps in front of an old apartment building, lazily shooting one another with water pistols. A gargoyle hunched over them like an angel. Beside them, a tiny garden in a tiny yard. Two sunflowers peeked over the black, iron fence. One said to another, what should we do? There's nothing for us to do, said the other. Nothing, nothing, nothing. I sucked the last drop of the banana orange juice from the Tupperware container. "Can I come over tonight?"

Ellie nodded. "Come at seven. Bring a toothbrush."

[CHAPTER 4]

Travis Many Fires lives on the fifth floor, the top floor of the second tallest building in Seymour. In the stairwell the air is sluggish, country smells of pork, sweat, roll-your-own Player's cigarettes. From each hallway, yelling and laugh tracks, children crying. Fake ferns and roses adorn the platform at the top of the stairwell – plastic stalks stuffed into styrofoam dirt – and someone has written *Seymour Sucks Ass* on the white wall with a black felt marker. Streaking and fading betray sad attempts to wash it off.

Travis wasn't in the phone book, but I found Many Fires Records under *Musical Soundscapes*. The voice mail featured Travis reciting his mailing address very quickly over gurgling techno music; an address leading to the Seymour skyscraper, a long, brown apartment building five blocks south of Rapid Shopping Centre on the way out of town. Six storeys high, it's almost as tall as the grain elevator, and just as beat-up. All the kids called this building Paki Palace when I was in school, and even though I don't remember anyone but poor white people living here, I doubt if it has another name.

Some deep but quiet bass hums through Travis's door – 527. I take a couple of breaths, choo them, and knock. The sound of a glass breaking at the other end of the hallway, a man cussing. Up here, the sluggish smells have been replaced by something sweet, dirty caramel. Although Travis and I were good friends in high school, best friends, I'm scared; scared in a numb and vague, reasonless way. If he foams at the mouth and licks the knob when I open the door, it will make a funny story. If he is brilliant and flawless, which is as possible as anything else, I might roast a little with jealousy. But in all, this fear is illogical, silly, maddeningly unavoidable. I hope he isn't home.

"Hold on."

I hold on. He hasn't seen me. I could leave, flee.

Travis coughs and opens the door, nodding absently to the beat, head as clean-shaven as it was at Gordy's the other night. I smile and nod too, and then we are both smiling, both nodding. Boom, boom, boom, boom. "Groovy," I say.

"You like? It's mine. It's what I do." A hint of pot eases out of the room.

"It's good."

When he begins to talk, he closes his eyes. He has always done this, so it isn't a dope thing. "Does well in the UK, raves are still huge out there. Huge. Not so well in Canada, except Toronto and Montreal. Not so well down south, but not so bad, either." Leaning against the door, he takes a pull of his water. Then he shakes the bottle. "Damn, look at you. What are you wearing there? Chinos? Look at you. A return to his native land."

If I felt more comfortable with Travis, I'd say, no, I'm returning to *your* native land. Travis is wearing a striped ski sweater with a bee on it, with some shorts. He still sports the Doc Marten lace-up boots, and in them he looks taller than on Monday night. I wonder if he is going to ask me in. "Congratulations," I say. "It's what you always wanted to do. How many people do what they always wanted to do?"

"It's wack, eh?"

I'm not sure if this refers to the music or him being a music-maker, so I just smile. On my tippy toes, I peek over him into the apartment.

"Oh yeah. Sorry, Jeremy. Come on in." He backs away from the door and closes it behind me. Sandalwood incense joins the pot, and it's dark because the only light in here comes from a computer monitor. It is early evening, and his curtains are closed. The music zooms from four speakers set up on top of a big computer table with two monitors, two turntables, and some mixing machines. On the monitor that is turned on, porno pictures dissolve into each other. I look and look away. In the back corner of the room are a blue velour couch and a red velour chair. Seventies stand-up ashtrays everywhere. On the wall are several bullfighting posters with large Spanish names underneath. Advertisements. The marquis item, above the couch, is a huge, black-velvet painting of a very red bullfighter giving a snorting bull the old *how's she goin'*. I sit in the chair. No TV. He walks into the kitchenette. "Drink?"

I want to sound relaxed. "Sure. What do you have?"

"Beer. Water."

"I'll have a beer."

His back is to me so I sneak another peek at the porno screen savers.

"Like those?" he says. "A friend sent them to me, from Germany."

"The screen savers, you mean?" I say, as neutrally as possible. *Porno – who doesn't love it?* is the message I'd like to convey.

"There's no place like home. There's no place like home." He clicks his heels together. "When'd you get back?" He sits on the blue couch, below the bullfighter, and hands me the beer.

"Aren't you gonna have one?"

"No."

The cap is off so I have to drink it. As I lift the bottle to my lips, he watches me as if this was an experiment. "I was just in the neighbourhood. Thought I'd stop by."

"You called."

"Yeah."

"I have one of those phones with call display, saw your number. You must have assumed I was home and not answering the phone. Did you assume that?" He grabs a toque from the floor and shakes some dust off it before pulling it hard over his bald head. It says *I love cops*.

"Why didn't you answer?"

"I don't know." He takes a remote control off the coffee table and increases the volume so it is very loud, a high, thumping business with sirens and Spanish guitar all looped up with some dingy bottom-end bass around it. Matches the incense. He crosses his legs, he sits back and he smiles. I smile back and I realize his smile is not friendly but threatening, fierce.

I take a big drink of the beer, looking at the porno some more. Then I look back at him and he is still smiling. "What, Travis?"

"I don't know."

The incense and music are making me sweat. How could Travis live in here? The screen saver has an overall red haze to it, giving the small room a log-cabin feel. A log cabin with thick, dusty curtains and techno and porno, and Travis's smile. "You wanna get out, Travis? I came by to see if you wanted to join me for a walk. I'm exploring."

"Sure, man." He downs his water and stands up. "Let's hit the road."

As he watches me in that same mad-scientist way, I finish my beer as fast as I can. He locks the door and bounds down the stairs, ahead of me. At the bottom, he leans against the mailbox and sucks air. I smile at him and he smiles at me properly; maybe he just needed to get out of that apartment. Travis was always a bit off, that's why I liked him. At the Seymour Composite High talent show he wore his mom's leopard skin jacket and cracked a whip a few times, screaming, as a Skinny Puppy song played over the PA. At the end of the song, nobody clapped. I didn't even clap. Finally some headbangers in the front row stood up and whooped and hollered, and Travis bowed. The first idea was for him and me to eat a can of *wet* dog food in front of the crowd. From the floor. From dog bowls.

Soon after I began watching the Plum House, watching Jeanette, I invited Travis to watch her with me. It was a sin to watch her from the railroad tracks with my binoculars – in her room, changing, sunbathing in the back yard or tending to the plum patch – so I tried to diffuse the sin by spreading it to Travis, my accomplice. We hid in the bush that surrounded the tracks and took turns with the binoculars. They were meant for sports. It's hard to understand how I was at that age, that day, so overwhelmed by the moment and what we saw that we both, almost simultaneously, began to jerk off. She wore short shorts. Afterwards, we did our pants up, looked at each other, and walked home in separate directions. That was the first and last time we watched Jeanette together, and we didn't talk about it afterwards. How could we? I prefer to think of it as something I couldn't help, something I dreamed. Something I did against my will.

Outside, catching his breath, Travis stretches. "Was Boston as good as you thought it'd be?"

"I couldn't have predicted it." It is a cold night, now that the sun is down. I should have worn a jacket.

Travis fishes around in the back pocket of his long shorts. "How about we go for a drive instead of a walk. I don't like walks. It's an old-people thing to do, don't you think?"

"Sure."

Around the side of Paki Palace, Travis continues to nod his head to the music. "Boston has seasons, like here?"

"Just not as severe."

"San Fran was one big season." He stops walking and shoots his hand out. "Here, man. Let's shake on it."

We shake on it, whatever it is. Looking into his eyes, I can see now that Travis is cooked. "Figure you should be driving?"

"Yeah, yeah. Why not?"

I just look at him.

He turns in a circle and throws his arms up in the air. Then he puts them back down. "Don't tell me you've found God or something."

"No."

"Then what's the problem?" He bends his knees, so he's even shorter than he already is, looking up at me imploringly.

"No problem." And there isn't, but I hope the dope wears off so we can have a regular conversation. "How's your parents?" Travis's mom was always very nice to me. His dad was nice too, quiet.

"Fine."

If he asks me about Dad, I'll say the same. Fine. I didn't see him all day because he was in New Sarepta, cooking hamburgers at a store promotion. He and Fred Carpenter are doing things for each other to prepare for Rodeo Days this weekend. "That's good."

"Yeah, it's great." He runs over and pounds the top of a brown Volaré. "Here she is. Connie, Jeremy. Jeremy, Connie." Leaning down, he says, out the corner of his mouth like a bad ventriloquist, "Charmed, Jeremy, I'm sure."

"Hi Connie."

Travis opens Connie and her passenger door creaks. Inside, he slides across the bench seat, so I get in too. Connie smells like dope. Hidden under the driver's seat is a CD player. Travis inserts it, starts Connie, and pushes play. More techno. Underneath the CD player, mounted to the floor, is a CB. The techno says, watcha-getcha watchagetcha, woo, woo.

"This yours too?" I scream.

He turns it down. "No, a friend did it. A Canadian techno compilation. It's an oxymoron, is the joke. Canadian. Techno."

"Oh yeah?"

"It's funny because Canada's not known for techno music," he says, very seriously.

"Oh." I wonder how many times he'll tell me about Canada and techno.

Out of the parking lot and on to 50th Street. Travis turns right, southbound, and we drive out of Seymour. Street becomes thin highway. There are a few farmhouses and the old, grey abandoned barn is still slumping into the ground at the town limits. It must sink an inch or two every year, because it looks slightly more pathetic than it did seven years ago. "Where you wanna go tonight, Jeremy?"

I just shrug, so Travis pulls over and turns off Connie. After pulling the CD player out and stuffing it under the seat again, he pulls a pack of cigarettes out of his shirt pocket and motions for me to get out. The driver's side door must be busted. Once we are out, he lights his smoke and jogs across the highway. Into the ditch, jogging east. I follow. On the railroad tracks he licks his finger, holds it up, and sits down. I sit down beside him on the smooth track, facing the prairie. The flat goes on forever, the short-grass fields still sloppy with melted snow, clusters of trees like skeletons in November football huddles.

His cigarette is a clove cigarette. Very sweet. Maybe this was the smell in Connie, not dope. I pat him on the back. "It's good to see you, Travis. Your own record company. Damn."

"Congratulations for being poor? Thanks, man. Same to you." He laughs about this, but we both know it isn't funny.

We look ahead, throwing rocks into the dark. I'm not sure why we stopped here. "Why did you come back to Seymour?" I say.

"Why did you?"

"Lots of reasons, I guess."

"Me too. The company I worked for . . . everyone called everyone else a musical genius, blowing moondust up each other's asses all day long. Even though they all truthfully hated each other. That's one reason." He scratches his toque. "It's obvious to me why I came home, but not so easy to explain. What I do know is I wish I'd brought some water out here. I've got a real thing for water, Jeremy."

"Water's important."

"I was lonely there, too."

I nod. "That part's hard."

"Seymour has soul, doesn't it?" he says, hitting two rocks together. "And you can't see it until you get away." Even though the rocks are big, he sets them carefully on the track. Then he stands and smiles and lines up some more rocks on the other track. This is something I remember doing as a kid, with Denton, propping up a few small rocks and hiding in the bush when the train came, giggling as the sparks flew, rat-a-tat like a Tommy gun. But we stopped doing that when a train south of Lethbridge derailed because of some rocks on the tracks, and a bunch of Americans and cows and horses were hurt and killed. I should remind Travis about this before he asks me to participate, because I couldn't live with killing a bunch of Americans and farm animals. But just before I open my mouth, just before I consider walking home because Travis and I can't be friends, not after so much time and not after he tries to kill horses, he kicks the rocks off the tracks and sits beside me again, and looks at me and claps his hands and rubs them together and points at me with his thumb and smiles, as if he knows what I'd been thinking. As if he were testing me. He laughs and shakes his head, and I laugh, but as usual I don't know what the hell I'm laughing at.

We look out as darkness descends completely and we are silent. Every few minutes I wonder what Travis is wondering, inventing variations of his inner world. He thinks I'm an idiot; he thinks about sex; he thinks about sex with me; he thinks about trains derailed, lakes of horse blood spilling over the field. A thin, cold wind blows over us and I hug myself. Travis must be freezing in his shorts. He sighs and elbows me, and I elbow him back. "Did you want a cigarette or anything?" he says.

"No thanks."

Then, straight out over the fields past the tip of the east-end neighbourhood where Travis used to live, the lights of the fair begin to flicker on. One by one the Ferris wheel, Zipper, Round-up, bright and hazy green and white and red and blue over the dusty fields beside the Black Gold Centre. Travis stands up and cheers, dancing around on the gravel, his striped toque flopping as he shakes his head. "Rodeo, rodeo." He picks up a handful of rocks and throws them straight up, and they land all around us.

I stand up too, and dance around some, because I have missed so many moments like these, when I might have danced. Moments I have regretted. Travis bounces and I bounce. We throw rocks all over.

The fair opens officially tomorrow, but I remember the line-ups every Wednesday night when 20 or 30 kids got to be first to ride, to sign waivers and test them for the rest of us. I throw a heavy rock as far as I can into a bluff not far from the tracks, and a deer runs out.

"Deer," says Travis, and starts running after it. So I run too and we're both chasing the deer as it bounds ahead of us, a perfect shadow, so much faster than a man can run, left and then right, behind and beyond big rocks and trees and into the night. In the mud and the mush we run anyway, laughing and coughing as the screams from the Round-up and the Zipper hover weakly over the field. The deer is nowhere now, so I orient myself by watching the rides. Where is Travis? After a jog I begin to run again, to test my heart. I run hard. Just as I think about slowing down, I step in an invisible gopher hole and go down hard, sliding a good four feet in the sludge. When I come to a rest, my face covered in mud, Travis appears above me. He laughs so hard he's silent, doubled over, teetering around and ready to fall himself. He lends a hand. "Real Ninjitsu reflexes there, Little." As he yanks me up out of the mud I have a strong urge to pull him down into it. But he's already filthy up to his knees and it'll be bad for Connie. "Man, you look funny."

Travis is having a bit too much fun with this. I'm wearing a sweater I like, and now I'll have to get it dry-cleaned. "Yeah. I'm funny all right."

"No, really. Still clumsy after all these years?" The smile has become hideous and annoying again.

"Fuck off," I say, pulling the mud off my sweater in clumps.

"Aw. Poor baby's slacks are dirty."

I kick Travis's legs out from under him and he's on his back. Then I boot some mud up on his face. "Aw. Poor baby's toque is dirty."

His face changes to angry. But as he wipes the mud from his eyes, he starts laughing. I forgot how good Travis's laugh was. He grabs my legs and I go down on my back too. And for a while we sit in the mud, laughing at first and then not laughing, just looking over at the fair. Happy to be in mud.

Walking back to Connie, we shake as much as we can off our clothes. "She's gonna be nasty," he says, when it's obvious we can't get anywhere near clean.

"Do you have any garbage bags or anything we could sit on?"

"Who carries garbage bags around?"

"I bet my dad does. I bet a thousand dollars he does."

"Well, he isn't here, is he?" Travis is suddenly realizing the implications of mud.

"We could walk back and change and I could drive you back here. In Denton's truck, if he's still home."

"Too cold." He's right. Now that the adrenalin's gone, the cool air and the soaked clothes won't be so comfy. "We're gonna have to take our clothes off."

A truck going north into Seymour honks as it goes by. The mocking, double honk. Travis pulls off his shirt and stuffs it on the floor in Connie's back seat. He pulls his shorts off over his boots. Because I don't see any other alternatives, I take my sweater off. The pants don't go over my shoes, so I take them off too, then squish back into them again. When we are done, in our wet underwear, Travis gives me a thumbs-up and slides into Connie.

Travis has a little pot belly and a hairless nut-coloured chest. Not expecting any action tonight, I'm wearing loose, baby blue briefs; I feel trashy next to Travis's tight Calvin Kleins. We are greasy in the non-light. He pushes the CD player into place and the Canadian techno starts up again, and I hope with conviction that we don't get pulled over by Chicken George or one of his toadies.

Before he puts Connie into drive, he turns on the interior light. He wipes his hands clean on the foam seat, reaches over me, opens the glove box, and pulls out a can of RAID. It's not really a can of RAID, though, because the bottom twists off and a little bag of weed falls out, with two already-rolled joints. "Fatty?" He pushes the cigarette lighter in.

"No. Thanks. It makes me crazy."

"Fuckin' A it does. We'll get crazy together. That's what crazy's for."

"No. Sorry." Travis's idea of crazy is not mine. I smoked a joint once in the back room of a bar one of Ellie's bosses owned. Ten minutes later, I had to back against the wall just in case someone attacked me. Nick Lozinski and Rory and all the Nicks and Rorys masquerading as Ellie's peers and mentors had been waiting for me to get messed up, so they could beat me down and piss on me. I was vulnerable, uncoordinated. They were gunnin' to get me. All the training was a waste, I discovered, pretending to laugh when everybody else laughed. I imagined Nick Lozinski walking in, everyone clearing a path for him. Nice try, chum, but you should know the Nicks of the world always slaughter the Jeremys of the world. Nature will win.

As we drive back into town, Travis smokes most of a joint. We don't speak until he pulls into our driveway. "Thanks for the good times," I say.

Travis nods.

"Give me a call. Remember my number?"

He nods again, and blows out some smoke. "I remember."

I grab my muddy pile of clothes from the back-seat floor. "Later, Travis."

"Check," he says, and backs out of the driveway, cranking the Canadian techno.

Ellie put together this list of books, to help me gain a more sophisticated understanding of the world and the hearts of men. One night two years ago, a cold and dark and snowless night in Boston, I was reading book number two on the list. The phone rang and I was happy to be interrupted. Ellie was working late, and I was bored with reading. It was Denton, and he was calling from the emergency room.

He had been wrapped in a blanket, sitting upstairs in the middle of the floor, picking at a bowl of Lucky Charms. Since he had a cold, Dad was outside shovelling the snow by himself. Shovelling the driveway is usually a two-man operation because the wind forces drifts on the hump between the street and the garage. One guy operates the snowblower and the clean-up man follows with the shovel. Instead of taking the snowblower out, starting it, letting it warm up, and blowing what he could before shovelling the rest, Dad decided to shovel. It hadn't been such a bad snowfall. As Denton finished his bowl of Lucky Charms, Dad walked into the house and stamped his feet.

"Hey Dad," said Denton. "Got 'er done?"

No answer. Still in his parka and still with his green and blue moon boots on, Dad walked into the living room, weaving, his right arm limp. He stood in front of Denton.

"Hey Dad."

No answer. Dad teetered and plopped himself into the rocking chair; he wiped his face and the gloves left a streak of wet. Snow from his boots melted in two circles. Hoping Dad was joking, hoping it wasn't happening, Denton put his bowl aside and stood up in front of him, smiling.

"What the hell, Dad."

Hockey highlights were on the sports channel and Dad leaned over to look at them as he wiped his face with his glove some more, so hard, Denton said, that it left red marks for a day. It looked as if it was 2:00 am and a boring movie was on, as if Dad were drifting in and out of sleep, drooling, eyes lazy.

"I'm having some cereal, watching *Sportsdesk*. The Oilers beat the Red Wings last night." Denton took Dad's hand. "Not bad, eh? The Red Wings."

Dad took his hand back and held his right arm, opening and closing his mouth as if a bad taste had gotten in there. "Just give me a second," he said. "I need a second or two to get things straight over here."

Clumsy then, like a drunk, he put out his hands as if to grab for something on the end table, and it crashed into the empty ashtray, breaking a full glass of orange juice. Supporting himself on broken glass, Dad stood up and leaned against the wall, smudging it with blood. Denton jumped to grab him before he fell on his face. "Don't fall asleep," Denton said, lowering him to the floor, and called the ambulance.

"Just give me one or two seconds to find myself."

Denton was not in good shape on the phone. He told me everything three times over. He cried. He told me I had to come home. Because Dad could die. The first thing I asked was if Jeanette was at the hospital. She was. Denton told me to grow up and think about this. He also told me, not crying any more, that if I didn't come home I was an asshole, no, worse than that. Evil. They needed me there. I told him I'd do my best and I hung up. I drove to the studio. It was the only night that Garret covered for me.

The intermediates were slapping each other's arms raw, trapping exercises. It was so cold outside the windows had fogged over. The class was small, but the regulars were there; Bobby Bullas was there that night. I told Garret he could go, and I had each of my students spar me to submission. Since most of them weren't so athletic, I did each of them in under 30 seconds. Even going half-speed. I choked a university student named John so hard that he never came back. It took me almost two minutes to beat Bobby Bullas, with the guillotine.

Once Dad regained consciousness, he offered to pay my plane fare home. There is no time in this world, he told Denton to tell me, to fight with the people you love. Ellie wanted me to go. I cancelled Friday and Monday classes and I was just about to call them, to make arrangements, when I changed my mind. I called Denton to tell him I had done my best but I simply couldn't make it, my work and Ellie's work, best wishes, etc. etc. Denton hung up on me. Every night, Ellie called to get updates on Dad's condition, and we had big fights about it. About what all this meant, me-wise. I was lucky enough to have a family. How could I? The last words she'd said to her own parents were, "Get me some treats."

If he had died, my last words to Dad would have been, "Fat chance." It was in the airport. August 1990. A dry day. Dad had a new haircut and his eyes were sore and tiny because he'd worked the night shift. He tried to slip me a hundred-dollar bill. He told me he was proud, that he'd write letters and send packages with towels and pajamas and snacks. He said we'd make plans for Christmas over the phone, after we all had some time to think. He moved to hug me and I stepped out of the way. "Fat chance."

Looking back from the terminal, I saw Denton put his hand on Dad's shoulder. It's all right. Jeremy doesn't mean it.

According to my horoscope in the city paper, today's winning colours are peach and hot pink. I could also make progress in my career if I speak up at critical moments.

The street lights pop all at once on these dark asphalt back roads that were gravel before I left; soft to walk on now, and if I drove, Cadillac-smooth to drive. People are laughing in their houses, sitting in kitchens with friends and too-loud country music. Rodeo Days, the unofficial long weekend, has begun. On 50th Street, Fas Gas buzzes in fluorescence and neon, pump boys spray and wipe the pumps down, watching the clock out the corners of their eyes. There are line-ups at the bank machines on the corner of 50th and 50th, and happy families walk out of Dairy Queen with recyclable bags full of beef and ice cream. Chicken George drives slowly by, makes eye contact. I wave and he shoots an imaginary gun at me.

The midway opens for the general public tonight, and it's cheap if you're under 14. Half the town will be riding the Tilt-a-Whirl and gawking at the rodeo horses in the temporary stables behind the Black Gold Centre, pointing, hugging their kids as the horses prance and snort.

West on 50th Avenue, the teenagers stand in the old Burnett Motors parking lot where excavations for something new seem stalled, smoking cigarettes and swearing amidst the temporary fences and deep pits full of rubble. The boys laugh tinny laughs and scrape the concrete with their skateboards. As I walk by with my paper, they stop talking and scowl a bit, like cool kids are supposed to when adults walk by. Poor teenagers, with their pimples and their new pubic hair, sneaking smokes in the morning when the folks leave for work, dope and beer on the weekends, burying smoky shirts under piles of other dirty clothes to hide the evidence. Mom and Dad so pleased that Billy and Sue are starting to pitch in, doing their own laundry like real troopers. Waiting for the lights to change, feeling them stare at the back of my head, ready to say something crappy about me when I'm out of hearing distance, I look through the national and world sections of the paper again, each article already fading into the cloud of irrelevance at the back of my brain, never to be retrieved again. Hebron gun, Algeria spy, Jakarta transvestite, Mexico jailrot, *Québec va séparer.* Goodbye Thursday, May 1, 1997. I'm going to my brother's bar.

In the last gas station before Gordy's, I buy a pack of cinnamon gum. Cinnamon because a smell expert on *Oprah* today said cinnamon makes people think of sex. Gordy's will smell like a cinnamon grinder tonight. Every bar in America, thanks to Oprah.

In Gordy's, I sit at one of the only free tables, under the worst TV in the bar. A playoff hockey game is on, and most of the guys are in front of the giant screen in the opposite corner, ya-ing and oh-ing. In a bright red shirt and a black apron, Denton brings me a pint and sits down for a minute. "It's Alberta beer. Pale Ale. Try it."

It looks like someone took a normal beer and mixed it in a blender with some whole wheat bread. I'm not much into dark beer. "I don't know." I look around, now that my eyes have adjusted to the dark and the smoke.

"Diane isn't here yet."

My whole wheat beer tastes like whole wheat beer. "It's a bit dark for me, Dent."

He leans over and grips my bicep with his big hand. "I'm really gonna have to learn you. American." Before he returns to the bar, he whispers in my ear, "Gwen's mentioned the weather seven times tonight. The weather." Then he punches the air. I give him a piece of cinnamon gum and wink, because we watched *Oprah* together this afternoon. "Oh yeah," he says, "sex."

The TV screen above me is so coated with tobacco resin the ice is a pale yellow, the home team, the Oilers, also yellow, and the Dallas Stars a dirty grey. I guzzle the repulsive beer and buy myself a Pilsner to wash the taste away. A thin, pink stream from a next-table cigarette runs straight into my nose. Since Edmonton is the only Canadian team in the playoffs this year, almost everyone is an Edmonton fan tonight, and the big news is that they've won. Under the big screen are high-fives and heads shaking, guys standing up and acting out the fights and saves. I listen to a conversation behind me, about someone *boot fucking* someone else. Two round-faced guys with gold Seymour grad rings.

So where is Diane? It's 11:00. Apparently she was in here last night, asking Denton about me, hinting that I should show up tonight. Bored and feeling like some kind of alcoholic, I regret throwing the newspapers away; I could have gotten one more skim out of it. Denton and Gwen are talking and it appears they're talking serious because Gwen is holding his arms. So I won't bother them. Where is my critical moment? My career opportunity? Merle Haggard is on the stereo now that the game is over, and a line from the Bible is mentioned. In-between my corner and the dance floor walled by video lottery terminals is a middle ground populated by obvious out-of-towners. Rodeo guys. Competitions start tomorrow afternoon. We went with Joe the same year he taught us to dance. Denton and me entered the greased pig competition, but Nick's older brother Ray won, and he got to keep the pig, a trophy, and $50.

Ah, Diane walks in. Gliding by my table with Tracy, she

plants her long fingers on my head for a moment. Then she walks by. Then turns, talking to someone, and looks back at me as she takes off her jacket. The black hair, tucked behind her ears again, frames her long face with some help from the tight t-shirt, also black, that says Perry Ellis AMERICA on it, in white. Tracy stands behind her, looking into the big screen. At least ten guys surround them, rocking back and forth from toes to heels, nodding and smiling and tearing at the bottle labels, stepping forward and back and turning around and around again when it's obvious they're being ignored, scratching at their shoulders and tearing at their bottles some more. There aren't any more tables but Diane and Tracy are given seats immediately. The two table-sacrificers stand over the women for a few minutes, leaning in on their conversation and smiling now and then, but soon they stand up straight and stick their chests out, and rooster to the bar, looking back over their shoulders now and then to see if the women are looking over at them. They're not. Sorry fellas. The sports channel is still on, now without sound, and male soccer fans in Italy jump and scream and spit and hit each other across the chest as the kickers score and sprint up and down the field, bashing into each other and hugging with a joy I might never experience. Next is ten-pin bowling highlights with a completely different crowd of men from the Italians across the ocean, from the crowd in here, but it wouldn't be hard to argue that we're all somehow interchangeable, us men. With this refreshing insight, I finish my beer and wave Denton over. He's busy so he waves me over. "I'm not a waiter," he says, as I approach the bar.

"You brought me the others. I figured –"

"Quit figuring so much." He slides the Pilsner over and I toss him a five-dollar bill, which he throws back at me before pouring tequila shots for the two spurned chair-givers. Who eye me suspiciously. Who eye me even more suspiciously when he pours me a tequila shot, and one for himself. It would be fun to tell them the drinks are free for me because I'm a *made guy.*

On the far side of him, straddling the sink island, Gwen mixes something with vodka and milk that looks as if it would make me throw up. I turn around and lean against the bar, surveying the scene. Between the video lottery terminals, a few couples dance to the Whitesnake song that's playing. The rodeo guys in the middle are getting drunk and beginning to shout at each other. The Seymour Composite High class of '90 alumni meeting in front of the big screen is as lively as ever, and Diane and Tracy have stolen my table. They aren't looking over at me so I don't know what to do. Is it an invitation? A challenge? I turn and look at the booze in front of the mirror, then I pretend to have something in my eye so no one can tell I'm staring at myself, hunting for resolve.

In front of me, a thin layer of sweat on her forehead, Gwen looks sideways into my right eye, the one I was pretending about. "Nothing in there," she says. "You're just drunk. Temporary psychosis."

"Hi Gwen."

"What jumps?" This is a Denton-and-me expression. We stole it from a cartoon when we were little and she stole it from Denton and now she'll take it to her next boyfriend. Of course Rob Palford says it all the time. Ellie! I'm home! What jumps, old girl!

"Not much. You?"

"I'm working at a bar, presently. So I don't have time to consider what might be jumping." She nods and adjusts her glasses. "So. You and Dents getting along? And Glen?"

I wonder what Denton tells her. It's a strange thing to consider, Denton and a woman. Denton having sex, say, with the lights on. "I guess so."

"Glen's a good man. I know you two'll patch everything up just fine. He's always been very sweet to me."

"Of course."

She looks at me funny for a second and adjusts her glasses again. I imagine Denton and Gwen and Dad and Jeanette on the deck some warm night, drinking wine and dissecting my way-wardness. "I was just telling Dents you should have me over for dinner sometime. Maybe you could invite Diane."

What the hell's going on here? "I barely know Diane. All I know is her and Tracy Lozinski stole my table. That's all I know." I take a long drink of my new beer, in defiance.

"Sure, sure. Why don't you go over there and talk to her?"

Gwen and I look back to see Diane and Tracy laughing at something, engaging in some form of inter-table communication with a group of rodeo guys. It's possible she doesn't give a rat's ass that I'm here, that I should go home and watch some videos to preserve some dignity.

"She's looked over here ten times in the last five minutes. Her and Tracy."

"No."

Gwen laughs, and Denton sidles up beside her, pours a third shot of tequila, and the three of us clink glasses and drink. Denton takes the glasses and throws them into the dishwasher, already dealing with another customer. Gwen pours me a rum and Coke, and slides it to me, with a napkin.

"No thanks. Too sweet."

"It's not for you, Jean-Claude. It's for Diane. Tracy drinks vodka and orange juice if you want one of those too."

"I don't know." From the end of the bar, behind Gwen's back, Denton watches us talk, and smiles about it. As Gwen fixes a vodka and orange juice, a drop of water splashes on my arm from the sweating pipes above us. Beery, smoky, cinnamon breath of us all. Like the bus window in Boston. I pay Gwen and take the drinks, the beer tucked under my arm, and Gwen smacks Denton with her towel. Just as I turn and walk to the table, a guy in a white cowboy hat, about Denton's size but thicker, bends down and kisses Diane on the cheek, then Tracy. Another one of Nick's hockey friends whose name I forget. It's not right. Not yet. The guy in the cowboy hat has ruined my moment. I turn around and put the drinks back on the bar. Gwen slowly shakes her head at me and then the ground. "It's not my fault, it's *his*." I point back at him with my thumb and shrug at Gwen and she shakes her head some more. So I pick the drinks up again and walk over to the table, to please Gwen and all she represents. Nodding, I put the drinks in front of the girls and take a drink of my beer, as coolly as I can. I nod at the guy. Again, cool. Smooth. Chet Baker smooth. Hello, ladies. Let's break a little heart.

"You the new waitress?" says the guy.

"Gwen says the drinks are for you. Two."

Both women thank me. Tracy looks away, at the terrible dancers who are doing the twist to an old Marky Mark dance song, bumping an old man on a stool who hunches over the little lottery terminal. "Get a chair," says Diane.

Might as well, I'd like to say, it's my table. I grab a chair from the corner and sit close to Diane. Silence. From the speakers, "Good Vibrations." I nod at the guy again and this time he shoots his thick, calloused hand out. Before I can get a good connection, he grips and squeezes my fingers hard. "Leonard."

"You know Tracy, right?" Diane says, lighting herself a cigarette.

"Of course." I give her a howdy-do smile before turning to introduce myself to Leonard but he gets up, tips his hat first to Diane and then to Tracy, and walks over to the hockey fan section without tipping his hat to me. He sits on the arm of a chair and looks over at the rodeo guys.

Tracy turns to the bowling highlights. Diane reaches over and gives my arm a rub. I get the feeling that Tracy doesn't think much of me, and even though it doesn't matter and oughtn't to bother me, it does all the same. To be sporting, I wave at Tracy. "Tracy."

"Yeah?" She doesn't look away from the bowler, who needs a spare.

"Sorry about Nick. It's too bad."

Tracy turns to me and claps her hands and points and laughs an evil laugh as Diane boots me under the table. She takes Tracy's arm and rubs it – does she rub everyone? – as Tracy shakes her head and gives a safer-looking smile. "Lucky you're new," she says.

Diane's pointer finger is in front of her glossy pink lips. "Shhh," she says, before I can ask what I said that was so wrong. She finishes her old drink and starts in on the one I gave her. Since Tracy drinks too, I drink.

"How you liking Seymour, Jeremy?" says Tracy.

"I don't know. I don't think I get the jokes any more."

"Hmm." Tracy nods at a little puddle of whole wheat beer I spilled earlier. "Well. I forgot to ask Lenny something. See yez."

I watch her go. Then I give Diane a *what the hell* look as she blows a cloud of smoke up and behind her. Straight to the pipes.

"It's all anyone asks her lately, Nick stuff. Pisses a girl off after a while. So earlier tonight, before we left her place, she said she's going to award a black eye to the first character who asks about Nick. Turns out you were the first character."

"Oh."

"So what took you so long, slick?"

"I was here a long time ago."

"Talking to Gwen, yeah. I mean, you saw us come in and it took you forever to come over. Looking around for better prospects or what?" The black AMERICA shirt really looks good on Diane. Her teeth are astonishingly white, for a smoker.

"I guess so." It doesn't please me to have to go through all this winking and nudging and cryptic, half-serious sparring before I can be with anyone again. There were times when staying home with Ellie seemed dull and unadventurous, a waste of my talents and energies, my youth, times when I ached to be *out there* meeting women, pursuing the stomach flip time-warp moment that precedes the first kiss. But now that I am here, essentially single, all I want is to be in bed with someone whose body I understand at the end of this night, looking forward to simple coffee and, ah, simple grapefruit in the morning.

Diane crinkles her nose at me. "I forgive you." The first notes of a country song I've heard at least ten times since I've been here. People say "Woo!" about it, and take each other's hands and move to the dance floor. "You want to dance, Jeremy?"

"Not really. Not right now."

Another drop, this time on my cheek. A worried drop, a drop of bad talk. Diane sighs and shakes her head. I feel what she's thinking. "You don't like me much?"

"Sure I do. I'm not much of a two-stepper, that's the problem."

Diane's cigarette smoulders in the ashtray, unsucked. She drinks and then slides her glass around. "All I'm saying is most guys, when they like a woman, they'll head to her table pretty quick or call them up. Or ask them to dance when a good song comes on. As far as I can see it, you haven't done any of that stuff."

There is no point in holding any allegiance to Ellie, in worrying about it and sometimes allowing myself to hope for some kind of Hollywood reunion, for staying up at night wishing I had made different moves at different *critical moments*. No point in missing the way our bedroom smelled in the morning, meeting her at my school during lunch break, when I had no students, when sometimes she'd take off her work clothes or I'd take them off for her, or she'd just take off her nylons and pull up her skirt, and we'd make love on the mats or against the wall or in a chair but mostly on the mats, and I'd have to wipe them off afterwards because sometimes she gushed when it was good, when our rhythms met and our skin and that, and *that*, and the smell of her, the smell of us, the smell of our bedroom in the morning.

I stand up and kiss Diane, lightly, on the forehead. Then I walk to the bar for two more drinks. Denton and Gwen high-five like frat brothers. Denton grabs my beer, Gwen pours the drink. "He works fast," says Gwen. We have another shot of tequila each.

"Undeniable sexual power," says Denton. "Runs in the family. That's seven bucks, Romeo."

I give him a ten and walk back to the table. The alcohol has eased its way into my legs. A heavy hum. "You want to go after these? Diane?"

"Where to?"

"Anywhere."

"Okay. I'll go with you."

Leonard and a few of his friends – faces I now recognize under the cowboy hats – move to the middle of the floor to lip off the rodeo guys. The rodeo guys stay sitting, which is smart of them. There's some talk of *fuckin' Americans*. They're semi-pro, so they must be used to medium-sized agricultural and oil towns, and the small group of assholes who live in these bars and taverns, listening to the same song list every night, feeling the same feelings. Dark, sad. Leonard turns to his seat, calling the rodeo guys a pile of chickenshit rednecks. Diane finishes her drink and rubs my arm, tipping her head in the direction of the door. I gun my beer and we're out.

We walk west, the long way home, along the shoulder of 50th Avenue, kicking at little rocks under the street lamps without yet touching. She tells me about Nick, about how he calls Tracy every night crying from jail. She smiles about that but I don't think it's very funny. I'd cry too, probably. Tracy's mom is living with her for a few weeks, and she's very upset that her daughter is in the bar every night when she should be home at this dreadful time. After Nick crashed into the Plum House and stabbed himself in the neck, Tracy dumped Hong Park. Tracy, Diane says, is hopeful about her and Nick even though she knows damn well there's nothing to be hopeful about. In a whisper, as if we're being followed, Diane tells me that she suspects Tracy is hopeful because it's safe to be hopeful, and it *looks good*.

Through the dark corridor under the overpass and into Seymour Gardens. Every after-dinner-mint house is sleeping, the newly planted saplings along the streets swaying in the weak wind. We walk five or six blocks into Seymour Gardens, under new street lamps, saying nothing, before she rubs the back of my hand. I read somewhere once that we touch people the same way we want to be touched, so I rub her a little bit too, wondering if this is something she does to her child. Diane tells me she swims every morning, and that she's trying to quit smoking. This won't be such a difficult task, since most of her cigarettes burn away without any direct contact with her lips. At one point, passing the first two or three manufactured lakes, Diane stops to tell me, gripping the collar of Denton's jean jacket, that time goes too fast. I agree, and we continue walking.

Here is the big, bright house where Nick Lozinski grew up. It still makes me think of modern perfection, all the things I wanted as a kid, new things, *just* enough money, suits and the smell of cigars and dry leaves in a big back yard in October. Across the street is a park with a little hill and a few tire swing sets. We sit at the top of the hill where it's dry because the tires smell and they're still full of snowmelt water. Diane takes my arm and puts it around her, and she moves in close as if I'm her boyfriend. The dirt smells.

"Do Mr. and Mrs. Lozinski still live there?"

"Yes, they do. They painted the doors and added a hot tub in the back. When his parents were away, Nick and Tracy would watch the house for them, and we'd sit in the hot tub and stay up late, talking and drinking. In the winter, we'd jump in the snow and then get back in. It's weird that all that's over, that Nick is in jail for good. I can't believe he did what he did. Why? Why do these things have to happen?"

For a long time I try to think of something to say. To explain myself, somehow. Diane rubs my leg. Since the forehead kiss in Gordy's I haven't done anything overt to convince Diane that I like her; even on the short stretch of highway without street lights we didn't touch, and the critical moment is – yes, fast – approaching. I have to do something or not do something, and I drank too much.

Garret, who did a BA in philosophy before initiating the Waterfront Warrior School, figured the world was divided into three kinds of people: the lookers, the touchers, and the penetrators. Lookers, the big group, watch life play out around them, engaging with it only insofar as the world engages with them. Touchers take more chances, but they spend most days in their heads, banking, creating, world travelling. The penetrators, the tiny group, they rule the world, and not with book-smarts, either. They do it with shamelessness. They *do*. It's a simple and easy way to look at something complex, and it's an attractive system. Especially when you're like Garret, absolutely positive that you're destined to be at the top of every social and evolutionary pyramid.

When the papers and TV began to say that I was Bobby Bullas's gay-bashing mentor, and things were falling apart with Ellie, Garret urged me to meditate myself into penetration. He said to write on little pieces of paper, *you know what you have to do*, and litter the house and studio with them. But I didn't know. Garret was wrong about me. I told him I was a looker and he told me he tolerated no lookers. This, I assume, was tough love.

The Lozinski house, where I spilled orange pop on the floor. Diane's dark, soft, straight hair. She notices that I'm looking at her, and she turns to me and smiles. "I'm sure glad I wore a coat," she says. "It's still cold at night."

What do I have to do? "Me too."

She rubs her hand along my leg one last time and then crosses her arms in front of her chest, leaning away from me. I was supposed to kiss her a few critical moments ago. When her eyes were shiny, when she wasn't thinking about the cold. We should be rolling around with our hands under each other's shirts. "What are you doing here, Jeremy?"

"In Seymour, you mean?"

"I mean right here, right now, on this hill beside me. But, sure. Why in Seymour?"

I pull a rock out from under me and toss it up into the air and catch it. "I had nowhere else to go."

"Why did you stay away?"

"Remember the year we graduated, when the Kravchuk house burned? That was my dad's fault and I was mad at him. And every year I stayed away it got easier and easier. You know what I mean?"

She doesn't say anything.

"What about you, Diane, your family? They're ranchers, aren't they?"

"I'd rather not talk about my family," she says, sitting up straight, her jacket crinkling. We are far away from that critical moment. This is a new one. "You didn't answer my first question. Why are you here with me?"

"I like you." This doesn't sound so good. I almost laugh, it sounds so weak.

She pulls a full mickey of rum out of her inner ski-jacket pocket, twists the cap off, and takes a swig. She hands it to me, warm from the inside of her jacket, and I realize taking another drink is the last thing I should do. I take it anyway, my first ever drink of rum. It burns like smoke. "What did Denton tell you about me?"

"Nothing," I say, and take another drink before handing it to her.

"Come on. Tell me."

What happened to that clean silence we had earlier? "We better get going, Diane."

She stands up, over me. Coughs a smoker's cough. "I'm not going anywhere, and neither are you, until you tell me what Denton said about me."

I snatch the bottle from her as I stand up, and take a long drink of it. "Okay, Diane. See ya." I toss the plastic mickey to her and make my way down the hill. First in the wrong direction and then in the right one.

She mumbles something, and runs down and around in front of me. I walk around her and she runs in front again. "Coward."

"I'm not a coward. I just don't like how you're talking to me. You're drunk."

"Is that what he said, that I'm a drunk? Huh?" In one drink, she finishes the last quarter of the mickey, and tosses it. Then, tough like that, she puts her hands in her pockets and stares at me. Stares at the ground. "Please tell me."

"No, Diane. He said nothing." The moon is half a moon, bright and crisp, the surrounding sky a sieve of stars.

"If it was nothing, you would have made a joke. You would have said something. Something means nothing. Nothing means something."

"All right. Nothing bad."

"I'd just like to know. I have the right, don't I?" Diane backs up a few paces, zips her jacket back up, and puts her hands on her hips. Her cheeks are red from the cold and the rum, blotchy under the street lights. She takes out her cigarettes and then puts them back in her pocket, without taking one.

"He said you have a kid."

"So what's wrong with that? You think you're better than me because I have a kid?" She pulls her wallet out of the same pocket as the cigarettes, and starts messing with it. "Do you know what my IQ is?"

A car honks from the road. Smoke blowing out the back. The Volaré. "Hey, Jeremy! It's me, Travis. And Connie."

Diane looks up at me and blows some air out her nose, some air that means *typical*, and steps back, more messing with her wallet.

I sniffle, amazed at this. My legs, now, are tingling. "Hey Travis. Connie."

"Hi Diane."

"Hi Travis."

With Connie sputtering, techno whirling out, Travis walks to us, smoking another clove cigarette. "S'up?"

"Nothing much," I say, feeling as if I've said it too fast, too naturally.

"Oh yeah? Where you guys headed?"

"Home. I guess."

Diane says, "Yeah. Home."

"Well Jesus. Let me give you guys a ride. Connie's all warmed up. Primed. I cleaned the seats after last night and everything. You tell Diane about that, Jeremy?"

"No. I didn't have the chance."

"So let's go. We could go smoke a bowl. I was just messing around on this internet newsgroup about *the end*, all these theories about the end of the world."

Diane looks at me and swallows. She holds a photo in her hand, of her kid, I guess. To prove something to me, something I don't need proved.

Travis takes a pull of his clove cigarette and offers the pack to me and Diane. I shake my head no, Diane doesn't respond. "A lot of these people have the same dream, of this meteor or comet – what's the difference between a meteor and comet? I don't know. Anyway, this thing from space hits the earth and the coasts sink."

Past Travis, I watch Diane look at the picture and stuff it carefully back into her wallet.

"If that thing hit, San Fran would go. Boston too, Jeremy. I was thinking: maybe me and you are *connected*. Maybe that's why we're here. Innerly, we knew the end of the world was coming, at least the end of the coasts, and we wanted to be safe. I was thinking about this and I had to get out of the apartment. I had to. What do you say, guys? Smoke a bowl? Come on, Jeremy. Diane."

"I don't know," I say.

Diane begins to walk down the hill, away.

"I better go after her, Travis."

"Oh, sorry, man. I didn't know I was interrupting. Check you later, Jeremy. Think about it, okay, what I told you."

"Okay."

The wind picks up, cold, as Travis gets into Connie. Techno-like heartbeats fade as he drives away, the Doppler effect. The Doppler effect is something I learned about in high school, sitting not so far from Diane. I run to catch up to her, concentrating on keeping the spins away. She stops.

I take her hands, but she doesn't respond so I let them go. "There's nothing wrong with having a kid. You just assumed Denton said something bad."

"What else did he say?"

"Can I see the picture?"

"No. He said other stuff too. Didn't he?" She rubs her eyes on the sleeve of her jacket; they are sore-looking, wet. Tomorrow, I decide, we can talk about this. I'm too drunk to talk proper. As I try to walk around her, she grabs me around the waist. I drag her a bit and she begins to yell.

"Let go. I'll tell you."

The wind is stronger now, full of dust. A plastic Safeway bag sails over the hill, swishing, and catches on the swing set. The little trees bend. Somewhere, guitar music plays, but soon it is gone. One hand at a time, Diane releases me and stands in front again, tucking her hair behind her ears, wiping her eyes. "Go on."

The taste of pumpkin pie comes to me. The dark filling, cheap after Thanksgiving. I have to say it. I have to say it because she wants to hear it, she won't accept anything else. "You drink, your parents support you. Trent has custody of the kid. You sleep around."

She looks down for a while without expression. Then she shakes her head and swings a slap at me. First, she cocks her arm back as if she's throwing a baseball. Then she makes a face and closes her eyes and twists her body a bit – but not enough – as the hand comes around; the classic Hail Mary swing. With training, you can see these coming and go through ten possible scenarios before you have to react. I don't want to hit her or hurt her arm so I just duck. I back up. "I'm sorry," I say.

"You fuckers, all of you," she says, and winds up again.

"Don't," I grab her. I hold her.

"It's a lie, you know. I hope you know that."

"I know."

She pushes away from me and starts walking down the sidewalk, in the direction of the second overpass; the overpass we go under to get to the apartment boxes and little houses that surround the Plum House. She picks up the empty mickey and stuffs it in her jacket. I wait until she's far ahead, and then I follow her.

Death.

Denton and Dad stand over me in their hooded robes, chewing toast. Sun, sun, sun, birds, acid in my mouth, the back of my head thumping with metallic poison. Pure evil. I tear at the high grass and close my eyes as hard as I can, searching for a dark, happy place. Giggling with toast in his mouth, Denton kicks at my legs. The ground is sopping wet and it smells old and sour, but it smells better than me. Won't something thin and icy come along and restore symmetry and balance, make things simple again, destroy this evil? As I turn over, Denton carefully slides a pair of sunglasses over my eyes.

Dad bends over me and takes a big bite of his toast. A small piece of crust falls on my stomach. "Oops," he says. Then he says, "I'm never gonna drink again. Please, God, make it stop."

"You look so pretty, Jer." A flash, as Denton takes a picture of me.

I am lying a few feet from the hole in the Plum House.

"Come here, Panther," says Dad. "Give Jeremy a nice, big kiss."

Denton drops the puppy near my face and he licks and pants and growls and paws at my ear. When I get to my knees, everything spins and I throw up. Denton and Dad stop laughing, throwing their toast into the high grass. When Panther begins to sniff at the puke, Denton picks him up. "You don't want that, boy. Stomach acid and alcohol aren't good for growing dogs."

A cellphone rings and Dad fishes it out of his robe. He walks to the sidewalk and talks to it and crosses the street.

I crawl a bit, towards the sidewalk, and Denton helps me up with his free hand. "What were you doing here last night?"

"I don't know." I really don't.

A prairie gull flies down for the piece of crust as we walk under the shadow of the red-ribboned elm and across the street. I'm dripping wet. Dew. "Home four days and you upchuck twice."

I remember waiting until Diane was in her building before starting home. After that, nothing. The thin clouds that often hang between here and the Rockies have burned away; all is clear.

In the bathroom I stick my finger down my throat and dry-heave a couple of times. I strip my clothes off, toss them into the bathtub, and wrap a towel around myself. My poor clothes, two outfits destroyed in two nights. In the spare room I find some plaid pajamas that used to be my grampa's. Denton brings me three Tylenols and a glass of ginger ale. In the living room I sit with him and watch *The Flintstones*, waiting for the drugs to kick in. It's the one where Fred and Barney build a swimming pool and then they have trouble sharing so they have to build a fence right down the middle of it. Denton and I used to watch this at noon and again after school. *The Flintstones* taught us about families.

"Go Freddy go," says Denton, peeling a banana, drinking a coffee.

Dad walks in from the bedroom, wearing his meet-and-greet Fire Chief uniform. "Jeremy. How's the head?"

"Thumpy."

"I wouldn't ask, but Denton has to work tonight. We're just a bit short at the beer gardens and I'd sure appreciate it if you could lend a hand, just pulling beer and taking money. Just standing around a few hours if you could. I wouldn't ask, but . . . you know, we could work together. Shoot the shit a little is what we could do. You know most of the volunteers I think. Little Aaron Dunphy, Jay Kang, Mason Fensky, Leonard Bucyk. Nick used to volunteer but he won't be there, of course. Some of them ask about you. You know what I always say?"

I can't believe he worked with Nick Lozinski. He *accepted* Nick Lozinski. "What do you always say, Dad?"

"Hell if I know."

Denton laughs. I look over at him and he doesn't look back. He smiles. "Barney said something funny."

"When they ask, that's what I say. Hell if I know. I guess I don't have to say that any more. I know now, don't I?"

"Yeah."

"It's only tonight. Carpenter's got it tomorrow night."

"What?" I can't concentrate.

"The beer gardens. Fred Carpenter's running them tomorrow night." Dad's been in charge of the Rodeo Days beer gardens since before I was born. I know all of this. I wish he would just stop talking. "Get there for 5:00 if you can. Sharp, if you can. All right boys, I'm off. Behave, eh?" He smiles and slaps the wall and leaves.

Denton throws the banana peel at me. Even though I see it coming, I let it slap me solidly in the cheek. "He's going to pick up Jeanette from the airport."

"That's nice," I say. But I don't think anything is nice.

"You want me to make a prediction?"

"I'd like nothing better, Denton."

"He's gonna move in with her. Soon too."

"Where?"

"She's got a nice house on the south side of the city. He'll commute. This'll be our house, mine and yours."

Too much information. What does she look like now? It's a long, boring commute. "I'm gonna take a nap, okay Dent? I gotta fix this headache."

"Okay. Listen, I got tomorrow off and it's supposed to be a pretty good night, not raining or too cold. Wanna hang out tomorrow night? We can ride the Zipper."

"That sounds nice," I say. Everything will be nice after this goes away, this hot and cold, dizzy, queasy pounding. Nothing else matters. I close the stairs door and the faintly cologne-smelling basement gives me hope. I'm not worried about last night, or about what will happen tonight. Often, before sleep, something rotten moves down from my brain and spreads to my entire body, and I worry about all the things I cannot change. But not now. No worries now. Now just thump thump thump.

[CHAPTER 5]

Mom died alone in the middle of the night. She was supposed to survive another month at least, and Denton and I were so used to the idea of our mom in the hospital where we saw her every day at 5:30, used to the idea that some days we were her sons and some days, because of the drugs, we were nothing but blurs or characters in a dream, that we both slept soundly that night. The phone rang at 6:00 am, an hour and a half before we usually got up for school, and the woman on the line said some very friendly morning greetings to me in a whispering and loving tone before asking if she might talk to my father. I put the receiver on the couch and knocked softly on Mom and Dad's door to wake him, but there was no answer. I knocked again and walked in. The bed was made and the fan was turned off; Mom and Dad always turned the fan on before they went to sleep. Although I was relatively certain that Dad wasn't working that morning, I told the woman he was, and she asked for his number at work. I told her 911 and she laughed quietly and told me she'd try the Seymour Fire Department, because she was in the city and the 911 was different there. A few minutes later, just as I was getting back into bed after some water and an oatmeal cookie, she called back, not sounding so pleasant anymore. It was an emergency and Dad was to call the hospital as soon as possible. I told her okay, and I tried to go back to sleep. Emergencies were common. Medication questions and cancer history questions that only Dad, who kept track of things better than a series of doctors could, knew. It didn't even occur to me that she may have died in the night.

When Denton and I got up at 7:30, Dad was in the middle of the living room, reading the paper. Since Mom had been in the hospital, he had been getting up in the morning, making scrambled eggs or peanut butter sandwiches and joking around with us about the stupid idiots running the NHL. It took me a few minutes to remember about the hospital.

Dad let Denton and me use our laps as a kitchen table so we could eat and watch cartoons in the morning. I remember the sun seemed to come up early that day, and it had snowed fresh the night before. Frostbite weather. Outside the front picture window, there were only two lines of footprints; one up our driveway and one in front of the Plum House. Dad's truck was on the street. We were halfway through *Astroboy* when Dad came into the living room and stood in front of the TV. I remember being a bit pissed off because *Astroboy* demanded one's full attention. He sat down.

"Hey Dad," said Denton. "You make a better door than window." This was one of Mom's sayings.

He started to say something, but said nothing. He just swallowed and walked into the bedroom, and closed the door.

"I didn't mean you couldn't stay in the living room. Jeez. Touchy." Denton tapped his cereal bowl with a spoon. "What's wrong with Dad?"

"Something about Mom." Even though Dad didn't tell us anything that morning, I felt a crookedness all day. It was so bright, so full of a dizzy, obvious clarity. The shine on the hallway between the home economics room and the counsellor's office, the noon announcements about the Seymour Jr. High Ski Club,

Mrs. Pottinger's brown dress with animals on it, Karen Young's superblue eye makeup, and Clint Somebody's Motley Crue t-shirt that a certain part of me coveted. The way I alternately cupped my cheeks and ears – I forgot a toque the day my mom died – on the way home. Dad had cleaned the house, washed the dishes. Sleeping when I got home, in their bedroom, smelling sweet, of booze.

When I woke him he sat on the side of the bed, mumbled something to himself as he looked into the mirror, and gave me a hug. He was sorry, Mom was dead. Then a long time passed when he said nothing, and looked as if there was something he was forgetting to tell me, something he didn't yet understand. He hugged me again. Would I be a big man and tell Denton, let him alone a while? I made some grilled cheese sandwiches and told my brother that our mom had died at 3:42 am.

A year before graduation, Joe Kravchuk discovered me in the bushes surrounding the railroad behind the Plum House, watching his wife. Luckily, I wasn't doing anything but watching her that day. Jeanette, who was lying back in a deck chair with her bare legs crossed, reading a magazine in the sun. And unlike other times, she was in long shorts and a t-shirt. Watching Jeanette had become a warm-weather habit, something I did, not because I wanted to but because I somehow had no choice. I knew it wasn't right and it wasn't fair, and at certain moments just before sleep, at prayer time, I felt diseased. But I couldn't stop.

I was looking through the binoculars, inspecting her feet, red painted toenails, when I felt a shiver. Crackling, footsteps, and close enough to suspend the possibility of running away. So I slowly lowered the binoculars from my eyes, closed them for a moment, and turned to the right. "Boo," said Joe.

He smiled and presented his hands to me, and I backed up a few steps. Then I realized he wanted the binoculars so I handed them over. He looked at his wife for a while, silent, and then he said, "Stunning. And she does it without effort."

I nodded. What else could I do.

"Do you know how old she is, Jeremy?"

"No."

"Jeanette is 37 years old. Do you know how old I am? How old do you think I look?" He passed me the binoculars. "Be honest."

Honestly, I figured 65. In the last three years his shaking had worsened and he dressed carelessly. Standing in front of me, his hair fly-away, his nose an overripe fruit, I wondered why, how. "Right about 50, I guess."

"Come on, Jeremy. Sean Connery looks right about 50. I'm 58 and I look it, every year of it. It's been eating at me, taking me down with it."

Some nights when Dad wasn't around, Joe would come over with a jazz tape for Denton and me to listen to, or a batch of plums that were particularly excellent. One night he invited us to sit in his Corvette, promising that we would each drive it one day. Joe and I had been friends, but strange friends. Beside me then, after discovering me as if I had been watching an ant farm, I felt something bizarre, grotesque, about him, between us. If he was done with me I wanted to go home.

"Have you seen her naked?"

"No." I answered quickly, and it was true. I'd seen her upper body, through an upstairs window, but she was wearing a bra that night.

"A 37-year-old woman is not a 19-year-old woman, but she is still as beautiful as . . ."

"Yes." I started walking, not around but away from him, the long route so I wouldn't have to walk through the bush until I got to the other opening in the fence a quarter of a kilometre away.

He followed me, tugged at my shirt, turned me around. "Jeremy. I'm not angry with you. I understand what you're doing here. I was a young man too, and I know what it's like to be frustrated. It's hard." Joe folded his hands above his waist and licked his lips. "It's rather hard."

I looked at his shoes. Blue topsiders, the skin of his ankles very white.

With his finger he lifted my chin and looked me in the eyes. "Would you like to *see* her?"

Behind Joe was the distant horn of the train, the ding ding ding at the north-end elevator crossing. "What?" I said, loud.

"Would you like to see her?"

Past the plum and cherry trees, I looked at Jeanette. Her magazine, *People*, and her hair. Strawberry blonde is what Travis called it. I didn't know exactly what Joe meant but I nodded, yes. Yes, I would like to see her.

The choices I made when I was 17, culminating in my decision to leave Seymour a year later, are foggy to me, confusing, shameful. How do I feel about what I did with Joe that night, and other nights? Looking back on it, I'm usually happy to have the fog roll in, another thought to drag in front, a more pressing, serving-the-future thought, something constructive that might serve the here and now Jeremy Little who must get on with his life, succeed, be a somebody. But some nights I am thankful to remember a time when sex was still powerful and dangerous, suffocating. A mystery. A time when I was absolutely obsessed with a woman 20 years older than me.

Joe ordered a pizza and the three of us ate it that night, on the deck chairs in the back yard. There was a light wind, lilac and the faintest hint of manure in the air. After some wine, Jeanette asked me about Tae Kwon Do and I demonstrated a couple of forms, even though I was still fat from the pizza. Like never before, I felt I was part of something delicious and sinister, and the glass of wine just made it worse; I couldn't wait for Jeanette to wish us our good nights and head upstairs for her nightly bath. Under the back porch light, I could see her nipples through the t-shirt. My knees bounced as I sat and listened to Joe's tales of the mistreated Ukraine, and of the Kravchuk connection to the bloodline of Jesus, a story that was becoming more and more convincing with each telling. An hour into the enigma of Pontius Pilate, Jeanette rolled her eyes at me. Proof of allegiance, I thought. She gave Joe a kiss on the forehead and squeezed my hand and walked into the back door of the Plum House. Joe continued talking, but he gave me a wink.

Their relationship was incomprehensible to me. Whispering under the sound of running water upstairs, Joe explained that because of medication he was no longer capable of *pleasing* Jeanette. As we sneaked up the stairs, I wondered why he watched his wife through a hole in the wall of his office. It was a perfect size. Although I never found out for sure, I suspect that she knew all along.

There were no bubbles in the claw-foot bathtub against the sloping white wall of the bathroom. Jeanette's breasts were wonderful in the clear water, her legs – which she had just shaved – shone. I would have done anything to be in that bathroom with Jeanette, in that tub with her, investigating the nipples that were far bigger than any I had seen in pictures. The triangle of hair I had seen in magazines was everything I had hoped it would be, and I wanted her to stand up over me; I knew what you were supposed to do there, with your tongue, to make the woman moan and claw at you and call your name. At first it didn't matter that Joe stood behind me as I watched, nothing else in the world mattered, there was only Jeanette, just that skin and that wet hair. Then he whispered something. I didn't hear him so he cleared his throat and said it again. "Do you want to be alone?"

I was so hard it hurt, and suddenly I remembered where I

was, what I was doing. "No, better go," I said, and tiptoed past him, into the hallway and down the stairs. The faces in the pictures on the way out of the house glared at me as if they knew.

Out the back door I paused at the patio table and took another small drink of wine.

For almost a year, I would be invited to the Kravchuks' once every two weeks or so, for dinner. Or a movie, because Denton had convinced Joe to buy a home theatre and a CD player. Since Jeanette had reincorporated Kravchuk Industries, the Plum House had reclaimed some of its earlier prominence in Seymour; there was an article in the *Star* about her achievements. After the first night, Joe left me to watch her alone, and I never stayed at the hole any longer than about five minutes because it verged on becoming dangerous. Several times I considered making a noise so she would be startled, so she would know that I was behind the wall, watching her. March 17, 1990: Jeanette masturbated in the bathtub, with her fingers. Curling her head over the back of the tub, she arched in the water, lifting her pelvis into the air, two fingers working inside her. Then she turned on the spout and positioned herself underneath it, still using her fingers. Her mouth opened wide, but outside of breathing she made no sound. The splashing of water. It seemed logical for me to go in there; she wanted someone. And I almost did. I have divined innumerable fantasies about that night, the things I should have or would have done.

I decided the day after witnessing Jeanette with fingers inside herself that I could never watch her again. It was doing things to me; she was all I could think about. I told myself that if I had any chance whatsoever with Jeanette – and it was possible, there were historical precedents – I couldn't be peeking at her through a wall, like Joe. I had to be a man, so I declined invitations to the Plum House for a while. When they came to see *Our Town* on the last night, it was the first time I had seen Jeanette in a couple of months. From behind the curtain, I watched her walk in. The same red dress she wore the first time I met her, the Indian night. She came alone. Afterwards, she said, "Jeremy, there wasn't a dry eye in the house," which was a nice thing for her to say, and she kissed me, twice, on the cheek.

Just as I was leaving the auditorium, there was a call in the office. Joe wanted to speak to me, something important. I told him we could meet at the back patio of our house in a couple of hours; a few of us were going for beers. Since I had lost my fight at the Canadian team trials, I had been going out a bit with my drama friends. And it was fine, the beer. We stars of the stage toasted each other and our futures, making predictions about each other. It pissed me off, after a few Pilsners, that I had to go back and meet Joe when the rest of the cast was jumping into a car and heading into the city for a big night of dancing.

Sitting at the table with his head in his hands like a kid at school, his long legs crossed, slippers. "What's up, Joe?"

"Jeanette thinks I'm sleeping." He wiped his eyes with a blue shirtsleeve, and stood up under the patio umbrella. The tie was twisted backwards.

"Can I get you something to drink?" I felt like a beer, even if he didn't.

"My father used to call me *the mess*. That was his name for me, Jeremy. When he said I would ruin the family business and humiliate our name, I'd grind my fist into my hand and tell myself, 'You just wait, old man. You just wait and see.' But he was right. He was absolutely right about me."

"Let me get you a drink, Joe." I opened the door but he held it and pulled me away, back out on to the porch.

Joe clenched his hands into tight fists, his arms shook. I was afraid he was going to cry. "I don't need another drink, son. I don't need that, or any pills. You must think I'm pathetic, less than a man."

"No. Listen, Joe, let me get you a drink and you can calm down proper." I tried to ease him down on to the bench, so he'd sit. His shaking made me nervous.

"Will you do me one favour and come across the street with me? There's something I think you should see. It will, I think, explain a few of the things that've been troubling me." Joe spoke as if he had come up for air and these were the only words he could say before being pulled back down again.

"Sure."

Leading me across the street, he said it wasn't fair, all of this, that God had stolen a chemical from his brain and forsaken him because of something his father or grandfather had done. That's why he couldn't concentrate without the drugs, why everything moved too fast and made it feel sometimes as if the back of his head were about to go up in flames. "When I was a young man," he said, "people respected me, admired me. Women found me attractive. I was intelligent and I knew my life was going to be a fine one. I was going to show my father. No one was as quick as I was. No one knew what I knew."

Over the carefully cut and perfectly green grass, glistening under the street lamp in the wake of a timed sprinkler system. Around to the back door of the Plum House. The door was locked so Joe opened it quietly, putting his shaky finger over his mouth to keep me shushed. We crept in through the kitchen and I took off my shoes in front of the wood stove in the main room. The house perfectly silent. In my socks I followed Joe up the steps, pausing every few seconds to avoid a rhythmic creaking. I whispered something to Joe. I wondered why we were being so quiet. He put his finger over his mouth again.

At the top of the stairs, Joe peeked into the bathroom and continued past it. The hallway was covered with a long, red Indian rug that helped muffle our steps. Lantern-style lamps shone warmly between the door jambs. I remembered that Joe was supposed to be in his room, sleeping. At his closed door, he pointed to Jeanette's door, also closed. "Go on," he said.

"No. It's Jeanette's room." My first thought was that she was in there, waiting for me.

Joe's arms were crossed over his chest, his hands on opposite shoulders. "She wants you to see. She told me so, Jeremy. She knows you watch her in the bathtub, she wants you to see." He covered his face with his hands.

I started walking away, not so prudent with the stepping any more. "Bye, Joe."

"Wait." Joe went into his room for a minute and then he came back out. Looking, I assumed, through another hole. Into her room. "Now is a good time to open the door. You have to look now, Jeremy. It's time." With the corner of his fist in his mouth, he walked to the end of the hallway and opened Jeanette's door; the one I had never seen, the one whose window faced west for a view of our house and the mountains. "See."

I should have been halfway down the stairs already. I should have had my shoes on. I should have been in the city with my friends, dancing at a meat market downtown and smiling at girls my own age, drunk, dreaming about my great future in Hollywood or wherever I thought my future would be when I was 18. I should have been sweating somewhere, talking, thinking: Oh man, would you look at all this! But I was upstairs on some thick red carpet in the Plum House, in the middle of the hallway, looking into Jeanette's room. Where they were standing against the curtained window, where my dad was pushing into her from behind, hairy, thrusting forward, hands wrapped around her. The skin on her hips shook; she gripped the thick brown curtain. Dad froze, and pulled out. He turned and grimaced and rushed out of sight, to the bed, I guess, where his clothes were. "Godammit, Joe," he said. Jeanette leaned forward against the window that faced my house, her ass that I had never seen heart-shaped and bigger than I'd imagined it was, her knees collapsing just an inch. Moving with her still-deep breaths, Jeanette swung her head down and around to look back at me out the corner of her right eye. I squinted at her and she began a smile that didn't finish.

Joe closed the door and ran for me, almost tackling me as I went for the stairs. Banging and crashing in Jeanette's room, Dad's voice. At the top of the stairs, Joe pounded the banister. I stopped halfway down. "Jeremy. It's been going on for years. They do it in my family's house! They don't even care that I'm here any more." His lips trembled, eyes huge. He gasped.

"Kravchuk, you son of a bitch," yelled Dad from behind the door. Stomping. I imagined that he was bouncing around, trying to get a leg into his pants.

"I've been keeping track. He has been inside my wife approximately 300 times. It started before your mother had passed. I wanted you to know that." He put his hands in the air and opened his eyes even wider, craning his head forward. He whispered now. "I have pictures. Proof. You understand what I have to do, Jeremy. Don't you?"

Down the stairs through the kitchen between the sprinklers over the grass and into the street. Without my shoes. Tiny rocks dug into the soles of the white socks my dad had weakened by bleach.

I went to stay with Travis for a while, without telling him why. Three days later, on a night I knew Dad would be working, I came home and told Denton what I had seen. Guess where Dad was on the night Mom died, at 3:42 am. Denton, the big confronter, wanted to stay up late and confront Dad about it when he got home, which would have been just after midnight. Our plan didn't work; we fell asleep on the green shag rug some time after the pilot for *Twin Peaks*.

It took Denton a while to wake me up, but by the time I heard the sirens I was already standing, looking out the picture window. The Plum House was on fire.

Glowing orange and statue-still, Joe stood just inside the house with the door open. The fire rumbled above and behind him like the origin of wind.

Denton and I ran across the street, screaming over the sirens, telling Joe to get the hell out of there. Past him, the stairs were on fire, each photo was a separate fire, walls and furniture burned in patterns. Flames licked out the window. Cracking and twisting of wood. The upstairs floor was still intact but barely. Joe was wearing the suit he wore on my 14th birthday, his best suit; his face and hair were blackened with smoke. The sprinklers were off but Joe seemed wet.

Alternating from foot to foot beside me on the Plum House lawn, Denton said, "What should we do?" I shook my head and shrugged, and he looked at me as if I had sprouted limbs from my ears. He ran to Joe.

I caught up to him and grabbed him by the shirt. "Leave him."

"He's got gas all over him. The house'll cave on him."

"Leave him."

At 15, Denton was already six feet tall and almost 200 pounds. He yanked his shirt out of my hands and pushed me back. Then he stood beside Joe and they yelled at each other but I couldn't hear; trucks wailed into the crescent. I was worried that Joe would burst into flames and Denton would too, because they were so close. Joe didn't struggle, he stayed stiff as a bass guitar when Denton grabbed him around the waist. Denton dropped the soaking wet Crazy Joe Kravchuk on the lawn, trucks pulling in behind him, and he looked at me and looked at the ground and closed his eyes to show how disgusted he was with me, with Joe, with Dad and Jeanette and maybe himself too.

From upstairs, a woman's scream. Fred and the firemen jumped off the two trucks and they pulled Denton, Joe, and me out of the way before disappearing into the smoke and the bright.

One of the firemen, someone I didn't recognize, stood and stared at Joe in wonder. They all glowed like TV ghosts under the street lights, fluorescent strips over grey coveralls and their yellow helmets. "Jeanette Kravchuk is still up there," I yelled to Fred, and Fred said, "Jesus H. Christ," just like Dad, and scrambled around barking orders to the jumpy and the scared who weren't already busy. "And my dad's up there too." Fred stopped barking for a moment and just stood and wiped under his nose with a big gloved hand. Nodded.

Any escape down the stairs was impossible. With the gas, Joe had made certain of that. By the time Fred and the petrified volunteers prepared the instantly inflatable crash mat that I always secretly hoped to jump into one day, Dad and Jeanette were waiting by the side window. The scream we had heard earlier had been a cry of pain, for Jeanette had broken the bone and ripped the skin of her ankle as she stepped through an almost-burned floorboard. They were both rushed to the hospital and treated for minor cuts from the broken glass of the window, superficial burns, and smoke inhalation. Jeanette's ankle was fitted for a cast.

In all the smoke, it had been hard to see them jump into the big red crash mat. But when they landed together, it sighed and collapsed around them.

Chicken George took Joe in. After two attempts at suicide before the trial, Joe was sent off to the Ponoka Hospital. I didn't visit him that summer. The upper floor of the Plum House was charred beyond repair. It stayed wet for weeks.

Denton shakes me awake. A pleasant discussion I am having with dream Ellie fades instantly. I slept too long; Dad is already tapping the kegs at the fairgrounds. My eyes adjust to the light and Denton sifts through my old junk drawer, wearing just his red boxer shorts, love handles sagging cleanly over the waistband. The headache has faded. Emptying my drawer on to the bed out of boredom, Denton finds U2's *Under a Blood Red Sky*, The Smiths' *Strangeways, Here We Come*, and two mixed tapes, one, if I remember well, Chet Baker, and the other John Coltrane. Further, he throws out a couple of Seymour Composite High drama handbills, scissors, some Dungeons and Dragons stuff, a bottle of black and white antibiotics, a hunk of petrified wood from the shore of Luna Lake, an out-of-date condom he thinks is pretty funny, matchbooks, poster putty, letters from my French class pen pal Gaston from Martinique, and two little Tae Kwon Do flags. Seoul, Korea, 1988. He pushes the Smiths tape aside and fills the drawer back up. Panther bounds on the bed beside me, waiting for a rassle.

Denton is leaving soon for dinner at Gwen's house. She invited him, for a talk. Since I haven't unpacked, he hunts through my bags for shirts he might wear, some outfit she hasn't seen, as I splash some water on my face and throw some clothes on in a hurry. I bound upstairs and Denton throws me the red sweater, the greatest red sweater in the world, because it's supposed to be a chilly night.

White and yellow clouds, purple in places, hang over the mountains. Unlike Boston, nobody carries an umbrella in Seymour, even when the clouds are purple in places. The wind is picking up. Traces of newspapers and slushie cups skim across Black Gold Drive, and the dust puffs along the fences, protecting back-yard swingsets and plastic pools from pedestrians and the multiple threats of traffic. Full cars and trucks shoo past steadily; city people like to come to Seymour for the spring rodeo because the pro circuit doesn't come through until July. According to a banner above the entrance, the religious school shaped like a cross on the other side of the Drive is hosting a choir contest today, and it must be over because uniformed kids and their parents in white dresses and blazers slouch out the doors. Next time, Cindy. You'll get 'em next time. Past the religious school are the frog-croaking football, rugby, and soccer fields along Belvedere Lake. The Kravchuks and other town founders decided in the twenties that the lake would be the best place to dump piss, shit, and garbage, so now it's more of a cesspool. In the study of the Plum House was a picture of the Kravchuks before Joe was born, posing in their oversized bathing suits on the shore of Belvedere Lake, kids splashing in the background.

The Black Gold Centre appears around the corner and hooray! – the Ferris wheel is wheeling and the Zipper is zipping. Kids' screams shift around in the wind and blend with the Cheap Trick song playing from the DJ booth in the Himalayan. Maybe Travis Many Fires is sitting in the middle of it with a microphone, sampling Seymour. An El Camino drives by, the guys in the back seat pointing at me. It slows and stops, halting traffic. The passenger rolls down his window, tosses his cigarette butt, and waves to me. I wave back. "Hey man," he says.

I walk towards the car, not certain of who it is because of shadows. Playing Radiohead in there, city guys.

"What's up? We're looking for the bar," says the passenger. Someone in the back seat says, "For tail!"

"Downtown," I say. "On 50th Avenue. Gordy's."

The guy in the back seat makes fun of the idea of downtown in a place like Seymour. I ignore them and continue walking. The passenger says something else but I don't hear it, and they all laugh. Clutch popped, tires squealed, they drive away, still laughing.

Cotton candy and the oil they cook those little doughnuts in. Cologne and cool air and hamburgers frying. The beer gardens is just beyond the midway, in-between the Round Up and the stage. It's only 5:30 but the band is already setting up, with red, white, and blue banners behind them. Molson and cigarette logos have been pasted on the bottom of the stage. Even though their hairdos aren't LA glam anymore, I recognize this band from high school; they played a Poison tune at the same noon-hour talent show when Travis wore the leopard skin jacket, screaming and cracking a whip over Skinny Puppy. The Jack Officers is their name. If Dad booked the Jack Officers, I hope he knows they're a glam metal cover band. He is sitting on one of the folding tables with Aaron Dunphy and Jay Kang. A bunch of other men and women I don't recognize sit in chairs behind the main table, under a grey tarp, drinking beer out of plastic cups. They watch me.

"Hey Jeremy," says Jay.

I nod and smile as Aaron looks me up and down, swinging his legs. "Didn't get near as big as your brother, did you?"

"Nope. Hi Dad."

"Better late than never." He is clean-shaven, his hair tucked into a stiff, yellow SFD hat with mesh at the back.

"Yeah. Sorry." I consider making up an excuse, but he is already looking away.

When he looks back, he scratches the top of the hat and says, "Bob Bélanger's daughter was here 15 minutes ago. She asked about you so I said you'd be working with me tonight." He takes a drink from his cup. "Might as well look around a while since you missed helping with the set-up. Be back at 6:00."

I sit up beside Jay Kang. Aaron leans over. "You dating Diane?"

"No."

Aaron nudges Jay and Jay gives him a look, so Aaron swings his legs some more and smiles to himself and takes a drink of his draft. Whistling, Dad slides off the table and walks over to the table under the tarp, where people in windbreakers and ski jackets are smoking cigarettes. A hockey mom I recognize stands up and they shake hands before Dad turns around and points to me and they nod. I look away. The sun is on its way out and the air is cooler than yesterday and I'm still feeling hungover and a bit fragile, so I make fists to warm my hands up.

"Test," says the head Jack Officer. "Test one two. Pantomime. Raspberry. Caliban. Newt. Song of Solomon. How's that?" This over *Cinnamon Girl*, playing out of the Himalayan.

"Aren't they the Jack Officers?" I say.

"No. Now they're Caught Using Purple." Jay laughs. "I love that name."

Aaron leans over again, his long, dirty-blonde hair falling in his face. "Glen says you had a Karate school in Boston. How's that?"

"It wasn't Karate. It was a mixture of styles, an integrated school. Bruce Lee's idea." A steady flow of people in front of us makes it difficult to make eye contact with Aaron. Pretty young girls with plucked eyebrows, women and guys I used to know, teachers. Jeans and jean jackets, cowboy hats, boots, fringed leather. Where are the colourful feathered roach clips that would transform an otherwise average young girl into the belle of the ball?

Jay rolls off the table and crouches in front of me with his beer. "Bruce Lee the actor?"

I nod, looking over him. The clouds haven't moved from the mountains. Not much of a sunset tonight.

Jay punches Aaron in the shin and says, "He was Chinese," and points to himself.

Before I can say anything about Bruce Lee, Aaron slides off the table and stands over Jay. "What about Chuck Norris at the end of *Return of the Dragon*? Was that not the hairiest chest and back you've ever seen? Now in all these new shows, no hair. Like in *Top Dog*. Hairless. Do you think that's electrolysis, or a wax job? Can you imagine how painful?" He shakes his head with serious concern.

"Have you studied anything, Jay?"

He looks down as if he's ashamed of his answer. "Not really. My dad studied Wing Chun too, for a while."

"Jay's a wimp, Jeremy, believe you me." Aaron is still standing over Jay. Jay stands up and they eye each other a bit.

"Does your dad have a wooden dummy, Jay?" I was hoping maybe he could tell me where I could get one.

"I don't know." Jay circles. Aaron jumps forward and strikes with a cuff in the back of the head. Jay moves in and they slap around at each other.

"I'll show you some white-man boxing," says Aaron, pulling Jay's jacket over his head. Jay gets Aaron's jacket almost over his head too, as they laugh and rough each other up. One tries to trip the other and they both go down in the dirt. Aaron is bigger but not by much, and they're quite evenly matched, huffing and puffing and rolling around on top of each other. Dad looks over at me from underneath the tarp and I shrug and smile. As quickly as it started, it ends. Jay rolls off and they both stand up, wiping grass from their jean jackets.

"Feel the Kung Fu blood of my ancestors flowing through me?" says Jay, swinging his arms around.

"Hoo," says Aaron, leaping on him again. This time it's only some pushing because they're both too tired. They sit back up on the table beside me and light each other's cigarettes.

After a while, Jay goes off to fill up his glass, taking Aaron's. Aaron coughs and wheezes and smokes beside me, cussing Jay and discussing his physical condition with himself, which is, I would agree, worrisome. Not wanting to interrupt him, I walk through the crowd. The closest thing I have to a conversation with my fellow townspeople is an "Oh, sorry, man," I get when a gangly teenage boy bumps into me. Lots of people I recognize from high school, in their mid- to late-20s, are standing around near the Moonwalk and the petting zoo, arms around one another, watching their children. My peers are shameless about growing old, giving in, building families and locking into long-term careers. And they look happy.

It's 6:05, so I walk on back to the beer gardens. A small crowd is gathering around the tarped table. Dad stands on a metal chair whose legs sink into the dirt. A few people laugh at that. "Listen up," he says, once the chair settles, wiping his hands on his jeans, his thing. When the whispering and laughing is over, Dad clears his throat. "First of all, thanks for coming. If the whole town goes up in smoke one night, your houses get saved first."

Everyone cheers. "Long's I get my insurance, Glen," booms Leonard Bucyk, in a cowboy hat again, one big arm around Jay and the other around Aaron. There is a Band-Aid over his left eye that wasn't there when Diane introduced me to him last night.

"All right, Len. Yours is last, so you can buy a whole new porno collection." Everyone laughs at that, and Dad continues, "Now. Let's please keep the drinking to a minimum. I know we're volunteering tonight, and for that I thank you and you deserve to partake, but remember this is for the benefit of the department and the whole town – so obviously, obviously we can't get so torqued that we're messing up with money and things. Okay?" Leonard moans. "Next, keep the free drinks for family only. The city folk are our main customers, yes, but if we gave all our friends free drinks, not a person from town would pay tonight. Also, we have to shut this thing down at midnight. George said that if he catches us selling a drop after midnight, he has to fine us."

"I'll fine Chicken George right upside the head," says Leonard, in his deep, forced voice, and everyone laughs again.

"Okay, Len. I'd also like to announce the new face, the new volunteer in the crowd who some of you already know or may remember. My son, Jeremy. Home from Boston. Say hi to everyone, Jeremy."

"Hi to everyone."

Everyone nods and smiles and says hi, and a few guys pat me on the back and say crappy things about Americans. The older men pump my hand and tell me I've sure grown up and ask me questions they're not so interested in hearing answers to, about what I'm doing now, about the Bruins.

A gust comes up and two bags full of beer cups go flying past the beer gardens and towards the stables behind the Black Gold Centre. I run after them because I'm happy to leave the welcome wagon. The bags hop up and down over the dusty ground and slam into the iron bars of the stable, the loose plastic whistling. I take the cups and watch the pen of horses, who watch me. I put my hand through the metal pen and one eyes me, shakes his head twice, blows out some air, and trots to within a few feet of my hand. He is shiny and brown with a black mane, eyes young and shy. Over the shit smell I can smell the horse smell, horse sweat, the smell you notice on them when they've been running, and just before a rain. Mom and Dad took us horseback riding near Banff about a year and a half before she died; Denton, who was nervous at first, rode with Mom and I rode with Dad. They were behind Dad and me, Mom telling Denton about when she was a kid and her dad – granddad, who we never met – took her to a ranch every summer. They would ride in the mornings and just before sundown, on the days that weren't too hot. As Mom told Denton stories about horses and our grandparents, I wanted to turn around and listen, but I was afraid to fall, so I asked Dad something. He told me to be quiet and pay attention. At the time I didn't know what I was supposed to pay attention to; the moist muscles of our horse's back, the bug in her mane, or the whipping tail of the one in front of us. I know now. At that time, he would have known about the cancer. He was watching everything, listening to everything. I got it wrong; I paid attention to the bobbing muscles. But Dad got it wrong too.

The horse inches towards me, sniffs at my fingers. The

announcer says, from inside the arena, "Will Vainter, folks, from Sandpoint. Riding Starjumper," and it echoes a few times. I reach and touch the horse's face and he jumps up and sideways, into the fence. I apologize to him and hurry away as a woman behind me says something, rushing over. Other horses clamour in the pen. I look over my shoulder and the trainer is up on the fence, saying soft words to her horses.

Seymour sings along to "Mammas Don't Let Your Babies Grow Up To Be Cowboys," a song I know all the words to. I'm leaning on one of the tables, the floodlights above turning my beer-soaked hands a dismal white. My shift is over and I'm just waiting for the fireworks so we can clean up and get out of here. Dad's behind me, torqued, as he would say, singing with his arm around one of his fireman buddies. Diane and Tracy walk up and stand next to me, and look off in the direction of Caught Using Purple. Clapping her hands without sound, Tracy sways to the music. Nods to me. After a while, Diane slaps me in the arm. "Hey."

"Hey, Diane." I don't want to feel nervous, and I don't want her to.

"Thought about you today." She moves hair from her face, where the wind keeps blowing it.

"I thought about you too," I say, but I'm not so sure I did. Not that Diane isn't worth thinking about, because she is. With the headache, it just wasn't the greatest day for thinking.

"Nice jacket," she says.

It's one of Dad's yellow SFD vinyl jackets; I put it on earlier because I was getting beer all over the greatest red sweater in the world. Since she challenged me about it, I consider taking the jacket off and unveiling it, but that would be an obvious and vain thing to do, an unattractive attempt at being attractive. Diane makes me feel twisty inside and regretful for last night, and I want to impress her, but not so much that I'm dripping in obviousness.

Even with the Chinook wind as bad as it is, the sound carries well. Caught Using Purple sing older-style country heartbreak songs, and they are winning me over; every song is good. In front of the band, the crowd sways, everyone drunk. Tracy moves in front of me, chewing gum and smelling good, messes Diane's hair and says she's outta here. After giving me a wave, she walks to the table where Aaron and Jay stand.

"I'm sorry about last night, Jeremy. I was drunk." She puts out her cigarette and unwraps a piece of gum for herself. Chewing, she hides her hands in the sleeves of her thick, blue sweater.

"People drink a lot out here. I forgot about that."

"We do." Caught Using Purple break into a Pogues song, so Dad and a woman I don't recognize polka around a bit. Others join in. Diane licks her lips and kicks at my foot. "The problem, I guess, is that I got a reputation a while back. And Colin, my son, doesn't make it any easier. So when I saw you and you seemed like a nice guy, I guess I hoped you wouldn't have these thoughts about me, these town thoughts. I'm not like that. I slept around a bit in college. But who didn't?" She shrugs, bobbing her head to the song. "But I changed my tune and got a serious boyfriend, Trent. It didn't work out but I got pregnant and I wanted to have the baby. I had him and then I had trouble with Trent, and one thing led to another and I got a reputation again. So shoot me. But I'm fine now." She looks at me. "Do you want to hear this?"

I rub her arm like she rubbed my arm last night. "Of course."

"I don't have custody."

"That's okay," I say, though it probably isn't the smartest thing to say.

"And that's that." Diane takes my hand. Dad grabs someone else and polkas her. Diane smiles at him. "There've been times when I wanted to move the hell away from here, but I don't know. I just want you to know I'm like everyone else." She points to herself. "The me that's beside you right now, *I'm* the me that matters."

"I don't care about any of that stuff," I say.

She is silent for a while. And then, as the song ends and the singer says some stuff about a lost cellphone, Diane grabs two handfuls of vinyl on the front of my jacket and kisses me on the lips. Cinnamon gum. It feels nice to be kissed. She backs away. "Will you call me tomorrow?"

"Yes."

Diane walks over to Tracy, they speak, and walk away from the beer gardens, into the dark.

I sit for a while, considering cinnamon and the way Diane's body felt in front of mine for that moment. As" Heart of Gold" starts up and everyone starts singing along, Dad stands over me. "How's my number one son?"

"It's okay."

"Can I sit with you?"

"Sure."

He takes his hat off and sits, and we look away and at each other and nod for a while, his head swaying like it always does when he drinks, one eye closed more than the other. "Thanks for your help tonight, Jeremy. Surely do appreciate it."

"No problem."

He smiles. "Your brother's turned out pretty damn good, hasn't he? All things considered?"

"He really has," I say. Dad's elbows are in some beer. They're already wet, no point telling him. "I'm proud."

"That's a good way of putting it."

No one is tending the beer table with the tarp over it. The fire volunteers fill their glasses by leaning over the public side of the table. This is a volunteer party now.

"Well, dammit, Jeremy," he says, suddenly, leaning over to

give my arm a grip. "Still wearing your mother's ring around your neck. That's nice."

"Yep."

"Certain times I figured, shit. Figured I probably wouldn't see you again. After the stroke for a while things were cloudy, and I told myself it wouldn't matter a bit even if you didn't come home. If you get me. But I'm glad you're here, son. Glad as hell."

I look away, but there's nothing much to see besides the rides and the people and the band. When I look back at my dad, his face has transformed. He isn't almost smiling any more.

"But I also feel that if you don't want to be part of the family, take off. I'm not gonna beg you to be in the family. I'm happy if you are, but I'm just living my life over here. Denton and I, we're doing good. Jeanette too." He takes a clumsy drink of his beer.

I sit here and look at my dad and try to understand him. I owe him that. But I don't see it. Why did he break our stuff and give the good furniture away and get rid of Mom's pictures if he was already happy with the woman across the street? And why did it have to be Jeanette? It's a big town. "Good for you, Dad." I take a drink of his beer.

"Families are more than a mental state, Jeremy. You have to *do*. You have to –"

"I get it, Dad."

"You get it." He pushes his drink away. Not too far away. "You get what?"

"I get what you're saying. Save it." A plane flies overhead, drowning the band a bit.

"So?" He shrugs, knocking his hat off the table.

"So what?"

"So do you want to *do* in this family, or what?" Terrible breath, head hanging over the table, the half-closed eye blinking slowly.

"I'm here."

"Godammit. You're here but you aren't here." The plane is

gone but he is still yelling. "How am I? Have you asked about the stroke? You almost lost your father, you big, ungrateful baby." Leering forward at me, he taps himself in the temple. "Think for once in your life, Jeremy. Think."

I think about popping him right in the slobbering mouth. "You done, Glen?"

He shakes his head, furious. Leaning down to pick up his hat, he mutters some stuff.

"Am I excused, Glen?"

He waves me away, so I stand up and start walking. I take off the jacket he gave me and I throw it back at him. "Hey!" he says, so I turn around. The fire people have stopped talking around us. "You can go all the way back to Boston, is where you can go. Go anywhere. Go away and find yourself another family, how about that?"

Instead of yelling, I sit again. He looks up at me with his head bent forward, as if he was actually looking down into the table. "Glen, think about this. Why would I *want* to be in this family?"

He points at me. "You are wrong."

"What you did to Mom, that's wrong."

"You shut up."

"How long did it take you to get from the hospital to Jeanette's bed? On the night Mom died?"

He stands up and shakes his head. "Stop, Jeremy."

I throw my chair back and slap the table as I stand up. The crowd has moved in around us. "Dad, you are a weak man. A small, stupid, weak man."

He leans forward on the table with his left hand and cocks his right back, as if he's going to hit me, but he stumbles back and opens his mouth to say something. Says nothing.

Then, very quietly, he says, "You're smaller, stupider, and weaker."

Someone pushes me from the side, hard, and I trip over the

chair. "You telling your own father to fuck off?" Leonard kicks the chair at me and I kick it away, staying down. "Arrogant little prick." He looks back at Dad. "You okay, Glen?"

"I'm fine, Lenny. We just had an argument, that's all." He walks around the table and takes Lenny's arm. "Jeremy didn't even tell me to fuck off."

"Fuck you," I say, standing up. "Both." I take off the greatest red sweater in the world and fold it on the table, unclasp the necklace with Mom's ring on the end of it and stuff it into my pocket.

A small group forms around Leonard and Dad. "Your dad's one of the best men in this town." Leonard shoots his chin out, puts his arm around Dad. "You insult him, you insult me." A few other people nod in agreement.

I lean down to tie my shoes as Leonard and Dad say some stuff to each other about how necessary or unnecessary all of this happens to be. Too late for that now. I pretend not to hear it when Dad pleads with Leonard to let me get away with it, to leave me alone, that he doesn't want me hurt, that I am his son. How many nights have I sat up at night, trying to shake and shiver off the certainty that Jeanette, who knew I watched her in the bathtub, told Dad, feigning disgust, that I had watched her?

Jay Kang pulls Dad away as Leonard takes off his jean jacket. Opens his mouth and pulls out some dental work, a bridge of false teeth, and smiles with his gums – his signature move? – before twisting his neck around and balling his big hands into fists. Song is drowsy, singer says, *put your arms around me*. There's lots of room, a square patch of grass and dirt between the tables. Leonard walks in, wide open, left arm forward to grab me, the right back and ready. Hockey-fight stance. Once he's in range, I fake a low kick and finger jab him. He covers his left eye with both hands and backs away, grunts and stamps, turns. So I move in and shin-kick the meaty part of his thigh, just above the knee, and he buckles. The crowd isn't so sure any more. Kick him again, same spot, and he covers it and cusses. Could finish it right now, he is unguarded up top, but no, this is fun, this control, the ground smooth and springy under my feet. He stands up straight, left eye watering, his hands not sure now because his brain told him they better protect his face and they better protect his sore leg. I could kick him low again, or give him one in the nuts, but I'd rather fight the way I've been trained. I'd rather let him show me. "Grab him, Lenny," says Aaron, to my right. "Just grab him." I put my arms down and stop moving. Leonard walks in and swings a wide, telegraphed right, so I give him a shot in the bicep as I parry it. I punch him square in the chest and he backs away and opens up again. Inside, driving straight inside I grab around his neck and headbutt him, put my thumbs in his eyes, knee him low, still holding on, elbow him across the face a couple of times, right, left, scissor, scissor before he grips my t-shirt at the waist and takes me down. As I hit the ground he punches me hard in the nose and I start bleeding right away, a flash of hot as always. I slither up over and on top of him in mount position and he squirms and bucks so I tie up his arms and drop a couple of elbows just above his eyebrows where the skin is weak. He bucks hard and rolls me over on to my back. The crowd cheers. My legs are around his waist, guard position, so I can keep him away with my knees, arching my back as he stands up over me to swing. His face is a mess. Over his shoulder, Dad looks down. I lock my legs behind Leonard and he goes down on his knees, his swings weak now, easy to parry. I pull him down into the top of my head and he sits up again, dazed, bleeding from the cheek and forehead and nose and mouth, puffing away, spitting. He pauses to look down on me in confusion, maybe disbelief; I don't think Leonard loses many fights. Finally he roars and grabs a clump of my shirt good and hard with his left hand. Arching, I move my legs up and hook them just below his neck. As he brings his right arm back to smash me, I twist on my left side and slide my right leg up and over his head, trapping his left hand on my shirt. Once my legs are over, I squeeze the left arm between my thighs and lock my right leg around the other side of his neck, inside. I begin to arch with his arm in place, and he lifts me up. His fingernails dig into my chest and I must look pretty feeble because the crowd cheers. I squeeze and arch all the way and Leonard drops with me, screaming. I take my time. I pull back slowly. He tries to punch at me a couple of times but the arm bar is locked in and he is in too much pain; all he can hit is the top of my head because my face is tucked away. The crowd is silent, the band between songs. Only Leonard cussing. Someone says, "Let him go, man." Finally, weakly, Leonard tells me he gives. So I pull back fast and his elbow pops before I roll back away from him. I get to my feet as he crouches on his knees, cringing and cradling his elbow. Aaron walks over to him and others do too. "It's busted," says Leonard, quietly now.

"It isn't broken," I say, wiping my nose with the already blood-soaked end of my shirt. My nose feels broken so I check and it's tender, throbbing, but not broken.

Everyone is silent or near-silent as I pick up my sweater and coat and walk out of the floodlights. My heart is hammering away and as I choo some air out and breathe I don't know what to feel, since I can't shake the certainty that Ellie would be disappointed in me. She would call this a small act, childish, a step back. Looking up, I walk through the second wave of the crowd; those who couldn't have watched the fight but who were interested enough to be here and to know, by now, that I was in it. And that I am a stranger, the bad guy. Most watch me as if my skin has been peeled away to reveal my alien innards. I look around for Chicken George, even though it was self-defence.

"Jeremy," says Dad, behind me. I turn and he just looks at me and I look at him. Part of me wants to go back and hug him; part of me wants him to follow me. But I know he won't, he can't. I shrug, and turn, and walk past the parking lot and into the darkness. As I reach Black Gold Drive, a violin solo distorted by the distance. A truck with a long horse trailer glides by, horses clomping around in the shadows. I try to smell them but my nose is bloody and sore, wrecked for smelling.

Just as I turn into the crescent, my heart finally settling, the band stops and the first fireworks explode over the Black Gold Centre. I know that Ellie would be disappointed, but she would forgive me if she were here. Without a thought of the blood on my clothes and face she would hold me and tell me it's okay. With her hand on the back of my head she would whisper into my ear that everything will work out. She would put a face cloth stuffed with ice over my nose, and we would snack on cheese and crackers and laugh about this before going to sleep. I don't look back at the fireworks because they aren't for me. Not tonight.

The house is silent, Panther asleep. Out the picture window, fireworks spray over the Plum House, illuminating it in bursts – spinning red wheels, blue fountains, yellow and green daisies. I close the curtains.

A few minutes after the last pop, the trucks and people begin to honk and holler down Black Gold Drive, driving drunk to Gordy's because it's only 12:30. Before I have time to consider it, the phone is in my hands and I am dialing Ellie's number, my number, even though it's early in the morning in Boston and the lovers will be awakened from their honey-scented dreams. Rob Palford answers, groggy, and I hang up.

Letterman is on, talking to a woman in a purple scarf. The time has come, she tells him, for Americans to re-evaluate all they take for granted. David makes a joke and the woman laughs, conscious, it seems, of taking herself too seriously.

Phone rings and I let it go. David asks the woman, who has a fine, dramatic voice, if she thinks all this is one big farce and she says, Oh yes, definitely, David. The answering machine picks up. Denton goes, "Say hi, Panther, speak," before Panther yips a little and Dad laughs in the background. Beep.

"Hello? Hi, Denton, it's Ellie. You called here, we have . . . one of those phones. Bit tired here. Is everything all right?" I love this tired voice. Part of me melts a little, scratches the arm of the pretty new chair, leaving dried blood. "Is your brother okay? I still haven't tracked him down over here, the operator has no clue, either. His phone has been disconnected. Out of service. Denton, why are you calling so late? Are you there? I don't get it."

I pick up the phone and the answering machine beeps and clicks off. "Hello."

"Hi, Denton. What's up? Is everything okay? Don't tell me something bad . . . please."

"It's Jeremy."

"Oh."

"Yeah, oh."

"What are you doing in Seymour? Why did you put that money in my bank account? Did you win the lottery or something?" She pauses. "Jeremy?"

"How's Rob?"

Sigh. Something clicks, a light. I know this light; it's on her side of the bed, a black stem with a red and blue stained-glass shade. She is sitting up now, wiping the light hair from the front of her eyes and looking down at her feet as they touch the dark, wood floor. "I don't need the money, Jeremy. You do. And the bank –"

"Is he naked?"

"Hold on." Ellie puts the phone on hold. And I know this is what she does: she stands up and shakes her head and slides her fingers through her hair, tells Rob it's nothing, go back to sleep. Turns out the light and tiptoes out of the room, pat pat pat. She grabs the cordless from the door jamb on her left as she walks into the kitchen, where the fridge hums, where the light from a street light behind the house shines in ghostly yellow. Before she touches TALK with her moisturized, coconut-smelling fingers, she grabs a banana from the counter and begins to peel it. "Hello?"

"Hi. Do you have a banana?" I turn off the TV.

She smiles and backs into the oak counter, slides down to the floor and hugs her knees to her chest. A night bus goes by in the rain because it is always raining in Boston. "Yes."

"How are you, Ellie?"

"I'm fine. I'm working on a big account. The client runs a national investment firm, and he told me over coffee that I should go independent. I could write off my car and a new computer and work from home for a while. Hire someone else. Maybe expand to a full-service communications firm." She pauses. "Sorry. Are you still there?"

"I'm always there."

"No, Jeremy, you're not." Another bus, or maybe a big truck goes by in front of the house. "You know, if I don't give this money to the bank, they might hunt you down and kill you. The money I loaned you was our money, not mine."

"Are you pregnant?"

"Jeremy, please. Do you want me to hang up on you?"

"No. I'm sorry."

"What are you doing in Seymour? How long have you been there? What's going on?" The line is very clear.

"There's a lot of love for me here. Everyone loves me in Seymour, that's why I came home."

"Is that sarcasm?"

"Yep. Are you pregnant?"

"No, Jeremy. I'm not pregnant."

Relief. Relief. I'm not sure why I can't be good about this, strong about it, why I can't suck it up like millions of others have. You always hear about people who have become chummy with their ex-wives and husbands and ex-boyfriends and girlfriends and sometimes, like Tuesday morning before Denton and Dad were up and the air was metallic and clean, I can see myself pure and plain like those people, laughing with Ellie and honestly hoping she is happy and pregnant like she wanted to be at this time in her life, and asking about Rob Palford in a decent way. "That's too bad."

"It's just fine. Everything is just fine, Jeremy, and thanks for asking this fine morning. Is there anything else?"

"I'm in Seymour." What else to say? I'm starting to forget what you look like, taste like, smell like and breathe like beside me in your bed. "It's Rodeo Days. The fireworks just finished. I got in this fight."

"Are you okay?"

"Yes."

"You won."

"I won."

"That won't do you any good, will it?" She sighs and takes a squishy bite of banana. "After all that's happened, between us and between you and Bobby Bullas, you're still convinced it's all about fighting. It's wrong, Jeremy, and it's stupid and selfish. My God, are you dense? How many times did we talk about this?"

"It was self-defence."

"I'll repeat it because you never listened and you're obviously not listening now. It's wrong wrong wrong. Fighting doesn't make you strong or sexy or a man – everything else about you does. I'd be more impressed if you sat down in the middle of a road and cried like a baby. That would be manlier than fighting. You're stuck, Jeremy." Again, she pauses, to let me say something. I choose to remain silent. But I can't.

"Fighting is beautiful, all the history . . ."

"You know that's not what I'm talking about. I'm talking about you, Jeremy, your brain. I'm glad you're with your family, maybe they can help you in ways that I couldn't. I want you to know, though, that nothing has changed. You can't make yourself a man by building up armour and dealing in blood. I know you're a good person, and if you'd let that come out instead of stuffing it deep inside every time you fist fight your way out of a difficult situation, well, then you'd be somebody. Cowboys and bullies are only cool in the movies, Jeremy. In real life, they're losers."

I've heard all this before. What does she want me to say? What can I say? I say, "Denton's in love with a girl here."

"Give him a hug for me. He's wonderful." She slides her heels down the floor, straightens her legs. "What's your response, Jeremy? What are your thoughts?"

"I don't know."

"Goodnight, Jeremy. Okay."

I don't want Ellie to go, ever. We are silent now, the thinnest crackles on the line. As she takes another bite of the banana, I want to tell her why I called. As she twirls the engagement ring on her finger—is there an engagement ring on her finger?—and looks up at the ceiling of the house she grew up in, the ceiling I know every inch of, I would like to tell her why I called. "Sweet dreams."

"Be careful," she says, and she is gone.

[CHAPTER 6]

This terrible cartoon.

As a kid, I swore to myself that I would never grow up to dis-like cartoons. How was it possible that Mom and Dad weren't interested in Bugs Bunny every Saturday morning, in *How the Grinch Stole Christmas* and *It's the Great Pumpkin, Charlie Brown?* Luckily, I have been spared whatever affliction they had contracted; I still like cartoons, love them. What's better than that feeling I get, that deep and roaring, almost overwhelming rush of good cheer when Santa, out of pure Santa goodness, brings Frosty back to life after the jealous magician locks him in the green-house? The simple messages, the songs!

Saturday-morning cartoons this Saturday morning are imper-sonal and diluted preachy things about not hurting the ozone layer, and Bugs and the gang don't get going until 11:00, so I put on some clothes and prowl out of the house. A bouquet of flowers, still wrapped, sits on the passenger side of Denton's truck, which is on the street. I take them out – the door is marvellously unlocked – and sneak them back into the kitchen. After cutting the stems, I arrange them in two vases, one for the wilted and one for the near-wilted. And slip out again.

Nothin' but blue sky, the warmest day so far. You don't often get five or six sunny days in a row out east, especially in the spring. Oh, in Boston, Ellie is just about to go on lunch break. I stop by 7-11 to pick up a couple of blueberry muffins, a coffee, and a city paper. In Alexandra Park adjacent to the Civic Centre, where the flowers will be blossoming soon, where the teenagers zip by on their rollerblades, and the single, divorced men eat their blueberry muffins and drink their coffees and read their papers in a wide, scattered semicircle around me, I eat my muffin, drink my coffee, and read the paper. Stern adult sounds, kid sounds trickle in from every direction; families are about. On the back of the World section, the weather page, it says Boston is overcast today, with drizzling rain. I wonder if Ellie remembered her umbrella, and then I vow to stop wondering about her. Families in sunglasses park themselves along 50th Street in front of me, with lawn chairs and bright vinyl bags behind them, bags full of ham sandwiches and little juice boxes and binoculars and sweatpants just in case it gets too cold for shorts. Today is parade day. Buried in the provincial section is a Nick Lozinski article; for some complicated and silly legal reason, he hasn't registered his plea yet. Another hearing this Monday.

The first muffin, the coffee, and the paper done, I lie back on my dry patch of grass where the sun has been shining all morning. When I try to cover my eyes with my forearm, I remind myself that Mr. Nose took a good shot last night, and I should be more ginger with him. Once you break a nose – and if you fight, you will break that thing – it becomes a tender and destroyed fellow that bleeds with the slightest urging. Did Leonard go to the hospital last night? Did he require stitches? Did any of the guys who laughed when Nick Lozinski pissed on my head happen to witness my triumph, with a hint of fear that they might be next? Ellie's tone last night brought me back to our arguments about fighting and my brain. Some people could be fighters but I couldn't because I couldn't separate the ring from every chunk of land or air in front of me. It's why I ran away from home seven years ago, why I could not adequately commit, why I couldn't consider a grown-up life with children and cars because then I'd have to protect them too. Usually I smiled when she criticized fighting. She just didn't understand. But when I was leaving her, and she was busy pointing out how she had been right all along, how I was a coward on the inside no matter how tough I made myself on the outside, I wasn't able to smile. I just wanted to hit something. And that made me want to smile even less.

"Steamroller," says Travis, and starts rolling up me. I sneak out from underneath him. Today, his bald head is shining, and it looks like he's trying to grow a goatee. He shifts to his knees and I realize that he – in huge, khaki pants and a striped shirt that says *Fuct* – is a 26-year-old skater. Must be the style in San Francisco. I hold out my remaining muffin. "Pour moi?" He rips into it, growling, stuffing way too much into his mouth, paper and everything. "So, what's the what?" he says, muffin flying out.

"Got a bloody nose last night."

"In Seymour? Say it ain't so." Again, pieces of muffin are airborne. I laugh as he extracts the slobbery paper, and I decide to let him finish before resuming anything like a conversation.

Girls play ring-around-the-rosey on the grass just beyond the trees, over and over again. They all fall down for the 20th time, and a mother in a lawn chair says, "Please, girls, please. Have a heart."

Travis stuffs the paper into his pocket. Perhaps he caught one of the cartoons this morning and learned a valuable littering lesson. After a long stretch, he pulls a weed out of the flower garden closest to us and sticks the clean end of it into his mouth. "Did you go to the beer gardens last night?"

"Worked it."

"Oh, yeah. It's your dad's show, I forgot. Some guy pop you in the nose for not giving him a free beer?" Travis chews on his weed, looking very Marlboro Man from the neck up. If Marlboro Man were a bald, Cree skater.

"Pretty much."

"Doesn't look so bad," he says, taking my cheeks in his hands. I back away a bit, by reflex, and he stuffs his hands into his pockets. "Gives you character."

I smile as warmly as possible. "I can use some of that." The Marlboro Man weed looks both tasty and rugged, so I lean over and swipe one out of the flower bed for myself. Not as pleasant-looking or as stiff as Travis's weed, but it'll do. It has a bored, vaguely smoky taste to it, like alfalfa sprouts that have been sitting on the counter for too long. As I lean back and admire myself for having this weed, I notice a bug on the end of it. If I were alone, I'd toss the weed and spit out what I'd already sucked, but instead I stay cool and look over at Travis, pointing at the bug. "Bug," I say.

"Hm. Parade should start soon." Travis looks at his watch and sucks his weed. Then, without looking over, he says, "I interrupted you the other night with your girlfriend. You should have said something right away."

"Ah," I wave at the air. The bug is really making me sick, so I throw the weed and stand up. Travis reaches for my hand and I pull him up like a Judo partner and we stand in the park, looking over at 50th Street, which is now cluttered with Seymourians.

"So. What now, Mr. Little? Any job angles? A military dictatorship of Thorsby? Anschluss New Sarepta? Marry Ms Bélanger and get respectable?"

This is my favourite question; I never tire of hearing it. "I don't know."

"You don't want to instruct any more?"

"No. I'm not a good teacher. I failed at it."

"If I stopped doing everything I failed at, my career wouldn't be Many Fires Music, it'd be Many Fires Self-Abuse, because whacking off is about the only thing I can accomplish consistently without failure. And even that's a chore sometimes. You know when you really want to do it and the moisturizer or Vaseline or what-have-you is way across the room, or you're in bed and you don't want to get it all over everything . . . I mean, that's failure. I don't end up whacking off at all sometimes, just because it's an inconvenience. My bed's too warm, say, for getting up. Ninety percent of my songs go unfinished. Is that failure? Maybe, but –"

"It's not something I need a pep talk about, Travis. If this is a pep talk."

"I don't know what it is. You were right to shut me up."

"I've gotta figure out something I can do, that's all." Rum a rum, lum lum, say the horns, and the drums of the high school marching band kick in too, so I take Travis's arm and we walk towards the street. On the curb I can't hold back a smile. I love the flat applause of the Rodeo Days parade; a safe, relaxed, and humble parade in contrast to those Ellie and me saw on August long weekends in towns like Concord and Lexington where everything important seemed to happen. Travis and I sit on this curb in-between two clapping families. Green and blue balloons drip down the street lights and from the trees hang white banners with stencils of a faded cowboy on a faded bucking bronco with the faded Rockies in the background, draped over the street, waving and twisting with each gust of wind. Little boys and little girls are cowboys and cowgirls. With plastic guns and with their hands they shoot at each other and at the marching band. All this even though the Canadian wild west was tamed by fur traders, Mounties, and Chinese rail crews.

Two thin girls, one with rosy cheeks and the other with painful-looking acne, both in the shortest of green miniskirts, twirl batons after the drummers. The ugly girl drops her baton, and when she picks it up she hits herself in the thigh with it, cursing quietly as she catches up with her pace-setting partner, who flashes the kind of smile you want pictures of, not missing a turn or a catch. Finding her step, the second girl throws the baton again and misses it again, this time jamming her thumb as the smiling partner twirls and spins, the deft silver baton now more than a baton, shining in the sun, now hope, future, strength. The second girl retrieves the baton from the side of the road, wipes the tears of frustration from her eyes and throws again, only to miss again. She stops and pounds the air with her fists, kicks the baton. The weak applause stops, and a couple of women and a man run out to the girl, the man demonstrating something. "Just don't throw it *so high*," he says. "You can do it." And the women encourage her and wipe her eyes, and she takes the baton and catches up to her partner, now past the railroad tracks. She throws it, this time only five feet in the air, catching it perfectly. The crowd cheers. Travis starts the wave and it runs right down the parade route, all the way around the corner.

The first float is a rancher's float. A big brown cow float with three couples on top in jeans and huge hats. "Beef!" says the wife to our left, a thumbs-up thrown triumphantly in the air, and the ranchers wave to her. Travis laughs and shakes his head. Two more cow floats follow, two trucks pulling smaller and less elaborately decorated Holstein cows. Kids sit in the back of the last truck, lobbing wrapped candies into the crowd as the truck passes.

Trailers covered in pompoms, old dump trucks draped with painted fabrics advertising old Kravchuk businesses like Seymour Pipeline and Seymour Truss, a truck like Denton's promoting the rodeo and the midway with Caught Using Purple playing an acoustic set – a Hank Williams medley – in the back, the chubby Shriners on their Masonic motorbikes, two police cars driven by younger cops flipping the sirens off and on because they never get to use them for real, the Seymour Karate Club with a triangle of kids and teenagers and uniforms, mostly white and yellow belts with two black belts up front, punching right left, right left, kiai! kiai! kiai! kiai!

The Seymour Composite High mascot comes by, a shabby-looking tiger that would have terrified me if I'd spotted him when I was five, and he shakes Travis's hand and my hand. "Hi, Travis," he says, muffled, "Hi, Jeremy," and walks away.

Travis taps me. "Look at the pisstanks." He points and laughs. Seymour Fire Department's finest are hanging off the sides of the old red truck Dad keeps around for show. Chief Glen Little is on top, waving gingerly. Those who don't wear sunglasses squint in pain. The Fire Department's role in the beer gardens is well known to everyone in Seymour – drink and sell, drink and sell. When I was young, they used to start with Scotch at our place early in the afternoon; this was before drinking and driving was the issue it is now. Men I recognize shout taunts at them: How's everyone feeling up there? Looking good, guys, real good. Top shelf, fellas! Little shaky there, Glen? Dad looks down on both sides, forcing a smile. When the truck gets to me, he hesitates before waving some more. The group around us begins to applaud. Most of the firemen notice me and double-take, especially Aaron Dunphy, who points and mouths something I can't figure out, something damning. Travis elbows me. "What's that all about?"

"My dad and I had a fight last night."

"Fucking families," says Travis, laughing. "Fucking towns." The truck rolls slowly by. I feel empty in the stomach, shaky, not as tough, as *c'est la vie* as I did a couple of hours ago. At the time and immediately after being vicious with someone, I can justify viciousness, roll in it, tell myself, Jeremy, you crafty asshole, because at least I'm not being a wimp, at least I'm not cowering, letting some Nick Lozinski piss on me. But hours later, when the guilt, when the forces of responsibility and goodness leak into me, like water into a faulty submarine, I am tempted to run and run and keep on running. Hanging on the back of the truck, covered in purple bruises and Band-Aids, is my good buddy Leonard Bucyk. His left arm is in a sling, not a cast but a sling – I told him it wasn't broken – and he doesn't wave because he hangs on with his good hand.

Travis waves at Leonard. "Hi, Leonard," he says. "Don't you have a wave for us? Come on, Lenny."

"Fuck you, wagonburner."

"Oh. That's a nice mouth with youngsters about. Very responsible, very forward-thinking of you." Travis elbows me and turns to the woman beside us, the one whose kids were ringing around the rosey. "I'm extremely sorry about that," he says to her. "Please accept my sincerest apologies, not only for my behaviour but for that of my curiously ape-like counterpart. The youth of today are a fiendish, blasphemous lot of disrespectful hooligans, fit for incarceration or worse, caging. Good old-fashioned caging."

She smiles at Travis and nods, pointing to the little cowgirls to her left. "You should hear their dad."

Aaron Dunphy whips an orange Halloween candy at us, which Travis catches, and the Chamber of Commerce people creep by in a red and white 1963 Corvette convertible. Joe's car. Jeanette must have sold it.

"You haven't been around, but Len Bucyk's turned out to be a real sweetheart of the rodeo." Travis unwraps his prehistoric candy and tosses it into his mouth. "Every time I see him, his knuckles are cut up. And he graduated two years before we did."

"He gave me the swollen nose."

Eyes watering, labouring away, Travis looks over at me, the Halloween candy a brown slab in his mouth. Some brown toffee juice drips down his lip and he smiles and wipes at it with his *Fuct* t-shirt. "Oh doe. Dirdy hell."

I had forgotten how much I liked Travis.

Imperious Arabian horses trot by, with shiny saddles and new bridles. "Wow," says Travis, almost through the candy. The man riding the horse closest to us, a Native man, tips his hat at Travis and Travis waves. He elbows me. "We're both Indians."

I nod, and laugh.

"Listen, Jeremy. I'm DJ-ing a show in Banff tonight, and they're giving me a hotel room and everything. Small expense account. I'm leaving at about 3:00 if you wanna come."

I look at my watch for some reason. "No. I can't. I told Denton I'd go to the fair with him tonight. I'll go next time, though."

"Yeah, sure," he says. Behind him the mayor, signalling the end of the parade, stands up with his wife in a rounded, black convertible. The mayor is a fat man with curly grey hair, in a cowboy suit with a bolo tie. Light blue all over. His wife is dressed in thin, suede leather, tanning-bed-orange face, hair dyed blonde and in pigtails: Pocahontas. Our leaders. How yez doin, everybody? says the mayor. Travis turns around and laughs a big, belly laugh at the mayor and his wife. They laugh along with him, and soon everyone around us is laughing. Then Travis suddenly stops laughing. "I've heard that one before," he says.

Travis throws his weed into the street and lights a stinky clove cigarette, and follows the mayor's car. He raises his cigarette like a hatchet and sneaks around behind the mayor's car. He looks back at me again to see if I'm laughing, so I do. I laugh.

Families gather their lawn chairs and bags, parents shouting at children and children reluctantly obeying. They had high hopes for the parade, and now that it's over they grumble, bummed. We missed ozone-layer cartoons for *this*? Sad hum and swoosh of traffic starts down the street again, dogs sniffing at things as masters yank hard on their chokers. Pretty legs. Tracy Lozinski, in a spring dress, so I stand up and clear my throat. Her son and daughter are holding her hands, one on each side, green and blue balloons tied to their outside fingers, perky with fresh helium in the light wind.

"Hi," I say, more to the kids than Tracy. They look away.

"This is Chad and Monique. Say hi, guys."

They mumble hi, tucking their little chins into their necks. Beautiful, blonde kids – fraternal twins? – dressed up in jeans and red plastic chaps, western shirts and matching plastic red cowboy hats.

"Hi Chad. Hi Monique."

Monique shakes her balloon string and then Chad shakes his. "So," says Tracy. "Heard you and Lenny had a disagreement last night."

I nod.

Tracy extends her hand and I don't back away. "You don't look too messed up."

I wonder how she got the mysterious, arced scar that makes her lipstick crooked. I remember it from Safe Grad. "My nose is bruised."

She nods. "Well, that's a pretty intelligent thing to do, all around. Get into a fight with the most popular guy in town."

"Lenny wasn't so lovable to me. Besides, isn't Nick the most popular guy in town?"

Two women come between Tracy and me, and bend down to fuss over Chad and Monique. Smiling to the women and giving Chad's cheek a quick wipe, Tracy pulls me away from the curb and in-between two trees. "He'll come after you. Or his friends will."

"He's in jail."

"Not Nick. Would you shut up about Nick? I mean Lenny's friends. It was a dumb thing that you did."

"None of his friends will come after me. You didn't see it, anyway. People who were there, they know I did the only thing I could do. He was threatening me."

"I heard you were threatening your dad and Leonard stepped in. You were about to hit Glen, is what I heard from the people who were there. You went crazy. Lenny gave up and you didn't stop."

"That's a lie. I'd never hit my dad." The wind gusts. She sounds like Ellie with her anti-fighting bit, and it makes everything feel hot and poignant for a second. Lecturing me here, among these bare trees and the warm wind, lends Tracy a lively, familiar air. She leans back against a tree, digging at the bark with her strap sandals.

"Lie or truth, Jeremy, it doesn't matter. The way people remember last night, the way they talk about last night, is the way you have to live with it. And you can't go around changing the story. I should know."

Her little dress opens at the neck. I understand why I kissed her ten years ago, without permission. Kissed her so Nick would piss on me, so I would need to fight and move to the USA and meet Ellie and wreck Ellie and me and wreck fighting. Here I am, ten years later, same spot on the cycle. I could kiss her again, without permission again, in front of her children and these women, against this tree, to see where it takes me, us, this time. Pulling Chad and Monique to our tree, the women tell Tracy how lucky she is to have such magnificent children, and they walk away, gripping each other's arms in that heartbreaking way senior citizens have. Chad and Monique return to her hands. Will they be fatherless? For how long? The sun goes behind a cloud and we are darker. The people are gone from the streets and sidewalks. "Gotta go," I say. "Thanks for the advice."

Kneeling, yanking a tissue from her pocket to give Chad's face a solid wiping, Tracy shakes her head in disapproval. About me or about Chad's dirty face? Both? "Good luck," she says.

On the railroad tracks that run parallel to Black Gold Drive, balancing on one track, then the other. A few minutes from home,

I sneeze. I sneeze again and my nose bleeds on yet another shirt. By the end of this week, my entire wardrobe will be ruined. I squeeze Mr. Nose, the sun comes back out, and in the distance, at the bottom of the colossal sky east of Seymour, the Ferris wheel begins to turn. I unpinch and it drips more. The smell of manure, sugar, blood.

A blue Eagle Talon with slightly tinted windows and a sunroof is parked at the bottom of the driveway. I stop and peek in the windows. Must be her long jacket in the back seat, her leather briefcase. Panther is on the deck, barking at me, unattended. As I take deep breaths to prepare myself for facing Dad and Jeanette, considering the option of a plane ticket to Mexico, Panther chews on the hand that isn't pinching my nose. When I open the door, he sprints into the house. "Panther, no," says Dad, as I take my shoes off. "Who's there?"

"Me." Over the sink, I unpinch and two or three residual drops of blood fall into a bowl half-filled with milk.

"Jeremy, call the dog. Put him back outside." In the living room, Panther is all over her, licking her face and crawling up her blouse as she tries to turn away. Heee, she says, panicked, as Dad extricates Panther from her and points his finger at him. "No," he says, and Panther barks as Dad drops him on the carpet. "The dog, Jeremy, now."

With a wet paper towel under my nose, I call Panther back into the kitchen and coax him outside. Whining, he jumps at the door as I close it. Damn, he must be thinking, do I ever want another shot at her. "Sorry, pal," I tell him, tossing the pink paper towel in the garbage. Just as I open the basement door to flee the scene, Dad calls me.

"Come in here a second, will ya?"

"I have some stuff to do downstairs. A pressing concern."

Jeanette sneezes and she says something to him, quietly, and he says no and not to bother herself with that. Then, obviously thinking I'm deaf and stupid, he says to her that I am a first-class shit. "One minute won't kill you."

Dad and Jeanette stand side by side behind the coffee table, holding hands, looking as if they just profited from a pyramid scheme. She smiles. "I'm sorry about Panther. He's a great dog but unfortunately I'm allergic. I get all puffy and sniffly around him, and uglier than I already am." Another smile, and another sniff. Dad hands her a tissue and she thanks him.

"Ugly," he says. "That'll be the day."

Of course she's allergic. If a believer were to convince me of the existence of God, the believer might well include in the argument that mighty attraction pets feel towards the allergic. God shows Himself to us in Jeanette's sneezing.

The light is behind them. In her dark, pinstriped business suit with padded shoulders, Jeanette takes her right hand from Dad's left and offers it for a shake. The look she gives me with the squeeze says: I *know* things about you. And this gives me a shiver. I know things about her; she is in the bathtub, they are in the bedroom. These scenes are the real story running through the living currents of this house, stopped-up in the cold system of wires and drains and empty pipes of the burnt house across the street. "How did New England treat you?"

I move forward a couple of steps in case she hasn't yet seen the blood. "Like a stepchild."

Dad clears his throat and sits, lightly pulling Jeanette down with him. "Let's cool it with that stuff."

Jeanette leans forward, looks at Dad and looks at me. "Your dad tells me you two've barely spoken since you've been home. I can understand why you'd be upset. Surprised, at this."

"I'm not surprised." My voice shakes as I say this, so I choo and step back. Relax.

Her hair is still strawberry blonde, bobbed just above her shoulders. A real tan, somehow. Diamond earrings. Did she buy this carpet, this furniture? The electronics? Or did she merely pitch in?

"Sit," Dad says.

"I'd really like to, I would, but I have some stuff to do."

"Jeremy. Sit."

So I sit in the rocking chair, close enough that I can see the lines in their faces but far enough away that I can feel and find some comfort in the distance. They open their suit jackets – hers blue, Dad's brown – and Jeanette smiles and nods and squeezes Dad's hand and shakes it as if to accentuate an important point. A bottle of red Chianti Ruffino on the table, two nearly full glasses.

"How are you, Jeanette?"

Dad laughs. He whispers in her ear, not really a whisper, that it's been five days and I still haven't asked him that question.

"Well, I'm honoured. And I'm doing very fine, thank you. The businesses I've kept in the industrial park are doing consistently well, contracts coming in." She knocks on the wooden leg of the coffee table. "Just had a successful business trip, in case Glen didn't tell you. That's why I haven't been about. I've opened a few hair salons in the city – one called To Dye For, if you can believe it – and three cafés around the university. People your age sure drink coffee."

"We sure do." I try not to change my expression. I'm stone.

She looks at Dad and sighs. "I'm living, now, in a beautiful house on the south side, with a gerbil. It's too big. Not the gerbil, the house." She looks at me for a few seconds. She lifts her wineglass for a sip, wine trembling. Dad takes a drink too, making a face as he does it. It must taste like the devil to his hungover tongue. He shakes his head and makes another face as he slides it back on the table.

The fireplace that is not a fireplace does not crackle, the stereo is off, the wind outside is not strong enough to hum through the trees. Outside the silence is only the classical music that seems to come through the floor. The back door bangs suddenly, Panther jumping at it. He barks. Jeanette puts a hand on the back of Dad's head and scratches. "Glen tells me you had some trouble with your Karate school."

"I did."

"Small business is tough, isn't it? All passion, no return. Losing a small business is like losing a . . ."

"Yes. It surely is. Well. I guess you two want some time alone, with Dad working tonight and all."

"And then tomorrow he's all mine." Jeanette takes him around the shoulders and kisses him on the lips.

Dad stiffens.

I'm torn between getting up right now for a hearty stomp out the door, and taking a long swig of that wine, straight out the bottle. Obviously she knows about last night, ignoring, like everything else remotely important, the blood on my face and shirt. "Nice to see you again, Jeanette." I stand up. "Have a pleasant afternoon." Out of the living room, wondering what they're thinking. Since they can't run away or ignore my physical presence, they are probably relieved that they have fulfilled their obligations to me. In the kitchen I open the fridge door and survey the milk and ketchup and sour cream and juice and leftover pyrogies and pickles.

"Jeremy?" says Dad.

"Yeah?" I close the door.

"How's the nose?"

"Perfect. He barely nicked it. Thanks for your concern." After closing the basement door I crouch at the top of the stairs and listen for a moment, the back of my head pressed against the wood of the railing. Though I can't hear them, I want to stay here for a minute, staring into the single bare bulb above me. When Mom was still alive and they had parties down here, when the basement was a basement bar, there was a tiki-man shade over that bulb.

At the end of that minute I stand up and take one step down. "I have to talk to you later," says Dad, just loud enough.

In my room, the clothes Denton borrowed are neatly folded on the bed. I knock on Denton's door. Nothing, so I push in without clearance. With a glass between his legs, Denton sits in the boxer shorts he wore last night, smoking a cigarette and tapping the ashes into a root-beer can beside his bed. Flipping channels. "You were upstairs?" he says.

"No. I came in through the servants' entrance."

He smiles briefly, without taking his eyes off the TV. The sound is off but classical music rolls out of the stereo. "So you had a chat with Jeanette." As he says this, I imagine the three of them coming clean about me; all the things I did, and saw. Another shiver.

The commercial must be over. When he drops the remote on the bed beside him, I recognize the movie, on TBS, *Ocean's 11*.

"Why no sound?"

Denton takes the glass from between his legs and fills it from the nearly full bottle of Southern Comfort sitting on the headboard behind him. He hands me the bottle. "I'm afraid Sammy Davis Jr. might sing another song, and I don't think I could stomach that right now. Earlier, he stood up in front of some tough guys in a garage and sang a song to them, just like that, in his coveralls. I don't know where the background music was supposed to be coming from."

"You shouldn't smoke, Denton."

"See Panther?"

"I guess she's allergic."

"Yep. Oh Jesus!" Dean Martin starts singing, silently, but Denton changes the channels anyway, from 2 to 54, 2 to 54. It hurts my eyes. Classical music. The chorus suddenly joins with the horns and strings and drums in the speakers.

"I talked to them for a few minutes up there. After letting Panther in without knowing."

"Dad's pissed at you, I guess." Denton is almost finished his glass.

"I guess."

"The firemen came into the bar last night, without Lenny Bucyk. Found out my brother beat up Lenny Bucyk."

"I didn't beat him up. I didn't start it. He started it."

"Firemen said you were about to beat up Dad and Lenny stepped in. Said you sucker-punched him too, threw dirt in his eyes. And after he gave up, you broke his arm."

I shake my head. If this weren't so stupid, it would be funny.

"Sounds like you went crazy."

"Either way, no one showed me any mercy when I got beat up. I got pissed on. They can whine as soon as they apologize for what they did to me ten years ago."

"Who, Jeremy?"

"All of those guys."

"Nick?"

"Yeah, Nick. And everyone."

Denton holds his glass out so I fill it with booze. Now my hands are shaking. The TV is on Superchannel. Eddie Murphy is on top of some woman, and you can tell by her face that she is moaning. Funeral chants, lots of bass now. Denton changes the channel and calmly throws the remote at his door. The batteries fly out, plastic chips off. I take another drink myself.

"Why are you sitting around in your underwear, smoking and drinking and watching TV with the sound off?"

"And classical music."

"And classical music? And busting remotes?"

He drops his cigarette into the can so it fizzes in the warm root beer at the bottom. "After I got all dressed up like a sore dink last night, I picked up the most expensive bouquet at Corinthia Flowers. Roses, tulips, lilies, some other ones. Extra baby's breath because Gwen likes baby's breath."

The TV says there is a 20% chance of snow on Sunday or Monday. "Snow?"

"It won't snow. It's May, and hot today. Don't worry, Jeremy, it won't snow." He lights a new cigarette, duMaurier Light, the same kind Mom smoked. The cards behind him have been rearranged. I would like to see the Ellie card again, to read what she wrote. I forget what she wrote. Denton blows the smoke up to the vent above. With the windows tinfoiled in here, it feels like midnight. "She took the flowers and the dessert I made – something with avocados and vanilla ice cream and instant coffee. She kissed my cheek, invited me in. I expected candles, wine, a sexy dress. I expected jazz music and low lights because she goes for that stuff. In the truck on the way there I was wondering if I was wearing too much cologne, if she would like the new underwear I was wearing. These ones," he says, pointing to his waist. "But there she was in the Harvard sweatshirt I brought back from Boston, and jeans. Her work outfit. She invites me to dinner and wears work clothes. I didn't know what to say."

"What did you say?"

"Nothing. I was embarrassed to be dressed up. All the lights were on, Muchmusic, no incense or anything. And she'd ordered pizza. Ham and pineapple. I don't even like ham and pineapple. She says it's no good for either of us to have a half-ass relationship, together and not-together and together and not-together. I say let's go all the way because we never actually gave it a chance. She's standing there thinking about that and I'm wondering if I should propose to her. I honestly thought it. Why not, I figured. We could die tomorrow, what's the point dodging each other when we might be happier together? And if it doesn't work out, at least we tried. You know?"

"But you didn't propose."

"After she stopped thinking she tells me she can't accept the flowers. That I can stay for pizza but only as a friend. A friend and a co-worker, as if it's supposed to be instant."

I take another good swig of Southern Comfort and jump on the bed with him so I can watch from his viewpoint. To cheer him up, I slap his leg. "I found the flowers. I put them in a vase upstairs."

"Thanks, Jeremy, but . . ." But nothing.

Since I don't know what else to say, I make that speech about it being fate, maybe. The right thing. I tell him he can't see it now because it hurts, but in a month or two he'll be thankful for last night, for Gwen's frankness.

"That's how you feel about Ellie?"

Wet snow or freezing rain, an Arctic front. It may miss us. It won't miss us. I know what 20% means. I take another drink of my brother's half-gone bottle of Southern Comfort.

Denton drinks too. "Hey, Diane called. Her number's on the phone, the call display. I need a shower, I guess. Thanks for listening."

"Are we still going to the fair tonight?"

He hops up and grabs a towel from his drawer. "If you aren't scared, I'm not."

"Don't worry about Leonard's friends, Dent. They can't hurt us. We'll be fine."

"We'll be fine." He whips the TV screen with the towel. There is a slight hobble to his walk, from drinking or from sitting around all day, or both. "It won't snow on Monday. Don't even think that, Jeremy. We'll be fine."

When the shower starts, he sings a Tragically Hip song. I can't remember the name of the song. The phone says Diane called two calls ago; it dials her for me.

"Yes?"

I laugh and take a drink, my last drink of Southern Comfort. "That's a funny way to answer the phone, don't you think?"

"I don't know. Is it?" There is a shakiness in her phone voice that I quite like.

"It is."

She doesn't say anything so I wonder if making merry with her is such a prudent idea. The Leonard stories must be bothering her, since I'm sure by now half of Seymour thinks I stabbed him in the back nine or ten times with a rusty knife and had sex with the wounds.

"So, Diane. Are we still going to the fair tonight?"

"Your brother said you're going with him. You made plans before."

"We can be a threesome."

"Hm." Quiet for a second, ticking something with her fingernail. I imagine she is ticking her teeth. "You know, Jeremy, I just wanted to tell you fighting doesn't impress anyone."

"Oh, come on. Not you too."

"It doesn't impress *anyone*."

"I know." But what I really know is that fighting does impress people; blood and guts and sweat in a world operated by computers and wimps. Even though people in Boston were disgusted by what happened with Bobby Bullas, some of the journalists who came by the school stayed extra long to talk with me about self-defence. They respected me. If people aren't impressed by fighting, why does everyone talk about it so much? People love battle, it's in their hearts. By the shake in her voice, I can tell Diane is impressed. She knows I won't be pissed on. "I don't care if it impresses you or not. I can't regret what happened. I protected myself."

"That's not what I heard."

"You wanna come over before we go out? Five or so?"

"I guess so."

"Denton's already half-corked."

"Oh, I heard what happened with Gwen, that poor little guy. He's –"

"He's fine."

She ticks her teeth some more. "I didn't mean anything by it."

"No, I know. Sorry for cutting you off. I just don't want people to think Denton's, you know . . ."

"Yeah. See you later, then?"

"Sure. Bye, Diane."

The singing has stopped, the shower has finished. The probability of flurries is down to 15%. The back door opens at the top of the stairs. Through the basement door, Jeanette yells, "See you, Jeremy. Bye Denton, sweetie. Talk to you."

"Later, Jean," says Denton, from the echoey bathroom.

Jean. Their feet on the driveway, Jeanette's heels and Dad's boots. How do they feel as they stand in front of the Plum House, as they see the charred upper floor? The big hole in front, the high grass and weeds in the front yard, the plum tree graveyard in back, the smell. Is it something they talk about, or do they pretend it's someone else's past, like a movie they've seen enough times to remember all the lines?

The pretty blue Talon hums out of the crescent.

Diane and I share a beer and eat dry Lucky Charms out of a shiny bowl as Denton dresses downstairs. All afternoon he has been stumbling around in his robe, making mean jokes about Gwen.

Done with the cereal, Diane leans back and tells me that her son Colin got a hernia while trying to climb a tree, that he is an uncommonly smart and handsome little boy, a heartbreaker for sure. When she plays rap music, her favourite kind of music, he holds on to the table and dances. I smile and nod and ask as many questions as I can think of, because she glows when she talks about her boy's misadventures. After telling me Colin doesn't even rip up his Dr. Seuss books, she bows her head, smiling, and tells me she didn't believe in God until Colin; there must be a God. She doesn't ask me what I think about that, which is good of her.

Denton clomps up the stairs and slouches into the living room wearing a Sloan t-shirt and his Stormrider jean jacket. Since he has just finished shaving, his face glows and he smells like icy freshness. In his hand, the bottle of Southern Comfort hangs from its neck, a mouthful and a half from being finished.

"It took you half an hour to figure out that ensemble, Versace?"

"Leave me alone, father beater."

Diane laughs. "How ya doin', Dentsy?"

"I'm demolished," he says, making like he's stabbing himself in the gut and twisting the blade around.

We lock Panther in the porch and suffer through his whining for a while, his pleas to make us reconsider, and we leave without locking the door. Denton finishes his bottle and tosses it beside the house. I tell him not to do that because I might plant a garden in there, and Diane asks if she can help because all she has on her balcony is a window box. Down Black Gold Drive we walk three abreast. We drink Pilsners as we walk, and Denton doesn't try to hide his when Chicken George drives by. When I tell him to drink his beer sneakier, he just laughs at me and says Gwen has demolished him.

Denton asks what it is to be molished. If he has been demolished, how can he get himself molished again? He is very drunk, slurring, yelling hi to all his buddies as we pass them.

We enter the grounds, and the smells and the sounds and the people swarm around us. Diane huddles up close and chews on her hair. "When I was a kid," she says, "I always thought Rodeo Days was magic. I looked forward to it like Christmas. If you're gonna get molished anywhere, Denton, you'll get molished here."

"You think so?"

"I know so," she says.

Denton holds her around the shoulders. "Could you answer me an honest question, Diane?"

"Shoot."

"Would you figure I'm a fine piece of ass?"

"Oh yeah."

And Denton walks ahead of us, past the Moonwalk and the bumper cars and the cotton candy guy, shaking that thing. He snaps his fingers and Travoltas around to make us laugh, right up to the Throw Your Loonies On Some Dirty Plates And Glasses And Win Whatever Dirty Plate Or Glass The Loonie Lands On. He tosses a loonie and it doesn't land anywhere. Then he ambles over to the betting wheel. When he loses two fins on the 20 to 1 spot, he calls the man running it a Freemason and we're off to the beer gardens.

Denton buys us a beer each and we sit across from where I fought last night. "Look at the Tilt-A-Whirl," Denton says. "We can't even ride it any more, we're too old. You know what kids think when they see me now? Old. They'll think that and the next thing you know they're my age and they can't ride the Tilt-A-Whirl any more, they'll be me, here, at this same table, demolished. And you know what I'll be then? Bald and fat. Fatter than I am now, full of margarine and ham. This dirty matter of Gwen won't bother me because I'll have lived another 15 years of demolishing by then. I'll just be sitting around, watching *Oprah* all the time, and she'll be skinnier and somehow younger than me."

The band plays a song with a violin, making all of this worse. Diane looks at me and rolls her eyes over her cup as she drinks.

"I'm serious, you guys. I'll be living in a trailer park down New Sarepta way, on welfare and selling blood and cum for booze money. Them will be the days."

As one of Chicken George's deputies runs after some kid with a stuffed dragon, Diane smacks Denton upside the head. "Get over it. Think if you were Nick, you big baby. You have a family and a good job, you're healthy and popular and you're not in jail. You have a lot to look forward to."

"Oh yeah? Like what?"

In-between songs, Caught Using Purple make some announcements about the ambulance lottery, and urge us all to check out the rodeo if we haven't already before breaking into three CCR songs in a row. After buying us the second round with my money, Denton tells us the fire dogs under the tarp said some shitty things about me, and that Fred Carpenter told them to keep their cakeholes shut. At Gordy's last night, Diane says some of the volunteers were lipping me off, but Dad kept arguing on my behalf, even bringing up the Nick Lozinski piss-beating.

Sitting here, talking, listening, Diane looks warmly at me and I look warmly at her. It's not the smartest idea to be on-the-verge like this, frivolous, with her being so sweet and black-haired and fine, a single mother with serious things like a boy who climbs trees and dances to rap music in her life, but the alternative seems lonely and desperate. Sure I love someone else. She probably does too.

I finish my second beer and turn the plastic glass over because I want to get on that Zipper. During a lull, I tell them to hurry. When the sun is gone and the lights make the midway more – maybe Diane is right – magical, the line-ups will be long. Diane finishes her beer but Denton just looks into his, as if it were a dead thing he once felt strongly about. "No," he says. "I think I'm gonna have a couple more here, to settle my nerves."

I remind him that he drank a whole bottle of Southern Comfort. Diane pulls me away, tells me to leave him alone. He's waiting for the molisher of his dreams.

Even though she buys a whole sheet of tickets, $25, Diane won't accept my money. In the Zipper line-up we listen to a group of teenage girls in front of us. They argue about a cute guy who's very cute but really quite an A-Number-One asshole. They have a vote among them and three think he's cute enough to override the assholeness and the other two figure he's too much of an asshole to be considered. In my ear, Diane asks me if I'm too much of an asshole to be cute. The midway lights flicker on and the good people of Seymour clap and cheer, "The Midnight Special" bumping out the big speakers in the field, and I consider reminding Diane that she was one of these girls in high school, pretty, loud, and that I was never the topic of any conversation she and her loud and pretty friends ever had. Reminding her that I always came to the fair alone. But it would be weak.

The girls look back at me now and then, as the line-ups thicken, as the stream of jean jackets and cowboy hats grows into a mob. In the middle of the circle, the girls pass a flask. "Hey," one of the girls says, finally, the one with an eyebrow ring who keeps looking, "aren't you the guy who fought Lenny Bucyk last night?"

"No. That was another guy." But I can't help smiling.

Diane turns away, drops my hand.

"It was you, I remember. It was rad."

I tap Diane on the shoulder. "Did you hear that? It was rad."

We don't talk for a while. In the dusty light, I stare at the mountains, at the grey rock and the snow up top, wondering how long it will take me to become comfortable enough in their shadow that I might ease into ignoring them, like I used to. The girls discuss the new movie with Nick Cage as they are separated into cars. The carnie opens the door and gives Diane and me the welcome-but-hurry gesture, a cigarette hanging from his cracked lips, and we step into our purple car. I hope it doesn't make you throw up if you've been drinking beer. Our lives in his hands, the carnie tips his black-and-yellow CAT hat to us. "Y'all locked in safe and sound?"

"Yes," says Diane.

He slams the door and the car jerks as we move up one rung. Even though we are belted in, Diane finds a way to bunny away from me, to crouch in the corner as if I'm contagious. I sigh, inside. Do I want this new bag of tension? New anxieties and contingencies and dependencies? At the top, our car rests upside down. It is suddenly dark. I don't want to have to say it but I do. "Don't be mad at me."

"I'm not mad."

"Yes you are."

"No. I haven't earned the right to be mad at you yet, Jeremy."

"You can be mad at me if you want." All the blood is rushing to my head. Diane's cheeks are red too.

"It just scares me that Colin might grow up into a drooling fool who has to kick the shit out of another man every few months to prove his masculinity to himself."

"You think I'm a drooling fool?"

"I don't understand why you have to be a tough guy. Most men are beyond it, aren't they? I used to think if people could just get away from Seymour ... I don't know." She shrugs, a very muscular gesture when you're upside down, strapped in by your shoulders. "Why, though? Why *do you?*"

Why? Why do I see it everywhere, the making of a fight? There are, of course, the soft and safe and sweet things, like our house at Christmastime when Denton and me were little and Mom and Dad were both alive, and happy. And I *do* want to provide that kind of love and warmth and safety for my own family, if I ever have one. But how can you be safe when other people are always looking for ways to hurt you? Do you have to move out to some faraway suburb where other people are scarce and there is only TV to hook you up to cruelty and danger? Seymour is no inner city – it's a tiny place with people who don't lock their doors at night. But Leonard Bucyk lives here, and people like him.

And I think, I realize, in an instant, upside down, that I am like Leonard Bucyk. Sure, little girls find it impressive, and it's more pleasing to give a black eye than to receive one, but is that what I am? Have I completely simplified my complexities, as Ellie would say? Have I been *that blind* to the world and the hearts of men? Aren't we all like this? Aren't we?

The Zipper rocks forward, creaking. We are right-side-up, upside down, at the top and at the bottom, whipping forwards and backwards. The belts dig into me, but I can't help but laugh and laugh. Diane laughs too, and screams, so I scream woo, hoo hoo hoo. After a few minutes, though, it becomes predictable and the creaking starts to bother me. I'd like to stop. I want to be back on the ground. When it comes to a rest, at the top, upside down again, I realize my throat is sore from yelling.

Diane smiles at me and I smile back. Then she nods and looks out the grate, adjusting her blue DKNY sweatshirt. We are high enough that over her shoulder I can see Denton in the beer gardens, sitting in the same seat, surrounded now by guys and gals. Poor, demolished Denton—someone is giving him a massage. The wind picks up and I get a whiff of horse. No need to ask Diane if she got it because she looks at me and raises her eyebrows. Yes. Horses.

The quarter lands in my glass again. Tracy and Diane are conspiring against me, because they are both terrific quarters players and I suck, getting worse with each chugged half-glass of beer they screw me into drinking. Not interested in getting smashed, especially if people are right about the firemen wanting me hurt, I only drink a bit and top it up as they laugh about how drunk I'm getting, or about how some chicks still wear acid-wash jeans and tease their bangs way up. I am more relaxed, more vulnerable than I can remember. Nothing seems to matter here, tonight. The table is flooded, the stench of last night's beer mingling with tonight's. Rodeo guys at the other end of the table are shaking it with their arm wrestling, an indication of Diane and Tracy's drinking-game talents. Solid bouncing even under conditions of chaos.

About an hour ago, Denton told me he was going to watch Caught Using Purple – who are now doing original songs, a mixture of country and folk rock with the odd waltzy thing thrown in so oldtimers can dance like they used to – so I have lost track of him. I bounce a quarter and miracle-of-miracles it lands in Diane's glass. She blinks at me a couple of times, right into my eyes; I hold the look as she wets her lips and takes the drink. It is late now, and we are past the point of flirting and hinting; it is obvious to both of us that we will be kissing later, breathing into each other's ears, saying crazy things, taking handfuls of fabric and skin. "Game over," she says, tossing her glass over her shoulder.

"I need a few more," says Tracy. "After tonight, the babysitter – Mother – is gone." She throws her hands up as she says Mother, so I assume it's Nick's mom. "Well, not till Tuesday, but I probably won't go out again. Mother won't let me."

"Don't tell me we're not going out Monday night, after the hearing." Diane slaps her arm. "It'll be good news, you know."

"I guess we'll probably go out that night too." Tracy's eyes open and close in slow motion. It looks like a lot of work to keep them up, her eyelids two spots of spilled milk.

Diane nods. "Make sure you get home all right, Trace."

"I will, honey." Tracy kisses her on the lips. "You two be careful."

"We will," I say, urgently.

Carnies pack up their fast-food trailers and sit in the shadows on humming generators, smoking dope. When Diane and me walk by, they stop talking and stare at us as if we're cops. We have authority, Diane and I. Once we reach the dark of the field, there are too many Stormriders and short haircuts to locate Denton, and we're not really trying too hard. We find a secluded spot on one side of a short bluff of tangled trees. The ground is dry. The front man plays a steel guitar and sings a slow song about insomnia, his cowboy hat pulled down so far he looks faceless. I lie back and Diane leans over me just as lightning flickers in the east, behind the band. Rain is falling on some small prairie house 50 kilometres from here, and Martha and Richard are hurrying to get the barbecue covered – help, kids! – because it will rust in the rain. She kisses me, a real kiss, wet and beer-tasting, cinnamon. Her lips are bigger than Ellie's, her tongue thinner. A hint of cigarette. Cheeks cool. She sits up and shakes her head and smiles. Looks at the band. Slides her cold hands up my shirt and I slink away and sit and watch her, and she watches me. Less than half a kilometre to the right is the darkness of Safe Grad ten years ago, where the plane crashed, where the ghosts are. Diane stands up and I stand up and the fireworks start hissing over us, popping loud. Seymour claps and cheers when a really big one goes off, or when a sequence of five or six little ones machine-gun in blue, yellow, red, white. Holding hands, we walk around the crowd, around the midway. Just beyond the beer gardens a crowd moves, some yelling as the fireworks finish.

"A fight," I say.

Diane squeezes my hand and pulls me in the opposite direction.

In the small kitchen I lean against the counter and inspect the pictures on the fridge. By the white night-light of the stove I can see little dark-haired Colin in a pile of leaves, wearing his tiny running shoes, denim overalls, and a Gap sweatshirt. Baby pictures, pictures of Colin and the grandparents. Another Diane and Colin and the man who must be Colin's father, Trent, sitting in front of the fountains at the legislative grounds in the city. Up top, a postcard picture taken near Seymour that says *if it ain't Alberta, it ain't beef.* Magneted to the side is a newspaper article on herbal remedies to relieve hypertension.

"Jeremy. What are you doing?"

"I just needed some water. I'll be there in a minute."

In her bed, Diane is naked. I am in the black underwear I wore specifically for this possibility. I expected to be here. What I didn't expect is that I would not be able to go through with it. At a critical moment in our pre-sex festivities, I got out of bed and ended up in here. I open the fridge door. A Brita. I pour myself a glass of water and bring it into the bedroom with me.

Diane sits up, over the covers. "Can I have some?"

In the ghetto blaster that sits on her pink dresser, the new Wu-Tang album. I imagine Colin bouncing up and down as it plays, his diaper crinkling. Diane takes one drink and looks at me, and takes another. The window is opened and her thin curtains sway and billow over her.

She tells me to get back into bed and I do. We kiss and I run my hand up these new legs and new hips, over her stomach and her breasts, across her neck. In this faint light she is so pale; when I open my eyes I can make out tiny black hairs above her eyebrows. She slips her hand into my underwear and asks me, in my ear, if I want to leave. I tell her yes and shake my head no, so she doesn't stop. As we kiss and move together, she moans and tells me things I pretend not to hear. When we are both naked, she slips me inside and rolls so I am on top of her. Lights from the next house shine down on her through the blinds. I can't do this. I expect Ellie's body, Ellie's sounds, Ellie's speeds. This is dangerous. "I can't do it, Diane."

"You're doing fine," she says, moving under me.

I try to pull out but she slides with me and I stay inside. "I can't. I'm not ready for this." I move back again but she holds me too close. She laughs so I put on a serious face. But it feels perfect, hot and cold and wet and wrong. "Stop, Diane. Please. I'm –"

"It's a good thing we're doing, Jeremy. Shut up and stop thinking," she says, and moves some more. Pulls my head down and sticks her tongue in my ear. "Do your job."

So I do.

At least three days a week Ellie would work late, and as I cooked dinner or attempted to watch TV, waiting for her, I would involuntarily invent grotesque scenarios of her capture and demise: an attacker in the back seat of her car, a bearded man with a rosy nose asking for the time outside her office, an asocial and sexually frustrated law clerk or student intern, gangs.

For the women's self-defence class I stripped away everything but the absolute essentials. Real fighting is ugly, so I designed the class along the primary objective of turning these women – Ellie – into walking nightmares. Into screaming, kicking, punching, kneeing, elbowing, pinching, clawing, head-butting, flesh-ripping, eye-gauging, balls-mangling monsters.

Since Ellie finished early on Fridays, it became a Friday-night class. On the fifth Friday, I taught them to pinch sensitive areas like the triceps, quads, nipples, inner thighs, and the handy genitals. Rachel was in the class so Garret came that night – the Sox were holidaying – to help me demonstrate and to act as an extra attack dummy. Using reasonable force, grrr, Garret and I *attacked* until one by one they screamed and pinched and clawed at us and we jumped off in astonishing pain, wanting nothing to do with them ever again. Men are especially sensitive to pinching and by the end of the class I could barely move and Garret was just as battered. The women – who had converted from shy, docile creatures on the first night into the dangerous brutes I promised they'd become – took pity on us and offered to take us out for a drink after class. It was an especially cautious non-drinking time for me, and certain women weren't interested in going to a bar because of the smokiness, so we went to a student's place on Storrow Drive where I watched Ellie and Garret and Rachel and Sandra – whose big, view-of-the-river apartment it was – and ten other women get nicely hosed. They were filled with adrenaline, bouncing in a state Garret and I knew well but in our pain that night could not enter, so we sat and watched and listened.

We took a taxi home, Ellie drunk and laughing her high, rising, infectious laugh in the back seat, slapping me and the ceiling as she repeated her favourites among the stories she'd heard from the women in the class that night. It was early winter, we wore scarves. At home we pulled the couch up and sat in front of the window together, with our feet on the heater, as she sipped herself a glass of wine and I sipped myself some milk. Astrud Gilberto on the hi fi.

As we talked, I considered her legs in the tight black pants she was wearing. I thought about how much I loved her and how glad I was that she agreed to take the women's self-defence class with me. The two most important streams of my life had come together; despite the bruises, that night was a pinnacle of comfort, safety. In a year and a half of living together, we had bought two chairs and a new TV, adopted an orange and white creamsicle cat named Frieda who was never around, stayed at Grandma's house on several occasions, and fought 11 times.

The women's self-defence class was a compromise between us, so she could better comprehend the myriad risks around her just as I had undertaken to gain a more sophisticated understanding of the world and the hearts of men. But just as the reading bored me, self-defence annoyed Ellie. The whole idea, according to her, of self-defence was ruining the country. Self-defence was not an adequate reason to buy a gun, to start an arms race, to break someone's nose. I had to trust. I had to believe. I had to be unsafe,

Choke Hold · 193

unprotected, undefended in order to live a true life, in order to be a man.

Ellie fell asleep in my arms that night, she even snored lightly, her after-wine thing. I watched the still cold of everything outside our window. The orange porch-lights of the apartments across the street, the ancient trees and 19th-century street lamps reminding me of time, small gardens dusted with snow. A woman in a BMW drove cautiously on the ice, gripping the wheel with her black leather gloves. She pulled in front of the building next to us, slid to a stop, put the car in park, and rested her forehead on her hands. I felt sorry for her.

One Wednesday night Ellie came home early with her portfolio. A man from one of the most prestigious advertising agencies in Boston had called – at work – to ask her out for lunch that Friday. He had seen some web pages he liked, so he looked into who developed them. She was ecstatic.

"This is everything I've always wanted. It's coming early too."

I was joking when I said it, I was, but I said, "He probably saw you in the lobby of your building. Probably thinks you're hot and wants a heavy affair with you."

"Right."

A design job at his agency would mean a raise of at least $20,000 a year. We talked about what that would mean for us. Over dinner, after a long silence of smiling and thinking, she said, "Who asks who to get married? Is it always the guy?"

I almost dropped my fork. Marriage? She had been talking about this, in hypothetical-future terms, for some time. I had never responded, because marriage was not an attractive idea to me. It didn't do my parents any good, or the Kravchuks. "What's the divorce rate in this country, about 60%?"

Her smile vanished. She swallowed and stirred her fork around in the the pasta. "I didn't mean that . . ."

"I'm not ready," I said. And as I said it I felt my heart quickening, like it did before a fight. It was unfortunate that I'd been curt, but I was being honest. I loved Ellie, but I didn't see any need to get married and have kids just so we could wreck it all ten years later. "I like the way things are now."

I had hurt her, and there was nothing more to say on the subject. Dinner was ruined.

For the next couple of weeks, her smiles were easy and perfunctory, like the ones you get at Wendy's. Then, slowly, everything went back to normal. She started at the new agency and she loved it. When she got her first paycheque, we celebrated with a night out at one of the fanciest restaurants in town, and at one point in the evening when she looked particularly beautiful and I felt I could not love her any more, I almost asked her to marry me. But I didn't.

One day at the Waterfront Warrior School, Steve Sutton called to let me know about a seminar in New York with one of Bruce Lee's original students. For New England Jun Fan certified instructors only. I could upgrade from Level One to Level Two without making a trip to California. And it came at a perfect time; I could get out of the house, breathe a little and give Ellie a long weekend to think about things, adjust. Ellie figured it would be a smart move for me, since I needed a holiday and a boost up the fighting pyramid; we didn't discuss the possibility that we might go together, as Steve had suggested. Promising to snap out of it, she even apologized for the way she had been acting.

It was early February, dogged winter with its ashy snow. It rained in New York, though, and it was great to do some guy stuff with other New England instructors. Since I was the youngest, I got more attention from the women in the bars. And it was a powerful feeling to walk into a New York club with four other guys, knowing that if anything went wrong, anything besides gunfire, we were perfectly safe. Nothing went wrong, of course. Nothing ever goes wrong when you're ready for it.

Day one of the seminar, the talking day, was all about eliminating boasters and braggarts, people who come in thinking *I'm gonna fuck somebody up!* from our classes. I didn't think any of my students were like that. The man told us how it is difficult, yet supremely effective, to disguise power, and I wrote that down to tell my class. We worked on Attack by Drawing techniques – tricking the opponent to open himself up, to give you a target and lend you a lot of beef for the counter-attack. Draw by feinting, by feigning fear, cowardice, ignorance. Keep your arsenal a secret.

Anxious and buzzing in the taxi from the airport. Ellie had been right; I needed charging up. Things would be better now, we had to talk, to reconcile and throw out the trash after the quietly frustrating time between us. We hadn't made love in over two weeks, so I was looking forward to a bit of that too. No more lying in bed beside her, staring at the ceiling, both of us awake with our own thoughts, thoughts impossible to share. I had bought a thin glass bottle of mango-smelling massage oil at a fancy store in New York, and I found a white dress with flowers on it that I knew she would love. In my head, she would be waiting for me, reading maybe, on a stool in the kitchen. Lights dimmed. Listening to something loud, with a beat. In the door she would pull me into her and we would do that thing on the Mexican blanket, long and dirty, love the silence away. Afterwards, a mango massage, kiss her all over, give her the pretty dress and remind her of things she may have forgotten.

I checked my watch, 7:18, and took a deep breath before opening the door. No music. Ellie wasn't on the stool or anywhere else. Even better, I figured, starting a fire before showering, shaving, and slipping into a soft blue suit she'd picked out for me the last time we were in New York together. The blue and yellow striped tie. Sitting and waiting, I went through three of her funk discs and a bottle of white wine before giving in and turning on the TV. No good. It was wrong that she wasn't home at 8:00, at 9:00, at 10:00, when she knew I was getting in tonight. I gave myself a stomach ache worrying about her. If she was working late – and of course she was working late, it was the only reasonable suggestion! – why hadn't she called? I couldn't try her at work because the phones at the agency frustratingly didn't take calls after 6:00 pm, and her cellphone sat on the kitchen counter, dead.

If there had been anything more to drink or some powerful drugs in the house, I would have taken them. Time was unbearable. Every time I reached the verge of imagining her with someone else, I transferred my thoughts to a sincere hope that her grandma had died. At 11:00 pm, after not really watching a newsmagazine show devoting a half-hour to Roswell aliens and another half-hour to ghosts in rural towns, I turned off the TV and slumped in the couch, stewing, drunk on wine, until sleep.

Only half out of a recurring bad dream about swimming to a shore that wasn't a shore but a long, thin piece of driftwood, I heard some fiddling with the lock. The door was opened so I yelled, "It's open, Ellie." There was silence then, so I considered the possibility that it was a robber. I jumped up, ready, eyeing the Kali sticks that hung over the smouldering fireplace. Because of some twisting during sleep, the tie was off to the side of my neck, and the pants and the jacket had become a roadmap of wrinkles.

In the doorway, she held a hand on her heart in a way I'd never seen before. "I thought you were . . . getting home tonight, Jeremy."

"Last night," I said, fixing the tie.

Taking her time, looking down as if thinking of an escape route, she closed and locked the door, stripping off her scarf and her hat and boots. There was a bad storm outside, the wind whipping white in huge circles in front of the window, the restored

Victorian gingerbread – the marquis property on our street – sad with dry February snow. A hint of smoke rose out of the fireplace. We stood staring at each other for a while, her face in a bit of a grimace. She squashed her hands together and backed hard into the door. "I'm sorry, honey."

I patted at my suit jacket, to get at some of the wrinkles. The stomach ache returned, my stomach seized. I swallowed and smiled. "Sorry. For forgetting I was getting home last night?" I wanted to pick up a glass or something pretty, and smash it.

"I'm so sorry. Let me –" She came forward.

I shook my head, stay away. "No."

As I moved away from her, to the window, she sat on the corner of the couch. "If I don't tell you, Jeremy, we might as well stop talking forever. I have to tell you why. It has a happy ending, this story."

I knew why. I fancied myself an expert in the whys and why nots, the ins and outs of this. Turning to the window, I tried to fix my suit in the reflection as she spoke. Past myself, the arms of the old tree pointed here and there in slow motion. Cars crept down our street, slipping at the stop sign beside the gingerbread. Pump your breaks, I thought, as Ellie talked to my back. Don't lock them up like that, you stupid Americans. These storms meant no school because the busses were down; they meant bundle up in comforters, kids, watch TV or movies or play Intellivision. Eat potato chips and drink ginger ale all day, invite someone over to play board games, play *Clue* because mystery is what we need, mystery. Teaching was rewarding on storm days and nights, when the heat was on. Students fought harder because there was nothing better to do. Hit the bag until you're dizzy and nauseous. Bend over and breathe deep and then hit some more. Harder, faster. Your muscles will recognize danger, students; your muscles will not give up. I listened without looking back, scratching the top of my head a few times, my hair messy in the reflection, fixing the soft blue suit jacket because it was stuck on the back pocket button of my pants. "Okay, Ellie."

"I want to be with you. I just had to know. If I hadn't, I never would have –"

"Okay, Ellie."

In the window I watched her approach, hug me from behind, kiss me. And because I didn't know what else to do, I kissed her back.

In the dark at night, when the distance receded, she sometimes asked me, quietly, if I was all right. If we were all right. Yes. And always I woke up the next morning in disguise, ready for a kiss. Ready to hear her plans for the day. Ready to smile through the smell of coffee and sliced grapefruit.

After classes, I trained alone. Spring came and summer crept in. Bobby Bullas stayed late some nights and we'd spar or work on sensitivity exercises for an hour or so, sweating all over each other. Admittedly, I kept certain techniques from Bobby because I was jealous of his talent, the effortlessness of his movements, his instincts; he absorbed everything like a perfect machine I plugged data into. Outside the odd joke or story about some sex deviant calling into the telepersonals company where he worked nights, Bobby and I didn't talk much. There was no place for it. Since my return from New York I had become rougher with the students, less patient and less anecdotal. Bobby thrived on it.

Garret considered himself an expert on matters of the heart because he and Rachel had successfully weaved through several acts of indiscretion. His advice was to shut the door on it, to get past *wrong* and embrace the animal nature of sexuality. Garret took an elder statesman tone when we discussed it, as if I was his apprentice in the art of love. We went out for lunch, to a Cajun restaurant on Cambridge Street.

"Just find yourself a fine thing and take her downtown," he said, digging into his shrimp, his hair now dark brown, parted at the side. He checked his shiny watch every few minutes. "Downtown! Get crazy with her too. Do all the stuff Ellie won't do. In public. Open up, Jeremy. Explore the anus. I'm telling you, it's gold, this advice."

And it made sense in an Old Testament way, but after some consideration I decided I wasn't that kind of guy. Did I want to be my dad? It was too simple, lacking in strategy. I figured on letting my brain sort things out for itself; no point getting anyone else involved.

One night after grappling class Bobby Bullas asked me if I had a minute. Because of the provocative tone in his voice, the first thought that popped into my head was that Bobby was gay, and he had a proposition for me. We sat down in the lobby with tea.

"I got these friends," he said. "Good guys."

"Oh yeah?" I was relieved.

"Yeah. And they want to get me into this fight. But I'm not so sure." He picked at the side of the couch with his fingernails.

"Well, you know how I feel about starting fights, Bobby. I've told you –"

"Oh, it's nothing like that. These other guys, they started it in a way. They got it coming." He picked harder. "I guess I don't know that much about it. I shouldn't be bothering you." He set his tea on the wicker table without drinking any, and gathered his jacket and bag.

"Just be careful," I said. "And either way, you're about the last person I'd be worried about in a fight."

He opened the door and held it opened. "I'm not afraid of getting hurt. I just don't know about it, that's all."

"When your friends need you, they need you," I said, sipping my tea, putting my bare feet up on the table, still happy about not having to deal with any gay issues. I suppose that would be irony.

"Goodnight, Sifu," he said, and went out into the dusk.

I didn't see Bobby again, not in person. That night, he and his friends waited outside the back entrance to a gay bar on Stuart Street. They had been drinking, and according to Bobby's testimony, "snorting just a little cocaine, just enough." A group left the bar and Bobby and his friends followed. Included in the group leaving the bar was a man who had come on to Bobby's brother at a party. It was revealed in the media that it was beyond "coming on," that the man and Bobby's brother had oral sex in the bathroom. It was a warm, late-summer night, a good night for a walk. Bobby's posse followed them to the Public Garden, surrounding them once they were safely off the road, secluded. The leader, Bobby's brother, Mitch Bullas – an awful name – asked them to surrender their wallets. The party guy stepped forward and said some things to Mitch about their bathroom adventure. Mitch hit him. A small, messy brawl broke out. By chance, a police car was on its way to an accident just a few blocks away on Boylston, and its sirens were on. Most of Bobby's group fled. Keith Hanson, an old pal of Bobby's who swore, "I didn't touch a hair on any of those faggotses heads," on TV, tried to pull Bobby off Jamie Anderson. "He was crazy, growling and spitting." By the time Bobby stopped hitting him, Jamie Anderson was unconscious. Bobby and Mitch and Keith Hanson ran away to meet up with the rest of their pals at Mitch's apartment, where the drinking and the cocaine continued. Drunk and high, Bobby bragged about his victory to his less successful brother and friends. Although most of the gay guys escaped with scraped knuckles and bloody lips or noses, giving as much or more than they received, Jamie Anderson hemorrhaged and died in the ambulance. The story was in the paper the next day and on TV that night. Bobby would confess to everything, including a few facts about my school. Where he learned to "take care of himself."

The reporters came without warning; I hadn't yet seen the papers or the news. They asked me what I taught and what I figured I was accomplishing by teaching gay bashers how to bash better. No matter what I said, it sounded guilty. For a week I was a celebrity, a stupid, unprepared face on TV, saying, "I was just doing my job." Jamie Anderson became a saint for a while; his life was profiled in the *Globe* and on TV, an anti-violence fund was set up in his name; his friends and supporters wanted the world to draw support from his strength and martyrdom. A woman who worked for a glossy magazine in New York interviewed me; she seemed sympathetic and intelligent about it at first, mentioning how in times like these it's rare to find someone so *devoted to the physical*. I agreed and told her I thought a lot about those kinds of things, and that I was just doing my job. She seemed to understand. We chatted a bit about how unfortunate everything was, and I agreed that Jamie Anderson sounded like a good guy, only 18, a boy. Then she asked me what colour my students were, if they were rich or poor – answering this question for herself after looking at my fees schedule – before making fun of the name of my school, the Waterfront Warrior School. I admitted it was a bonehead name, but Garret had urged me to keep it because it costs money to change names and signs. She didn't care about that. "So the warriors are white, upper-middle-class *men*, spoiled young men. And you teach them how to kick ass, right? How to kill." I told her I teach self-defence. She asked me who people like that, people like me, the privileged, need to defend ourselves against. I told her my family was poor but she wasn't listening any more. "Who threatens you?" she said, not angry but something, her tape recorder whirring on the table in front of me. "Who threatens you, Mr. Little? Who?" Everyone, I said. She sat silent for a moment, smiled, shook my hand, and left. I didn't buy a copy of that magazine.

Ellie was sweet and comforting, but I wouldn't have any of it. Everyone had failed me, everyone and everything. One by one, the students stopped coming. By the time Bobby Bullas and Jamie Anderson weren't on TV any more, I had three students left. One night, a Thursday night, I did a three-hour class with them, pushing them hard, before thanking them and telling them not to bother coming back.

Since Ellie fronted me so much money in the beginning, the bankruptcy was tangled. I gave the bank a chunk and emptied the rest of my accounts. The night I closed the school, Ellie left work early to make me a candlelight dinner. Beeswax candles. Manicotti with wine and bread; there was a dessert but I can't remember what it was, something with peaches. She wore the white dress I had bought her in New York, new underwear.

No matter how beautiful that night looks and smells in my memory now, and how strange and broken my actions seem, I understand how it was for me; I was doubly poisoned. There was no talking myself out of it. I wasn't hungry, wasn't feeling sexy. Although Ellie was frustrated, she served the dinner smiling, doing her best. At one point, when dinner was finished, she cried and asked me if she could help because she wanted so badly to help. I said no. No, Ellie, you can't help.

Garret came by the next day, the Friday before Halloween, with a pizza for lunch. It was clear that he had been sent. He informed me that these were days of reckoning, a critical time, a crossroads, that the decisions I made would be the most important in my life. As if I didn't already know it, he told me a man was defined by his actions. He wrote something out for me, called the Categorical Imperative, and had me sit and think about it for a while. The school was nothing, he said, people would forget about Bobby Bullas in a month; I could start that over. Losing Ellie would be for keeps. Once his mission was completed, he left. On his way out the door, he told me I'd better not disappoint him.

That night was her agency's Halloween party. We would get dressed up and go out for falafel sandwiches on the way, my suggestion. Ellie seemed very happy, and it felt as though we were on our way out of the rut. She danced around as we got ready, the stereo thumping. Since we hadn't planned on going, due to sadness and troubles, our costumes were last-minute deals; she went as a gangster with a hat and a pinstriped suit and painted-on stubble. I was a clown, because she had some clown stuff from a party in college.

The floor was decorated with orange and black paper, cobwebs. Office doors made to look like gravestones. ELLEN DONNELLY, R.I.P. Although I told myself I wouldn't fixate on the man she had been with, Steven, a vice-president, I stared at him from across the room. He was Batman. When he walked in, Ellie pulled me aside. "He's nothing to me, Jeremy. Remember that." I smiled and nodded. But Batman. How dare he? "He might try to talk to you. He still thinks it's a big secret. Don't . . ."

"It's okay," I said, and kissed her cheek, my clown nose poking her in the side of the eye. She rubbed it. "Sorry. Don't worry. I'll be good to Batman." Steven was an inch taller than me, and a bit stockier. Even with the mask I could see he was a handsome man, mid-30s. And there I was, a clown, wearing fat-guy hippie pants and old boots spraypainted red. After eyeing me up a while, forcing me to pound a couple of gin and tonics, he walked over and introduced himself. "We've all heard so much about you, Jeremy. Too bad about that terrible stuff with your student. Blatant media distortion." He looked where I was looking. "She talks about you incessantly. Incessantly."

"Oh yeah?" I made sure my nose was on straight.

"You two've been together quite a while, haven't you?"

I nodded and turned away from Steven. In front of a big plant near the window, the city lights behind her, holding a drink in one hand and her red plastic gun in the other, Ellie raised her eyebrows at me. She aimed.

"Listen, Jeremy," he said, "we have a squash league going here at the agency. You might want to get involved. It's a blast, actually, and we get into a bit of wallyball too when we're hankering for a change. You played squash? Gets your mind off things. What do you think, guy?"

Batman smiled at me with wet lips, winked, tipped his drink in the air. Thick arms and small dark eyes. I could hear him breathe, sense his chest expanding and shrinking, heart beating, that breath coating the inside of his glass when he brought it to his mouth, closed his eyes, and drank. Scotch. The room went silent. That breathing and where it had been. Those little eyes. Steven was on the floor in seconds, his drink spilling down the shiny Boston hardwood, and I was locking his wrist way up in the air, my thumb digging into the back of his hand, my clown foot planted on his shoulder for support. He swore and swore again, called Ellie. I pulled my foot off and dug my knee into Batman's neck as I asked him how she was, how he enjoyed my fiancée.

I didn't sleep in Ellie's bed that night.

[CHAPTER 7]

It rings and rings. The answering machine picks up and hope is restored until the phone rings some more. As the fifth round begins, I get out of bed and answer the damn thing. Denton.

"Brother?"

"Yeah. What time is it?"

"Early. I woulda called earlier but I didn't know. Thought Dad might be up but I guess he isn't and I can't really call later. Or maybe I can. Haven't asked." He breathes deeply a bit. "I'm a bit messed up, Jeremy. I don't wanna be here any longer than I have to be and . . ."

I take the phone from my ear and shake my head. It's so dark down here I can't tell if it's 10:00 am or 5:00 am. English sparrows chirp outside but they start pretty early, as a rule. It's Sunday, I know that. I know also that I sneaked out of Diane's apartment after we slept together, after we sobered up and she told me *they* think she is an alcoholic and that is why she doesn't have custody of Colin. "What's going on, Dent? Slowly."

"Had some trouble. I hate to ask you, Jer, but can you come get me out of jail? I'm in the tank and you have to pay to get me out."

"What –"

"I'll tell you later. Hold on." He asks somebody how much it's going to be. He says, "Jesus," and asks if there's any tax on that. "Jeremy."

"I'm here."

"It's $185. You got it? I could pay you back later."

"I'll get it on my way. Should I drive?"

"Take my truck. Keys are on the rack in the kitchen. Thanks for this, Jeremy."

The streets are empty because the whole town is busy sleeping off its hangover. It's good to drive again, at 6:15, with this acoustic guitar music and the windows opened. I can smell the snow coming. One truck with a woman pulling a horse trailer creeps slowly along Black Gold Drive, bouncing, the two brown passengers standing patiently. One looks like a pinto. The music is good and I'm too tired to be in a hurry; Denton sounds safe, so I wait for the woman and her horses before I turn in behind the trailer. She waves and smiles and I wave back. Candy wrappers and busted balloons sit in the dry sidewalk drains of the parade route, glinting in the sun, with tiny Seymour Rodeo – the cowboy and his horse – flags stuck in the grass beside. A jet rumbles overhead, its stream the only cloud in the sky.

At the bank machine I take out $200 without looking at the statement; it's far too early for that. I am extra careful not to lock the keys in the truck as I park at the police station. The grass here has already been cut, and someone has been doing some work in the garden. The statue of a soldier commemorating Seymour's soldiers who died in World War II has an enormous, silky black raven on its head. The raven looks over at me, silent, unafraid, feathers ruffling in the wind as I jog by.

The station door is locked. After I buzz the buzzer, a muffled voice comes from somewhere. "Yeah. Morning."

"My name is Jeremy Little. I'm here to pick up Denton Little."

The door buzzes some more and I push through. Antiseptic

smell, off-white walls, humming fluorescent lights, a hospital that doesn't help you. I climb the stairs in the entrance, scanning the press releases, bulletins, and pamphlets tacked to the particle-board wall. The grey-coloured man at the top of the stairs waves and takes a drink of his coffee. His uniform is too small so his little belly pops out and his white socks show. Big, familiar ears and sandpaper hair. "Jeremy Little?" he says.

"Yes."

"My name's Arthur Laine. We played hockey together years back, Pee Wee."

I nod and smile. Of course, Arthur. "First year Pee Wee, the green jerseys. You played goal."

"I was the goalie."

"That's right. That sure is something."

He puts down his coffee, claps his hands, and gives me a shake. "Small world, eh? I heard you were in town."

"Sure is." I think about this for a second. Why wouldn't Arthur and I run into each other in Seymour?

"How the hell are y'anyways? Keeping busy, or?"

"Bit tired right now." I smile, to probe. "It's always kind of a shock in the morning to have to bail your brother out of the tank."

He smiles and swipes at the air. "Ah, it's small potatoes, Jeremy. Everyone's in here some night or other. George hauls you in, no matter what, when, or who. Even if you didn't start it. Coffee?"

"Start what? Was Denton in a fight?"

"Coffee?"

"Was he in a fight?"

Arthur Laine unlocks a door and I follow him down a set of brightly lit yellow stairs covered in brown plastic dirt-catchers. "It's Rodeo Days so you never know, exactly, how things went. But it's no big deal. I've been here over two years now, and I can't remember three assault charges that stuck." As he turns back to me I swear his ears wiggle. "They never stick, is the thing. People never go through with charging a guy because of all the liquor and illicits that's usually involved. Once everyone's sober and they realize it was just one big party and . . . and damn if there ain't a fight in this town every night. As you know." Arthur clears his throat and makes like he's bringing up a big load of snot, but whatever he brings up he swallows. "So where you been, Jeremy? Living in the city now, or?"

"No. I was in Boston the past seven years."

He stops walking, sniffs. Hands out in supplication, he turns around. "No shit? Wow. Boston's fair big, isn't it? Well, small world, eh?" He backs against the wall, gives his ears a wiggle, and looks down as if he's giving something a serious contemplation. I wish he'd hurry up. Denton's in jail. "Jesus, the Bruins sucked ass this year, didn't they? First time they didn't make the playoffs in a coon's age, wasn't it? Man, when they lost Cam Neely they went straight to hell. And those new jerseys are just ugly. That bear head. Wow. Boston, eh? So I guess you're an American now?"

"No." We stand in front of another grey door. It's cold in here. Through the thick frosted glass near the top of it, I can see a bright hallway. Arthur scratches his arm, troubled by citizenship questions and the Bruins' poor luck. I clear my throat. "I'm sure Denton's anxious to get sprung."

"Oh. Oh, of course. Thinking about hockey'll do that to a guy. It can take the brain right out your head."

"It sure can."

Behind the grey door, the floor is olive green and the doors are silver, all very clean. Arthur takes out a card with some scribbles on it. He counts off, "One, two, three, four . . . okeedoke, your brother's in six." He unlocks the door and walks inside.

Covering his eyes with his forearm, Denton lies on the little bed with one leg on the floor. Blood on his shirt. On seeing the blood, my first instinct is to hunt and destroy anyone who hurt my brother. "Wake up, Dent," I say, my voice actually shaking. I help him up and hug him. "What the hell are you doing in here?" He pulls away from me, uncomfortable with hugging in front of Arthur.

"Follow me upstairs, boys. You aren't gonna give me any trouble, are you, Denton?" Arthur winks at me. "We'll get a guy taken care of here so you can get some sleep in a real bed. How's that sound?" He winks at me again. I have no idea why.

"Fine."

Arthur enlightens us about the Boston Bruins a bit more as he leads us back into the lobby. He decides, handing Denton a small pile of forms to sign, that if he was going to live in the States he'd want to live in Wyoming because it's such a decent name for a place. He says it a few times, to demonstrate. Wyoming. I give Arthur the $200.

"Thank you kindly," he says, counting it. "Missouri's not such a bad name, either, you know that? Missouri. Miz-oo-ree. And here's $15 change. I lent Denton an extra fiver last night. It's usually $180. Right, Denton?"

Denton nods. "That's right, Arthur. Thanks again."

"Okay, boys, take 'er easy, eh. You got all your copies, Denton? In court June 12th. 1:00 pm. If it goes that far, which it probably won't. God, I can't wait for June. My birthday's in June." Ears wiggle. "See yez!"

Denton staggers a bit when the sun hits him. "Agh. Can you drive?"

"Sure."

"Thanks, Jeremy."

"No problem."

As I turn the key, the radio blares. Denton turns it down. "I don't know why the radio always does that," he says, opening his window to investigate himself in the side mirror. "It's freezing out." He has the early puffiness of a shiner on his left eye, the same eye where I gave him one. The thought of this, with the air, makes me shiver. I wonder if he's thinking that too, right now.

"What happened?"

He points ahead of us, to a broken beer bottle in the road. I swerve around it. "It was sick. I have to move away now, and quit drinking."

I nod. It's probably a good idea all around, for everyone.

"We'll go Christian, how about?" he says, and hits my arm. The knees of his jeans are grass-stained. Outside his knuckles I can't see any wounds to account for the blood on the front of his shirt. As I turn down Black Gold Drive, Denton dry-heaves out the window. His body tightens up and he hugs himself around the front of his jacket, groaning quietly. "I barfed earlier."

The sun hits the window dead-on and I wish I had sunglasses. Denton stinks. How close to an average week has this been for him? Why didn't he hug me properly? When I'm not around Denton I assume that everything is perfect between us, that we're best friends and he knows everything about me without ever having to tell him, and that I know all his confusions and doubts and joys too, without any trouble or uncomfortable confessions. I wish it were true. "You gonna tell me what happened?"

He wipes his eyes, watering from the retch. "I got into a bit of a tussle."

"Well, I figured that. With who? Why?"

"Ah, with lots of people. I'm sure everyone in town will be talking about it, about me, this morning. Me and the horrible things I did."

"No. They're still too busy talking about Nick Lozinski smashing into the Plum House."

"I feel for Nick right now." He scratches at the crusted circle of blood on his t-shirt. Little flakes fall on his jeans and he doesn't wipe them off. "Did you see Gwen last night?"

"No."

"Louis and Charlene worked so she got the night off. Went to the fair with her bitch friend Alice who hates me."

"Did you talk to her?"

"There she was, dancing. Celebrating getting rid of me, I guess."

"You got pissed off and picked a fight because you saw Gwen having fun?"

"All decked out, lipstick and everything."

"So you said something to her?" I turn into the crescent and drive slowly.

"I did. And it wasn't nice, either."

"What did you say?" The truck is nearly stopped.

"Let's go. I can't remember. Get parked."

The paper delivery boy rides by on his bike, wearing a toque and a parka, peering in at us on Denton's side because we've been going so slow. He gives us an annoyed, inquisitive look.

"I'm ashamed to tell you," says Denton, as the front tire hits the curb.

"Don't be."

"I did something awful." He scratches at the blood some more. "I followed her around for a while at the end of the night, because she hadn't seen me. Like a detective. She was flirting with every guy she saw, and it wasn't just the normal hi-and-bye stuff, it was arm touching and giggling all over the place. I work in a bar. I know flirting when I see it. So when I couldn't stand it any more, I ran in front of her. I said something like, 'You couldn't have even waited a week . . .' You know the kind of things people say. I might have called her a whore."

I go up into the driveway and put it in reverse.

"It all came out. And after I said the things I had to say, she started screaming at me. It wasn't fair for me to do this and that to her, and I'm a son of a bitch and a woman hater. Alice yapped too, fuckin' Alice. They called me a woman hater, I remember that."

I wait for him to continue as I back out of the driveway and park on the street. He doesn't continue. "Then what?"

"Then the fight started. Put it in the driveway, please. Back it in."

I do, veering too far to the right so the thick arm of the pine tree claws over the cab, probably scratching it up. After powering through it, I apologize and turn it off and get out. I go for the basketball and throw it to him but he just catches it and drops it. I walk over to put my hand on his shoulder or something, but he turns and shakes his head no. "It'll be okay," I say.

"I don't know why people say that all the time, when things are about a thousand miles from okay. I'm in trouble. That's the truth."

"No, you're not. It was just a fight. Arthur said it won't stick."

The town is still silent, and very cold. He backs up against his truck and donkey-kicks the door. He kicks it again, this time harder, and it dents. Looking down at his damage, then, he slides down and crouches beside the front tire, fingers under his chin. "I hit Gwen."

I grab the basketball and take a shot. Air ball.

"We were right by the beer gardens, in-between the Moonwalk and the beer gardens. She wouldn't stop yelling, and Alice was there and she knows how I feel about Alice, and I was this woman hater in front of everyone. The fireworks were going off. The band was done. And you know how drunk I was. Everyone was watching, everyone who wasn't watching the sky. What could I say? What? It frustrated me so much. Why couldn't she just see herself, yelling like that? It's our business, you know? Not Seymour's."

I can't say anything.

"I didn't *want* to hit her. I'm not violent, you know that. I'm really, really not a violent person. I'm not saying she deserved it but she was wrong, yelling like that in front of everyone, about us."

"You punched Gwen?" I imagine something hard and fast, the sound, swak, not like in the movies. Real fighting is ugly. Gwen falling.

"No. Nothing like that. I started to walk past her and I pushed her in the forehead. My hand was open. It made a slap sound, though, and people yelled. I realized it was too hard and I tried to apologize but she punched me in the face before anything else happened. I think she busted her hand."

"That's where you got the shiner?"

"Yeah. Then her little brother James jumped me. Just a little guy, your size, so I tossed him. I'd sobered up a bit with all the yelling and that shot in the face she gave me, and seeing her there holding her hand and crying, all I wanted to do was go to her. But when I tried, Alice and some other chicks took her away. James got back up and Mason Fensky grabbed him and they started going. It got out of hand a bit, but it was mostly just a few of us. I cracked a pretty big kid a few times because he wouldn't shut his yap, and I was frustrated and mad and hammered. I'd seen him in the bar before, from New Sarepta, never liked him. I caught a bloody nose and a fat lip from him or someone. Then Chicken George came in, swinging his baton. He didn't take anyone but me. Seriously, there were tons of other people to take and he only took me."

"Why?"

"He doesn't like Dad, some town thing. And one of Gwen's friends told him I beat her up."

"You didn't, though. You just pushed her head. Once."

"I told George that. I told him I wanted to see Gwen and apologize but he said to shut up. Not to make matters worse for myself. And you know what he said? He said, 'You Littles got a real nose for trouble, don't yez?' Can you believe that?"

I smile down to him. Pushing someone in the head isn't so bad. It wouldn't be pretty if Denton did something really bad, because I'd have to support him anyway. "She charged you with assault?"

"Chicken George charged me. I'm not so worried about the charge. It's what people'll say. All I have to do is tell George to file against her and she'll refuse to testify and that'll be that, both'll be dropped. I called information in Boston last night, to get Ellie's number. I woke her up. Remember how her dad was a lawyer? Well, of course you remember. She told me not to worry, that if the Canadian system is anything like the American system, it won't go to court in a million years. I can get witnesses to say she was freaking and just about to get violent so I had to keep her at a safe distance with the palm of my hand. Proof is that she cracked me so hard. I have to call a lawyer tomorrow morning, and get pictures of the shiner at its shiniest. I could even touch it up with make-up, Ellie said, to make it uglier. I told Ellie I wanted to call Gwen and let her know that her case won't work but Ellie said not to. Because we shouldn't let her know our strategy in case it does go to court."

"Did Ellie say . . . much?"

"The reason you had to pay five extra was because Arthur let me use his calling card. He's a good guy."

I guess he didn't hear my question. I'm afraid to ask again. "I played hockey with him."

"That's what he was saying. Yeah, so Ellie basically said to doctor the story up a bit if we have to. Everyone was so pissed up. My friends'll say whatever."

I fake a cough. "That's a relief."

He goes for the basketball, sinks one with a sky hook. "I just hope she wakes up this morning and realizes I'm not a monster or a woman hater. I'm not, Jeremy."

"I believe you."

Fade-away jumper. "But after someone calls you that, says that about you, sees you push someone in the head . . . don't you think I'll be a woman hater now, to the town?"

"No. People'll understand." Maybe I'll ask about Ellie later.

He sinks one from the deck as I walk in the house and down the stairs, peeling off my clothes. I put pajamas back on and close the door. As I hop into bed, a knock on the door. "You asleep already?"

"No." I turn on the lamp.

"Sweet. Jammies." He runs out of the room and returns a couple of minutes later in his own pajamas, with rocket ships on them.

"You wanna talk, Dent?"

"Could do," he says. "But I don't have to or anything. I feel better already, after telling you about it. I think Ellie's right, too." He jumps on the bed beside me. "But it's hard not to think of it in an awful way, as if I'm a bad person."

"Whenever you can't stop thinking of Gwen, think of Disneyland."

"I'm not a woman hater. I'm a woman lover."

"I know. You're the best guy."

"You have to say that 'cause you're my brother."

"Maybe. But Arthur Laine said it was gonna be all right, and Gwen hit you even harder. I bet she feels as shitty as you do. Besides, it doesn't sound like Ellie —"

"Jeremy, she didn't ask about you."

I look over at the wall, count the fake planks of wood on the panelling.

"I was waiting for her to ask but she didn't. But she was all business about the charge, so that's probably why. And she was pretty tired."

I turn off the lamp.

Denton sniffs. "But you should call her up anyway."

"Why?"

I can hear him shrug. Why not? We are silent now, in the dark, Denton smelling like beer. Our breathing is at the same pace, both too fast to sleep. After a long while, Denton says, "I'd give anything to go back in time."

"Don't talk like that," I say.

We just have to do it right next time.

Denton doesn't snore. Curled up with hands clasped under his chin, he breathes deeply and smoothly beside me. The light above the stairs leaks into my room, and on to Denton's face, which is, in this light, an angel's face. I imagine I can hear his heart beating as he breathes, as he works his troubles and desires out in his dreams, and as much as I feel a simple wonder for life in watching my brother in the process of living, it fills me with a dread for time passing, the weakness and fragility of our bodies, the fight against death. For as much as I am aware in my head that Denton will someday die, that I will, in my heart I cannot accept it.

Without disturbing him, I sneak out of bed and into jeans and a t-shirt. After messing with Panther on the balcony awhile, shocked by the sudden cool in the air, I walk down the driveway and sit on the curb in front of our little house. From the collection of rocks in the gutter at my feet, I take the biggest one and throw it into the jungle of grass and weeds growing in front of the shrinking Plum House, only two shades darker than the sky. The bright blue of this morning has been replaced by thick, low cloud. It's too cold out here for jeans and a t-shirt, but cold is the least of my concerns. I *would* give anything to go back in time. To amend past decisions.

In the hazy, golden light of the photographs that lined the stairs of the Plum House, I can see dancing parties 50 years ago, big dinners before that. Music, smoke, languages I don't understand. White and black tuxedos, long dresses. A band playing in the back yard, a fountain. Poor Kravchuks. Royal blood descending from Jesus himself, getting messed up with the peasant family across the street.

I walk across, inside. There is a layer of glass and mushy black bubbled wood, dust, and dirt on the floor, tire marks from Nick's Jeep Cherokee. Where there is any white left on the walls, crosses of all sizes have been burnt – the Seymour Satanic club. A few broken tables sit in the study, and the scorched chandelier hangs lopsided over me, over the foyer. I can see through the ceiling, old lattice-work, up into Jeanette's room. As I put my weight on the first stair, something gives and the house shifts over me, echoing creaks and snaps. The smells of wet wood, dust, hair, old fruit, and coals. Up the stairs and the house continues to whine and resettle. A Chet Baker song jumps into my head.

The thick red carpet with the pattern is still up here, and the bathroom looks all right, waterless but cleaner than the rest of the house. The window has been planked and a pile of broken glass sits in Jeanette's claw-foot bathtub. Someone has taken the toilet seat. Past the bathroom, the floor of the hallway has been destroyed by fire; the second level rumbles, loosens, threatens to disintegrate as I near the cavity. I could attempt to navigate over these great holes, but falling would mean a 25-foot drop. And I'd be taking a good collection of jagged lumber with me, nails . . .

I can't get to Jeanette's room. What did she keep in her closet? What did her room smell like, where did she keep her favourite things? I hold the railing and step on two solid-looking boards. One of them begins to crumble immediately and the railing wobbles so I throw myself backwards, the floor shifting now like in California earthquake movies. Black blisters on the walls; these rooms have been boiled. Chunks of wood fall through the holes and crash on the first floor as I pick myself up and walk carefully down the hallway to the top of the stairs. The Plum House is crumbling. I hurry down the stairs, past the gasoline snakes of black burned into the wall where the photographs of handsome Kravchuks once were, over the glass and filth as the boards continue to crash and bounce behind me, through the hole Nick made. Safe. With my shoes on.

In our house, Denton is making pancakes with sliced apple in them, coffee brewing. I close the door behind me and choo some.

"Coffee, Jer? You look freezing."

"It's gonna snow." In the living room I look out the picture window, and though I look closely I can't tell if the Plum House is moving. It might be my shivering.

"Mr. Rhinehold from Gordy's called. He wants to know if you need a job."

Should I tell Denton what I just did? He would ask me why, and I would have no good answer, and he would shake his head and think.

"Scott and the other bouncers have trouble taking care of business without breaking glasses and tables. Hurting people too. He wants a cooler, an expert. I told him you were an expert."

The house is still. I rub my eyes again. The Plum House is still.

"Jeremy!"

"I hear you, Denton. Why are you up?"

"The phone rang twice. Gwen called and Rhinehold called. So I called Rhinehold back."

"He isn't gonna fire you?" I approach the kitchen. The Plum House is still.

"Why would he?" Denton is still in his pajamas. A slice of apple hangs from his mouth.

"You and Gwen work together." I take a slice of apple too. "Can I have pancakes too?"

"They're for both of us."

"Did you call Gwen back?"

He takes a drink of coffee and makes a face, picking some grounds off his tongue. "Cheap filters. No, I know what she's gonna say. It's all on the machine. That she isn't really pressing charges. Bitch Alice wanted to, and told Chicken George some story about me being physically and mentally abusive throughout the relationship. Gwen also said she's quitting Gordy's and she never wants to see me again. I don't think I should call her back. As much as I want to. I'll let her cool off, is what I'll do."

"How's the hangover?"

"Four Extra Strength Tylenol *kickin' in*. What about the cooler job?"

"I don't know."

"What don't you know?"

"I don't know anything. I don't know if I should be doing that."

"What?"

"Fighting."

Denton slices a new apple into four, cores it and peels it. Another drink of coffee, licking his arm to get the grounds off his tongue. It looks like he's been gardening with his mouth. "If you're leaving Seymour, leave now. Otherwise, you'll need a job. And you don't know how to do anything else, do you?"

"Leave me alone about it for five minutes, Denton." I pour some coffee, straining it into the mug through another filter. We could use some music.

"Me and Dad figure you have to decide if you're gonna be in this family or not."

"You and Dad."

"That's right. Our family."

I take a drink and open the back door. The mountains are obscured by the snow clouds. Denton lifts two pancakes off the frying pan and drops them on separate plates. Even though it is covered in newspapers and envelopes and flyers, he slides the plates on the kitchen table. It must be the first time anyone has eaten at this table in years.

"I can't *not be* in the family, Denton, wherever I am. Even if –"

"Yes, you can. You haven't been in the family. When Dad was sick, Jer, you should have been here. All you wanted to do was fight. Everything was fighting."

I drench my pancake in syrup. Unbalanced on a pile of paper, it runs off the plate. On the fridge is a picture of Denton and Mom and me; it wasn't there before. We are on her lap. She looks like a hippie. "You're right. I regret that, Denton. I should have been here."

"Dad loves you, Jeremy. He's your dad."

I nod.

"You have to talk to him."

I nod.

After two new pancakes are in the frying pan, Denton sits at the table across from me. He smiles, digging in. It's hard to keep the syrup evenly distributed on the plate. As I crumple the soiled newspaper, my fingers get covered in syrup. Everything I touch, now, will be sticky.

According to the ad on TV, it's cheap night for long distance. Call a loved one, it's Sunday. The grandparents light up as rain falls out the window, lovers quake out of their loneliness for each other, Mom eyes Dad coyly as the college student asks for money. It is dark outside, and cold, and the commercial gets to me. I could call and thank her for being so kind with Denton last night, when he was afraid. I could ask her how things are going at work. Rob, I'm sure, is doing something spectacular as usual, and maybe she could tell me about that; he is a fundraiser for a Boston cancer institute, a childhood friend turned – now – lover. I'd like to hear about Frieda our absentee cat, about any new disks she may have bought. How are Rachel and crazy Garret? Have my deceived creditors been calling me? Is her blonde hair still the same shade, the same length? Has she changed perfume? Any plans for the summer, renovations for the house?

I could apologize for the other night, declare my allegiance to compassion and empathy, display my new understanding of the world and of the hearts of men, swear off fighting forever. I will go back to university, like we discussed. Become an architect. Beg her to forgive me, reconsider me. Admit that I am broken. That I can be fixed.

Without picking up the receiver, I dial her number on the digital phone. Our number. Before I can convince myself to pick it up, Dad's truck rumbles into the driveway. He stamps up on the deck and opens the door, tramps in, boots still on. He stands behind the TV and smiles, waves, wearing mittens, looking chilled in his windbreaker. I erase the number. "Hi Dad."

"Your voices sound exactly the same," he says. "Like twins, you two. Seven years didn't do much to change that."

"Nope."

"What are you watching?"

There is a *Dukes of Hazzard* rerun on, but I haven't been paying attention. The house is very warm because Denton turned up the thermostat. The burnt-dust smell I remember from Nick Lozinski's house floats up through the vents as the heater kicks in. "The Dukes."

"Don't forget to turn the heat down before you go to bed, Jeremy. Tell your brother too, if you're gonna have the heat on." The truck vrooms in the driveway, and idles lower. He turns and shakes his head. "I told her not to do that. Is it a good one? The Dukes?"

"Pretty good."

He nods. "Well. I'll let you get back to it, I guess." His boots are loud on the hardwood when he walks into his and Mom's room. A sound I remember.

"Dad."

"What?" He walks out with his wallet in his hand, clearing his throat. "What, Jeremy?"

"How are you, Dad?"

With a smile, he passes the wallet into the inside pocket of his thin jacket. "Fine, thanks. How are you?"

"I'm nothing, somehow. In-between, in flux."

"We're always in flux." He stands and smiles some more, pulling his mittens back on.

"Sorry, Dad."

"Oh yeah?" He leans against the door jamb in the entrance to the hallway leading to their room, scratching his back on it. His boot scuffing the carpet. His smile is a satisfied one. He is a handsome man, my dad.

So. Did Jeanette buy this carpet? The furniture and the home theatre? Are we a rich family now? "I just wanted to tell you that if I could do it all over again, I'd do things differently."

"Suppose I would too. Thanks for that, Jeremy. It's nice to hear you say it." Dad looking at me, swallowing like this, embarrasses me.

I stand up to shake it off, and look around, kick playfully at Panther. "I'm sorry for being rude to Jeanette too."

"You should be. And you know what, tell her that yourself. She's out in the truck right now. I bet she'd be real touched to hear you say that."

"Can't you tell her for me?"

He shrugs and scratches his back on the corner some more.

Then he wipes his hands on his pants and looks at his watch. He picks up a balled-up Kleenex from the dining-room table and looks at it sadly. "No."

"Tell her for me, Dad. And I'll talk to her next time. From now on —"

"You'll sit in here and tell me sorry now and then? After you do some hell of a thing like call me every name in the book in front of the whole town?"

There is a well-trained muscle in me that wants to tell him to go fuck himself if this is how it's going to be. The rest of me is confused. I know what Denton or Ellie would have me do; and if there was one move that could salvage it all, I'd make that one move. But this is going to be long, complicated, and painful. "I'll talk to her."

Dad takes Bugs Bunny from the rocking chair and throws it for Panther. "You'll talk to her like a human being?"

I walk past him, without looking. He's wrong too.

"Better put on a sweater, Jeremy. It's damn cold out there. Snow, if you can believe it. I'm grabbing a couple of sweaters right now, for Jeanette and myself. We're going to the drive-in tonight, her bright idea. The drive-in in the snow." I throw on the jean jacket I wore the other morning, and a pair of Denton's cowboy boots that are way too big for me. The tension leaves his voice. "We all have to make sacrifices. You know what family means. Just yesterday, I was sayin' to your brother . . ."

On the deck I stare into the superbright halogens of Dad's truck, and wave. I can't see Jeanette but she can see me. Is this enough? The electric window slides down. "Jeremy."

"Hi."

"Come down here so you don't have to squint."

Panther is out here with me, so I grab him up as a buffer and walk down the stairs, on to the driveway. The heat billows out of the truck. The smell of Jeanette. I make Panther's paw wave. Joni Mitchell on low volume.

"It's really so nice to see you back here, Jeremy. I'm not surprised to see how wonderfully handsome you've become. You
three must be the three best-looking men in this town. I'm in
good company around here."

Even though I don't want to, I smile. She's giving me sugar, a
look I remember. "No, we're in good company. Jeanette Kravchuk,
the queen of Seymour."

She laughs. "You see what that boy did to our house?"

"Yes. It's too bad."

We both look back, as if we could see the house from here. An
opal earring dangles as she turns her head. How old is she now?
Adjusting the side mirror, she says, "I'd like for us to get along,
Jeremy. It's best this way." She puts her hand on my hand, the one
that holds Panther, and looks hard with her small, serious eyes.
"Can I ask you to please be understanding with your father and
me? We might as well get along, because you'll never get rid of
me." She waves me closer. Simple-minded. Does she have a secret
to tell me? Is there something in my teeth? She reaches for me with
her pretty hands and takes me softly around the back of my head.
Jeanette moves forward and kisses me on the side of the mouth.
Panther squirms and gnaws at my hand. I almost kiss her again,
but she moves back. A friendly kiss, a woman-to-a-boy kiss.

I stand back with the dog. Sick of being held, he growls. Wet,
heavy flakes of snow begin to fall. The wind has disappeared.

"Goodnight, Jeanette. Have a fun time at the movies."

"In the snow. It was his idea, you know. Pay attention to your
father, the hopeless romantic. Take notes."

Up on the deck, I back up and smile into the headlights.
When did they first see each other, Jeanette and Dad? First meet?
First decide they had fallen in love? I stand in the snow and
Jeanette says out her window, "Jeremy, Joe would want to say hi.
He's doing okay at the hospital, in his way. I'm planting his plum
seeds, the very best ones, at my place in the city." I tell her to say

hi to him for me, and Panther and I go into the house together, catching Dad with the fridge door opened, drinking milk from the carton.

"Was it so bad?" he says, wiping his white moustache.

"No. It was kinda nice."

He hands me the carton of milk and bolts out the door. With the snow falling and some dragons crawling out of the mental state of this family, I sit in a kitchen chair and think: it is a fine thing to see my dad bolting.

The power is out this morning, branches have fallen from their trees. The inflatable golf dome in the city has toppled under the weight of the biggest one-night spring snowfall in 80 years. No school today, Seymour is a powerless playground. No TV, no stereo, no *Doom* on Denton's computer, no fridge humming or alarm clocks buzzing, no eggs frying or coffee brewing or toast popping. In their drenched snowsuits, the kids are out screaming in the street.

Denton lies on the couch, a forearm over his black eye, mumbling the lyrics to a song I haven't heard before. It is warm now, the snow already melting, falling in massive clumps from the roofs of our neighbourhood. Streams are forming in the fields of clean white. Three branches have broken off the ancient elm in front of the Plum House. Last night, after the lights flicked off, the whole neighbourhood cracked and snapped, the Plum House roared under the pressure of the snow. I sat with candles, eating peanut butter sandwiches and listening.

Since Dad got here ten minutes ago, he has been shovelling the snow on the back deck. I asked him if he wanted me to do it, but he said no, and refused help. It's not as if I'm going to have a stroke, he said.

Denton sits up suddenly and squints out the front window at the kids playing in the sunshine snow on the street in front of the Plum House. The house itself, with its flat sections of roofing, looks as though someone deliberately tried to bury it in flour. Then he sits back down. "Those kids' parents are gonna have to hang their snowsuits over the bathtub," he says, and covers his eye some more.

The cellular phone rings in the kitchen. Denton jumps up and runs for it. He opens the back door and tells Dad, "Phone!" Then stomping and more stomping, outside and then inside the kitchen, before Dad's talking to whoever it is.

As Denton sloths back into the living room, wiping the condensation from a blueberry yogurt on his t-shirt, pouting because the call wasn't for him, I ask him, in a whisper, if Dad knows about the drunk-tank thing yet. No, he tells me, and we shouldn't worry his fragile heart about it. The back door is opened, and the cool but somehow warm, scentless air sneaks in. Panther, who had been playing outside with Dad and the snow, walks in and shakes a few times, so violently he falls over. He jumps on Denton but Denton pushes him away. "Wet dog stink!"

Dad stamps and leers at us for being loud while he is on the phone.

"Who's he talking to?" I say, eyeing that yogurt.

"The *Star*."

I back up a bit, to hear. "Historic day in Seymour history. That's right, that's right. It's overshadowed all of us, that's right. Touched us all, certainly. Been with us almost the whole century, the good and the bad of it. The evil and the . . ." He covers the receiver. "Jeremy. What's the opposite of evil?"

I walk in. "Good?"

"No. Bad and good. Denton! Evil versus what?"

"Gwen. Gwen's the opposite of evil. Angelic perfection is what she is, the gift of the magi, the eighth wonder of the world, the

Hope Diamond, a Polish princess." He waves his spoon in the air, standing up. As he's about to say something else sarcastic – now I remember his sarcasm face – he tips the yogurt cup and it plops blue on the light brown carpet. Stinky Panther pounces it, and Denton kicks at him to get away. "Son of a whore!"

"Dents. I'm on the phone here, with the *media*. You wanna watch your damn mouth, or?" Dad uncovers the phone. "Hello, Barry? Yes, the evil and the heavenly. No, heavenly. The Kravchuk place has seen the good and the bad of this century. The evil and the heavenly."

"I don't think that's the right word, Dad. Tell him you wanna change it." I don't see how a house can be heavenly, especially the Plum House. And I think it's a sneaky move for the paper to ask Dad about it. Out the back window, some clouds are rolling in. Round two of the spring storm?

"Hold on a sec here, Barry." He covers the phone again, kicks the cupboard. "What now? You don't like heavenly? Talk to your brother, he suggested the goddamn word."

"I did not." Scooping, Denton tries to keep Panther away from the yogurt spot.

"He said angelic, and that's no good, either." I walk over and close the big door; the crisp air is exciting, but without coffee it's too exciting. I don't know what the opposite of evil is, and I'm not so hopped-up about the controversy that I'm willing to hunt around the house for the thesaurus I used for writing papers in high school, but the word 'heavenly' just isn't right. "Maybe virtuous?"

"No, not virtuous," says Denton, on his hands and knees now, wiping at the yogurt with the hang of his t-shirt. "That's what virgins are. And if virgins are virtuous and virtuous is the opposite of evil, I guess that would make sex evil." He stands up again, waves the spoon some more. "If things continue as they are, I'll never get any ever again, but I'll tell you one thing – sex sure as hell isn't evil."

"Jesus H. Christ you two! Barry's waiting here. He's liable to hang up on me. The guy's working in a dark office. All he wants is a paragraph from a bunch of people in town here. My paragraph's not even so important. What's it gonna be? Evil and what?"

Is it something about motives? We can't be perfect; we can't be virtuous or heavenly or pure or clean like the snow today, but we can be the opposite of evil. Bad and good lack mystery, unlike evil and its opposite. Maybe the opposite of evil is safe mystery. And it's exactly what I want, safe mystery.

"Honesty," says Denton.

"Honesty can be evil," I say. "It's not honesty."

"You pack of wild animals," says Dad, marching like a four-year-old who has to pee. "I've had him waiting since creation. Ah, shit. Okay, Barry, tell ya what. Just say the good and the bad, screw the evil stuff. Leave it at that. Yes, I know, I apologize for that. Oh, the power'll be back on real soon. Fred and the boys are working on it. With the power people. Sure, Barry, bye." He hangs up and shakes his head at us, very seriously, slipping on his boots. Outside, he sweeps snow off the deck chairs. Tonight he is in for a busy shift, with all the snow damage.

Out the screen door I watch him for a few minutes before asking why they're doing a story about the Plum House.

"It's dangerous. We're doing a controlled burn, taking it down."

The truck snakes all over the one lane that Black Gold Drive has been reduced to. A mixture of rain and snow plops on the windshield in clumps, like sour milk. Dad is driving me to the Gooseberry Inn for a meeting with Denton's boss, Mr. Rhinehold. Denton was supposed to drive me because he set up the meeting, but Gwen called on the cellular, and he wanted to be private about it. Neither of them trust me to drive alone in this weather.

I haven't mentioned the controlled burn of the Plum House, which I am thinking about, because Dad has been talking non-stop about how funny Jeanette was last night. Thanks to the snow, the drive-in shut down, so they went out for dinner instead. Apparently she caught her jacket on a door knob at the restaurant, and it ripped. So right in front of everyone she bent over and slipped out of the jacket, took her keys out of the pocket, and left it hanging on the knob. He says these things and sighs, and looks over at me. The truck spins out, goes sideways, and rights itself. Then he punches my knee with his free hand, a nervous thing. He is just about to say something he thinks I won't like. I know my dad.

"You thinking on staying in town a while, then?"

I nod. "At least a while."

"Because you know the house is paid for, since last year." A car moves slowly toward us, a Honda Accord knee-deep in slush, sliding all over the lane. Dad drives up on the curb, beside the junior high school, so we can wait for it to pass. "And it looks like I'll be moving in with Jean, is the reason I say it. Big place for one gal, alone. She's funny to ask, I suppose. But it isn't right to be doing like we've been doing, here-ing it and there-ing it like teenagers. So I says we get married first and she says yes, so . . ."

"You're getting married."

Dad waves at the Accord guy as he passes us. "Not that I ask for your blessing. I just wanted you to know, since you're back home here."

"Well –"

"And you and Denton can have the house, for as long as you like. Forever, if you like." Holding the wheel, he flaps his elbows like wings, peeking over at me as we glide back into the lane.

I wonder how long they've been engaged. Were they going to

seek my approval if I hadn't come home? My cheeks go hot. Although I should have seen it coming, I didn't see it coming. Of course, they're getting married. That's what people do when they're in love, when they want to sleep in the same bed all the time. I make an effort to nod and seem quietly pleased, as if it's natural. My voice cracks as I say, "Congratulations," so I say it again. "Congratulations, Dad."

"Hell," he says, and looks over, and smiles. Blushes.

At the lights, Tracy Lozinski stands perfectly still, in a yellow raincoat. With a newspaper opened over her baseball-capped head. Dad honks and I open the window. "Ride?" Dad and I should talk about this a bit more, though I guess there will be time for that.

"Why not," she says.

I open the door and jump out to help her in, so she can be in the middle. Tracy gives me a look about it, as if she didn't expect such a classy move from a rat like me. But I may be wrong in my interpretation of the look.

"Hi, Glen." A whisper.

"Tracy," Dad says, slapping the steering wheel, "what are you doing out in this shit? You could call any of us for a ride, you know that. Any one of us could pick you up."

"Little Taxis?"

"That's right."

I don't look at her. I look out my window and smell her buoyant perfume blowing off her, mingling with the vague warmth of the truck defrost.

"Where you boys off to this morning?" she says, her voice small, folding her newspaper absently, with shaking hands.

"It's afternoon, dear. I'm driving Jeremy because he's got himself an interview over there with Denton's boss."

"Rhinehold?" she says, leaning ahead to turn on the radio. After pressing a button that doesn't do much of anything, she sits back. The front of her baseball cap says Riggers, the Junior B team Nick and the other guys skated for when I left Seymour. "For what?"

Dad pulls on to 50th Street, honking at a car plastered with wedding pompoms. "Don't tell me someone's getting married on a Monday. A Monday like today. That's enough to make a man cry in his sleep."

"A security job. Bouncing, I guess."

"He must have heard about you and Lenny."

"I don't know."

"Why would you want to do that?"

I hesitate a moment and then ask, "So where you headed, Tracy?" Dad's still shaking his head, obviously concerned with the implications of a wedding on a Monday. I'm more interested in what Tracy's doing walking around in the slush.

"I can get off with Jeremy. That'll be great, Glen."

"Sure? I can drop him off and take you wherever you need to go. Music, you guys?" He turns on the radio, CIKN Country.

Tracy shakes her head.

The smell is making me ball my fists up, making me wild and jumpy in the stomach. She bothers me. Her white pants are soaked and the muscles in her thighs move with the music; she is wearing a traditional-looking wedding ring, maybe Ukrainian. I hadn't noticed it in Gordy's, or at the fair.

Dad clears his throat. "You know, it's really too bad what happened with Nick, Tracy. He's a good guy. I got to know him a bit, him volunteering."

I almost laugh out loud. My dad is worried about the boy who hit me and kicked me and pissed on my head. He sighs, about Nick Lozinski. I almost laugh out loud, and then I do laugh out loud. The burning in my cheeks gets worse as Tracy looks at me. I don't look at her. Everyone has forgotten it, no one cares but me. And it's about time that I stop caring.

The kids are everywhere, jumping and rolling. In the driveways and the yards, on sidewalks. As Dad pulls into the Gooseberry Inn parking lot, gravel underneath this cream, the most slippery place so far, I wish for a moment that he would turn around and keep driving somewhere so Tracy could stare at the side of my face some more. It's safe mystery.

Four or five people are in the process of pushing their cars out of impossible bowls of snow. Dad shoves it into park and looks around. "I'm gonna see if I can help," he says, and hops out. As I open my door, he is already armed with a shovel and a bag of sand from the back of the truck, on his way through the crème de la crème to help the first victim. I offer Tracy a hand and she ignores it. "Good luck, son," Dad yells, ripping open his bag of sand.

Slipping but not quite falling, Tracy hurries away from me. I take the paper out of the truck and close the door again, before running after her. Once I get beside her, I take her arm and she yanks it away. "Tracy. Your paper."

She stops and slips and backs up, righting herself in a pocket of gravel before I have a chance to help. The awnings of Gordy's and the old craft place are only a few feet away, but we stand for a moment in the snow and rain. My hair and pants and the top of my tie are already wet. Water drips from the brim of Tracy's cap. "I only laugh because of what happened with Nick and me. I don't even know him. I was thinking that it really doesn't matter any more. You know?"

Raised eyebrows.

"Where are you going, Tracy?"

She snatches the paper from my hand and holds it awkwardly over her cap. "That's a real good question."

I notice she isn't wearing any makeup, that her eyes are red, and I remember that Nick's hearing is today. "Did the hearing go well?"

She laughs and takes a big step before walking away. I won't ask any more questions about Nick, because it's probably obvious to her that I don't have any loving feelings toward him. What would I do if I saw him? The best thing, overall, would be to shake his hand and tell him I'm sorry about his luck. As Tracy walks, I realize she isn't actually going anywhere. Or doesn't seem to care where she goes. She stops and turns around, waves me over. I take big steps over the truck tire ruts in the snow, feet squishing wet in my shoes. "There was no hearing. Nick tried to off himself last night."

"Oh."

She wipes her eyes. "Yeah, oh."

"That's awful."

"The puny bastard. Where does that leave us?" She turns around and kicks at some snow. "Huh?" to the west, to the invisible mountains.

"I don't know."

"This is a great talk we've been having, Jeremy," she says, and shakes my hand. And walks gingerly away, past Dad and all the cars he's rescuing. They wave to each other, Dad and Tracy. And suddenly the street lights pop on, the red and blue OPEN in the window of Gordy's, the big turning neon strip-mall sign that says *Gooseberry's Means Magic*. Everyone in the parking lot cheers.

I hop under the awning and fix my tie in the reflection of the glass door. In the manager's office I sit in the lobby a while, in my wet suit jacket and pants, reading an article on the people who make computer viruses. They have cool names like Striker and Dirty Arrow. Eventually, Mr. Rhinehold calls me in and offers coffee. I accept. My past. My security past, my criminal past. He asks about my history of violence and as I make up some stuff, I consider my history of violence.

Did I like university? Did I like Boston? Why did I come back? Can I be trusted? Can I stop a large attacker, multiple attackers, Vietnamese gangs who might try to infiltrate rural

Alberta? Am I a team player? Motivated? A leader? A forward thinker? A man who is comfortable with his place in the world, his realistic goals?

As I answer, I watch his handlebar moustache. There is a little spot of white powder on the corner, and a mole on his forehead I long to erase. Mr. Rhinehold plays with his watchband, his wedding ring. He is nervous, I think.

Mr. Rhinehold tells me I can start Thursday night, and I tell him I've changed my mind. I am a forward thinker.

The bottom of Jeremy Little is what Diane says she'd like to get to. The machine is full of messages for Dad and Denton. One from Jeanette features her calling us "the three sweeties." Diane, in her shaky phone voice, says we can get together tonight if I want. She says she wouldn't mind bringing over a bottle of tequila and four lemons, so we can get to the bottom of Jeremy Little. She will call back later.

On the fridge a note from Denton.

At Gwen's. Wants to talk. Gwen does, not me. (Well, I do too.) Denton. ps Carl Kang dropped off a pile of polished wood for you. Said his dad wanted you to have it, no charge. Just practice sticking hands with him sometime??? Denton.

Downstairs, I change out of the only suit I own. Since I walked home, it is drenched and will have to be dry-cleaned like everything else. Dad is still in the parking lot, saving the day. If this isn't a sweatsuit afternoon I don't know what afternoon is, so I put one on – my black Waterfront Warrior School sweatsuit. In the garage, I wipe off the pieces of the future Carl II. His torso stands up against one wall of the garage for now, under Dad's pre-fluorescent grey fire uniforms, in-between filthy old fire-hall shovels and rakes and axes. I wriggle his arms and legs into place. Once he is set up, looking confused and asymmetric, I back away. Moving in quick, Bruce Lee style, I give Carl II a bong sao and his arm falls off. The torso slides down, bouncing, wood on concrete. I will have to build a proper stand for my wooden man.

It will take a couple of weeks for my body to readjust to daily training; the body loves to rest, to calcify and grow, to stay inert. To stop and look around. When I closed the school, I felt weak and nauseous for two weeks, very anxious. My body was angry with me for not training, Now I must recompute, start anew, feed it some of its old addictions, sweat.

I do a warm-up and a long stretch on some strips of cardboard. The garage seems oily with the door opened, the wet outside. I pull the heavy bag down and start in on my boxing combos before some light kicking. Then footwork drills. The Wing Chun straight blast, called the Jit Chung Chuie, is a series of one-over-the-other vertical fist punches. I practise these for when you see a wide opening, for when you've trapped your opponent's arms, and you want to hurt him and end the fight quickly. These aren't the powerful punches of a boxer, with the hips and the shoulders; these are superfast, on-centre-line, rolling punches thrown with fierce forward momentum that keep his hands down, disorient him, confuse him, open him for your finishing move. Fighters stay up nights dreaming of a chance to perform a gorgeous finishing move, even though going for the neck, like an animal, is always the smartest and most economical move. From there, elbow, knee, head-butt, eye-gouge. Ugly. I practise my Jit Chung Chuie and my knuckles bleed, just a bit. And for the first time, as I stand and stare and lick at my bloody knuckles, I understand how I have been stupid about fighting. Seeing the squared circle everywhere, and structuring your life around it, prevents you from really living. Ellie was right. I have to be undefended.

My dad and my brother, they like to have a cordless phone in the garage. I wipe my knuckles on some coveralls and pick up the phone, press talk. Dial tone. After listening to dial tone for a moment, choo, I dial Ellie at work before I can convince myself not to. As the phone rings, I freeze up. Why call? What do I want to say? The faraway rings keep ringing. After ring four, I breathe, I can move again. The secretary answers. She recognizes my voice. She'll give Ellie the message.

Please come watch my father burn the Plum House down. You know, I can sometimes hear the rain beating down on the silver garbage-can lids below our bedroom window. Hi to Rob and Boston and thanks for Denton, Ellie, I'm okay here in Seymour. I'm not okay in Seymour. I miss you in Seymour.

Slush turns to rain. A plane flies over. The paper delivery boy, hours late, slides around on his bike. The kids holler everywhere red rover red rover let Lindsay come over. The shh-ka shh-ka of paved driveways and their no-work-today Monday shovellers. A *Seymour Star* K-car pulls up and a man with a beard – Barry? – gets out and lifts his glasses at me before turning around to take some shots of the Plum House. He writes a few things down, the umbrella somehow rigged to his shoulder.

The phone rings.

The pain of loss and change and heartbreak, the dull thud of a fist upon a face, all defeat and humiliation carries with it the bleary hope of a more perfect tomorrow, a time of utter completeness and safety. This symmetry exists. Proof is in the picture of my mother and me in the dirt at the side of this house, with the fender of an old car gleaming. I trust in training, in the hunt for the more perfect tomorrow. And if I plan carefully enough, if I am truly prepared, nothing can hurt me. Yet, the dream of the perfect finishing move, the interception of everything but symmetry, has pushed me to overlook the simple moments – rain beating down on the silver garbage-can lids below our bedroom window – that are, really, the best a man can expect. The moments he will long for. The ones I long for.

The phone rings.

Empty pop and beer cans have been poured into garbage bags for a trip to the depot. Now I sit in a puddle of stale beer that has escaped from the bags, and two cold and certainly confused bees won't stop buzzing my ass. I consider this.

The phone rings.

The phone rings.

Inside, the machine picks up. The dusty garage echoes and then we are as silent as we can be, me and the bees. This beer, these bees, the possibility that it wasn't Ellie at all but Diane, Travis, or a magazine telemarketer just about my age, single, on the verge of losing his hair, obsessed with sports he never played, prone to bouts of marijuana abuse . . . *this*, all of this adds up to asymmetry, imbalance, resignation, hope; it might be her, or her, she might be talking to our empty house. This is sad. This is mute. Potentially fine. Fine.

The phone rings. And I run for it.

Other Titles by Turnstone Press

Summer of My Amazing Luck, a novel by Miriam Toews
    Nominated for the Stephen Leacock Award for Humour

This Place Called Absence, a novel by Lydia Kwa

In the Hands of the Living God, a novel by Lillian Bouzane

The Drum King, a novel by Richelle Kosar

Driving Blind, a novel by Steven Benstead
    Shortlisted for the McNally Robinson Book of the Year

Madame Balashovskaya's Apartment, a novel by Martha Baillie

Thirteen Shades of Black and White, short stories by
    Michael Bryson

Home Free, a novel by Wayne Tefs
    The final novel in the trilogy including *Figures on a Wharf*
    and *The Canasta Players*